I0738193

The Library of Unfinished Business

The Library of Unfinished Business

Patricia Bell

CLOUI INK

First published in 2022
Published by Cloud Ink Press Ltd, Auckland
P O Box 8988, Symonds Street, Auckland 1150
www.cloudink.co.nz

ISBN number: 978-0-473-58203-6

Poetry acknowledgements:
"And Yet the Books" from The Collected Poems 1931-1987 by Czeslaw Milosz.
Copyright © 1988 by Czeslaw Milosz Royalties, Inc. Used by permission of
HarperCollins Publishers.
"Do Not Go Gentle Into That Good Night" (four-line excerpt) by Dylan Thomas,
from The Collected Poems of Dylan Thomas: The Centenary Edition. Publisher:
Weidenfeld & Nicolson. Reprinted by permission from David Higham Associates.
(Worldwide permission excluding US)
"Do Not Go Gentle Into That Good Night" (same excerpt) by Dylan Thomas, from
The Poems of Dylan Thomas, copyright ©1952 by Dylan Thomas. Reprinted by
permission from New Directions Publishing Corp. (US only)

Cover, internal design and typesetting: Craig Violich (www.cvdgraphics.nz)
Printed by: Ligare, Auckland

This book is for:
My father, the book hoarder,
And my daughter, the story lover.

And yet the books will be there on the shelves, separate beings,
That appeared once, still wet
As shining chestnuts under a tree in autumn,
And, touched, coddled, began to live
In spite of fires on the horizon, castles blown up,
Tribes on the march, planets in motion.
"We are," they said, even as their pages
Were being torn out, or a buzzing flame
Licked away their letters. So much more durable
Than we are, whose frail warmth
Cools down with memory, disperses, perishes.
I imagine the earth when I am no more:
Nothing happens, no loss, it's still a strange pageant,
Women's dresses, dewy lilacs, a song in the valley.
Yet the books will be there on the shelves, well born,
Derived from people, but also from radiance, heights.

– Czeslaw Milosz, "And Yet The Books"

Contents

Part One
The End and the Beginning

1

On the day I died, I was running happily late for work. I still grasp at those final splinters of memory: the squeal of tyres, the slice of sun on metal, a brief but vicious clutch of agony, and a detached sense of glee that I was going to miss the start of the Monday morning staff meeting.

But I'm getting ahead of myself.

I hadn't slept well, and at 5.50 am, ten minutes before my alarm was due to go off, I gave up trying. I harrumphed my way to the side of the bed and banged on the radio. A mediocre host was swaggering his way through the traffic report. I walloped it off again, sending it skittering across the bedside table and onto the floor. I cursed my way to the toilet and through to the kitchen.

The sun was making a half-hearted attempt to limp over Bressington Hill as I stood, scratching, staring out the window at a pile of stinking rubbish. It was strewn all over the pavement, in the gutter, and down the shared driveway. Milk cartons and eggshells and expired TV dinners (mine) and dozens of chocolate bar wrappers (not mine) jostled messily for space. The bloody dog from 66A had obviously knocked over the wheelie bin I had trundled out to the kerb the previous evening during a brief attack of efficiency. On the downside, I thought, I would have to clean it up before Mrs Hardy had a fit. On the upside, this might mean I would miss the Monday morning staff meeting.

I snapped on plastic gloves and spent as long as I could scraping crap off concrete. Then I hosed it down. Lace curtains twitched. I gave them the finger and for a moment was tempted to hose rotten eggshells into Mrs Hardy's kitset carport. I ended up leaving them stranded on the grass strip that marked the boundary between our two properties. It was a statement, but an easily retractable one.

By the time I left the house I was running thirty minutes late. Humming an old Bee Gees tune, I was just slowing down to turn left onto Preston Road when a silver hatchback barrelled through the red light, flipped, and performed a surprisingly graceful pirouette on the edge of its front bumper. It then crashed back down and skidded, on its roof, into my front windscreen. It was going so fast the impact was a sonic boom. I didn't stand a chance.

At least Andy wasn't with me. Sometimes she hitched a ride, but on my last morning on earth she had stayed in bed. I had yelled once from the kitchen that I would be leaving soon, to no response, so I had scribbled a note and slipped it under her door:

Dear Andy,

I had the strangest dream last night. I dreamed about a daughter who actually listened to me and was grateful to be offered a free lift to class. Then I woke up.

Dad
P.S. We're out of milk.

For years Andy and I had adhered to an unspoken agreement. I would pretend not to notice she was becoming more and more like her mother – unbearable – and she, in turn, would treat me like a pile of excrement. So that was working out pretty well for both of us.

I did care about her, of course. I loved her more than life. It's just that when I was alive, I was never very good at it.

But let's not get all hand-holdy just yet.

To recap: I was in the car, running late for work, a pirouetting hatchback crashed head-on into my windscreen, and the last things I remember were the squeal of tyres, the slice of sun on metal, a brief but vicious clutch of agony, and a detached sense of glee that not only was I going to miss the start of the Monday morning staff meeting, I was never going to have to attend one again.

I think I may have also wet my pants.

And then, for an indeterminate period of time, nothing.

2

I can't fill in the blank between dying and arriving at the gates of Heaven. In my dreams I chase ephemeral silhouettes of mist, and a light, and a period of waiting: for what, I'm not entirely sure. My dead relatives lined up beyond a rainbow bridge, perhaps, beckoning me to join them. Or a trumpet fanfare and a posse of angels fluttering around me like a twitter of hairdressers around a bride. God himself even, throwing open his arms, gathering me to his bosom at last. The fact that I was a deeply committed agnostic wasn't going to deny me this cosy tableau.

My first clear memory is of the mist and light suddenly *making sense*, abruptly coalescing and forming meaning like those Magic Eye optical illusion books, the ones where each page is a sickening swirl of nonsense until your brain does its job and reveals the hidden 3D picture.

I sensed ground beneath my feet. Temperate air. Possibility. I heard brisk footsteps.

A pony-tailed young woman dressed in a short yellow skirt and polo shirt, clipboard in one hand and a bunch of skipping ropes in the other, bounced into view, beaming. Her teeth gleamed. She wore a giant badge in the shape of a wing, which read:

Hi! I'm your Heavenly Host! Have a Nice Day!

"Ooooh, super!" she squealed, looking me up and down. Her eyes took their time on my stomach. "We needed another hefty chap for

Michael's rowing regatta. Now, let's see…"

She flipped through a few closely typed pages on her clipboard, cleared her throat, and began to read.

"Welcome to Hippy Happy Heaven, your afterlife home away from home. I'm delighted to be your Heavenly Host. We were sorry to hear about your recent death, but are confident that you will find the accommodation, services, and activities more than satisfactory here in your own little slice of paradise." She looked up and winked. I stared.

Hefty?

She continued. "In a moment I will show you to your accommodation. Please make yourself at home and take the opportunity to freshen up before the day's excitement begins. Meals are served in the Hallelujah Hall: breakfast at nine am, lunch at twelve, dinner at six. Please arrive promptly or you may find your selection of meal is unavailable. The Boogie Bar is open from four pm to ten pm every day, serving non-alcoholic beverages as well as wine, beer, cocktails, and … spirits." She looked up. I stared again, perhaps a touch wildly. She looked down.

"An activity schedule will be posted outside the Hallelujah Hall every morning at eight am. Please do make the most of what we have on offer. We invite you to join us for Cocktails with God every Tuesday evening at five pm on the Cocktail Lawn. Your friendly Heavenly Hosts – " she tapped her badge " – are more than happy to assist with any queries you may have." She slapped the pages back to the beginning. "We hope you enjoy your stay with us!"

I registered that my mouth was hanging open. It tends to do that when I'm either blind drunk or bewildered. The former had occurred sporadically over the previous few years; the latter is still not uncommon.

"For God's sake close your mouth, Dad. You look like an idiot," Andy used to snap at me. I tried to do so now as my guide turned and hurried off, holding a yellow flag high above her head. "Follow the flag to find the fun!" she trilled over her shoulder. I stepped forward, noticing as I did that I was wearing my old green and red tartan slippers, a Christmas gift from Andy several years previously. They scuffed and flopped as I followed Little Miss Sunshine towards an enormous set of yellow metal gates with a large sign curving above them, which read:

Hippy Happy Heaven Welcomes You!

A squat yellow cabin sat just inside the gates, the open window framing an excessively handsome man dressed all in white. He was speaking briskly into a telephone tucked under his chin as he flicked through paperwork, but he looked up at me as we passed. His hair, pulled back into one of those ghastly man buns, was a glossy panther-black, his dark eyes enormous and wide above cheekbones that were almost feminine in their precision. Mid-thirties, I estimated, and one of those men who would just get better with age. I detested him immediately.

The young woman seemed to walk faster, her gaze fixed steadfastly ahead. "Morning, Peter!" *Flick flack* went her flag. The man didn't reply.

We made our way along a wide, smooth driveway. On my right was a tall hedge beyond which I could see nothing. To my left stretched an expanse of brilliantly green, perfectly coiffed lawn dotted evenly with triangular trees, each one head-height and identical to the next. A group of men and women holding eggs in teaspoons were jumping in yellow sacks towards a stretch of tape strung between two poles. A perky instructor clapped and cheered.

A little further on, a dozen or so people were shuffling to the beat of an 80s pop track straining from invisible speakers, urged on by another instructor in yellow chinos and T-shirt, his face open and sweaty and excessively cheerful.

"That's it! And *right* one two three and *left* da-dum *da-dum* two three four … We're doing this as a *team*, people! You've got it!"

My guide slowed down just enough to turn a perfect pirouette, calling to me as she spun, "Morning jazzercise. That'll be you soon!"

She twirled and skipped forward again.

I scuffed after her. I can't remember thinking or feeling anything at this point. I was numb, and my slippers were a temporary distraction as they repeatedly made me stumble and lose footing. I had only ever used them in and around my house. Clearly they weren't intended for brisk walks in the afterlife.

We followed a gentle curve round to the left, passing several puffing joggers – mostly middle-aged men with paunches – and a fit young guide wearing a yellow sweatband to match his shorts and singlet. As they passed, he threw a brief but disturbingly wide smile in my direction. "Welcome!" he panted, with a jerky wave. "Hope you'll be – *pant* – joining us – *pant* – soon!"

It'll be a cold day in Hell, I thought, before the existential implications of entertaining this thought in my current setting made me swallow a sudden gob of nausea.

A two-storey office block came into view. We paused only long enough for me to read the sign on the front door:

Welcome! Please ring for service (Business hours only)

"Closed for now. Let's keep on!" My perky psychopomp resumed the relentless pace, leading me past the building and straight on to where the driveway funnelled to a narrower path lined on each side by trees identical to the ones I had seen earlier. The tall hedge on our right dipped lower and lower, then ended abruptly as we emerged onto a circular concourse paved with terracotta tiles. In the middle of the concourse a shrub crouched in a terracotta pot next to a giant signpost sprouting seven wooden arrows, each pointing down one of seven paths: **Citizen Cabins, Hallelujah Hall, Lake, Reception, Boogie Bar, God (500 metres), Toilets (6 am – 6 pm only).**

I craned my neck in an effort to catch a glimpse of the bar. I wasn't going to risk looking for God. I was apparently dead and in some sort of afterlife. My tenuous belief system was under enough strain.

We hurried on in the direction of the Citizen Cabins. The path led to another, larger concourse, this one surrounded by small prefabricated cabins of the kind set up temporarily at construction sites, in which workers would drink bad coffee and flick through porn magazines. Several paths led off from this concourse to, I presumed, more cabins.

Flick flack went my Heavenly Host's flag as she led off to the right, until she stopped at the third cabin. On the front door was a laminated sign bearing my name, along with the words "Car Accident", the date, and the number 291.

"Well, here you are!" Beaming, she dug a key from her pocket, bounced up two steps, turned the lock, and threw open the door, ushering me inside. "I trust you'll be comfortable. You'll find extra blankets in the wardrobe and toilet paper in the cupboard below the bathroom sink." She sniffed and consulted her watch. "Feel free to have a shower before breakfast. You have ten minutes, so – " she clapped her clipboard briskly against the door jamb " – chop chop! Have a nice day!" She handed me the key, which was attached to an enormous tag in the shape of a crown, then skipped out the door and started back in the direction we had come.

For a moment I could do nothing but stare at the picture on the wall opposite the front door. A black woman with bananas on her head stared off to my left. Her dress was an ochre and yellow riot of swirls, checks, diamonds, and dots. She looked pissed off.

My palm ached. I had been gripping the key tag so hard it had left a coronal indent. The tag read:

I WILL GIVE YOU THE KEYS OF THE KINGDOM OF HEAVEN
(Lost keys will incur a charge)

Next to the banana woman another door stood open, through which I glimpsed yellow tiles and a shower stall. Against the cabin's far right wall was a kitset wardrobe. To the left of the bathroom, filling the rest of the space, were a double bed, a chair, and a bedside cabinet with drawers. The bed, complete with yellow quilted duvet, looked comfortable enough. A small sign perched on the pillow, exhorting me to save water by reusing my towels. A glance into the bathroom, which was so tiny I would have to mimic a contortionist in order to sit on the toilet, revealed the usual accoutrements: a packaged shower cap and cheap detergent poured into small plastic bottles to pose as shampoo or body wash. The only thing that set the cabin apart from other anonymous motel rooms was the giant sign above the bed, which read, in Comic Sans:

WELCOME TO PARADISE! HAVE A NICE DAY! - GOD

The banana woman glowered.

I opened the wardrobe. Hanger upon hanger of yellow shellsuits crowded next to a narrow built-in shelving unit, which displayed various items of undergarments and socks. A full-length mirror alerted me to the fact that I was dressed in what appeared to be a paper gown. It was brilliantly white with a frilled collar, and it hung loosely about my body as if reluctant to be there. I raised an arm and sniffed. I stank of sweat and copper, faintly tinged with smoke. I gently touched the skin on my face, which appeared unblemished, if a little dusty. A solitary smear of dirt stretched from my left ear to what was left of my hairline. With some trepidation, I patted myself down, furtively opening the gown to assess the damage. My body was whole; unscathed and unscarred.

I was still wearing the tartan slippers. Had I forgotten to take them off that morning? And there were more pressing questions, such as: Why were there egg and spoon sack races in the afterlife? Would I really have to jog? Could I change the artwork in my cabin?

Is this all there is?

A slap of dizziness made me grip the edge of the wardrobe door, and my stomach jiggled apologetically from a sickly belch. I was, I decided, either deceased, or trapped in a nightmare featuring me as the main character in a Mitch Albom novel.

I didn't know which was worse.

3

My father is dead.

I can see the sun struggling, slow motion, limping its way across an empty sky. I can see beyond the sun, beyond the stars, beyond everything.

There's nothing there; nothing at all.

Maybe if I'd got up instead of ignoring him. Maybe if I'd gone with him and insisted on stopping at the dairy for a strawberry milk. Maybe if he'd washed his coffee mug instead of leaving it on the bench for me to wash like he always did. Maybe if I just lie down and go to sleep I'll wake up and it will fade like a bad dream, fleeing and screeching, daylight snapping at its heels.

It's cold, so very cold. My ice breath rises from my mouth, up and up, then pours back down, anointing my head, clutching at my heart, whispering along my arms to my fingers and through my pen to these words, making them crawl and scratch and bleed across the page.

My father is dead.

4

I couldn't be bothered showering, despite (or because of) the exhortation embossed on the shower stall door:

Remember: Cleanliness is next to Godliness!

I dressed, splashed water on my face, brushed my teeth with a small packaged toothbrush and toothpaste that tasted like chalk, and took a few moments to smooth down what hair I had left. I swept recalcitrant strands to the left, then the right. I could never make up my mind which side the part should be on. I sniffed again under my arms and decided I should have taken a shower after all. Death was no disinfector. Two quick swipes with an unfortunate flannel and I could put it off no longer. I slipped the door key in my trouser pocket – the crown made for an interesting landscape across my groin – and ventured out.

People were emerging from their own cabins and making their way, I presumed, to breakfast. Every single person, including me, was dressed in a yellow shellsuit. Plastic sweat catchers, I used to call them as I sneered at fat Americans spilling out of the cruise ships that docked at the port for two or three days during summer. I would vow that no matter what happened, no matter how sartorially desperate I became, even if all my clothes rotted away and left me naked and blinding in all my pasty glory, I would never, ever surrender to them.

The swish-swish of my thighs was deafening.

People walked around the concourse deliberately, silently. There was no interaction, no easing into a new morning with friendly greetings and yawns and gentle observations about sleep and the weather.

The air was precisely temperate. The light was strange, as if it were bottled. A vague, barely distinguishable tint of yellow wove its way through the blue expanse above. It was as if God had dripped just one or two pregnant pearls of yellow watercolour off the end of a giant brush, leaving them no avenue but a clandestine sigh across their azure backdrop.

When I was young, I had always wanted to look directly at the sun, despite being told by parents, teachers, and various white-coated scientific experts that it would ruin my eyesight and cause cancer. I would fashion a pinhole camera with two pieces of cardboard so that I could at least see the sun's projected image.

Here, I could stare straight at the ball of light and hold it in my sights without squinting or (hopefully) risking retinal damage. I could swear I saw flames leaping and curling and spitting off the surface, suspended in brilliant red and orange explosions of heat and gas. For a second, I was thrilled. Heaven had momentarily fulfilled its promise.

I drew my eyes away from the shock of the sun, back to the dead people around me. There was an even number of men and women, and everyone was looking straight ahead. Various ages were represented, although most were my age or older. I saw no children. One young man with hair to his shoulders, which were stooped in an apparent effort to minimise his considerable height, turned his head to look at me. *Around Andy's age and probably just as ghastly*, I thought before his eyes jerked away and he dug his hands deeper into his pockets. In front of him an elderly man and woman walked carefully together. The man reached for the woman's hand as we emerged onto the sign-posted concourse and made our way towards the path leading to the Hallelujah Hall. It struck me as a reach for safety rather than affection.

A few idling metres on smooth stone bordered by grass clipped to a dizzying precision, then the path dipped steeply and we were cocooned in an impossibly perfect tree tunnel, through which I glimpsed, on my right, a lake. The strange sun rippled and distorted in water just roused enough by a breeze for tiny laps to lend the surface a gentle relief. I would have found it almost pretty (although I wasn't a nature-loving man – too many enthusiastically ignorant people in khaki shorts and sensible boots for my liking) if I hadn't spotted the building squatting apologetically by the water's edge.

The single-storey Hallelujah Hall resembled a small-town community centre: wooden and last-resort. An obviously unused deck covered with rippled plastic roofing ran along the side adjacent to the water. It was dotted with tables and chairs and collapsed umbrellas, faded and stiff from sunlight and neglect. As we emerged from the tree tunnel and followed the path around to the front of the hall, which faced away from the lake, the smell of rubbish bins and burnt toast mingled with the faint strains of a keyboard and fragile drumming. What appeared to be an outhouse was tacked on to the building on the side that hadn't been visible from the path. Steam coughed from misted-up windows. The kitchen, perhaps.

The front door of the hall was crowned with a flashing neon sign, which shouted:

HALLELUJAH! (Mind the Step)

"Listen up. Do what you're told. If they ask you to get up and speak, just do it. Don't eat the pancakes, they taste like cowpats. And don't stare at the naked people."

The young man I had spotted earlier was suddenly walking beside me, looking straight ahead as he whispered out the side of his mouth. Around nineteen, lanky dirty-blonde hair, extremely large feet. He smelt of unwashed clothes and sweaty armpits. At least I wasn't alone in that regard, then. His yellow jacket crackled as he walked, and a disproportionate number of pens peeped out of the breast pocket.

Naked people? My mouth opened with a question, but he put a spindly finger to his lips and shook his head almost imperceptibly.

As we joined the queue approaching the door, I had a sudden flashback to a cruise I had once braved with my ex-wife. It was a few years after we were married, before Andy was born. The cracks had begun to appear in earnest, so like any good married couple we decided the best course of action was to pretend they weren't there. We booked an exorbitantly expensive holiday on a cruise ship in the unacknowledged hope that the structured activity and lack of escape routes would at once force us together and preclude any opportunity for deep and meaningful discussion.

The most vivid memory from that holiday – apart from the over-abundance of stupid American shuffle boarders – was the house band in the smorgasbord restaurant. It comprised a pianist, a double bass player, a drummer, and a singer (and I use the term loosely). They were all about ninety and wore black tuxedos, the shoulders of which were shiny from bad ironing and speckled with dandruff. For the entire duration of every meal, the singer shuffled and finger-clicked his way through a selection of cruise-ship standards (i.e. music that can only be played at sea because no continent would put up with it). As we disembarked on the last day, more estranged and unhappy than when we had boarded, I thought to myself that even if my marriage was flushing itself down the toilet, at least I never had to listen to that fucking house band ever again.

And so, it was with a sense of horrified déjà-vu that when I crossed the threshold of the Hallelujah Hall, the first thing I saw was a geriatric house band on a stage at the far end, tottering its way through Burt Bacharach's "Close to You". The singer seemed the only citizen immune to Heaven's wardrobe requirements: he sported a tuxedo jacket striped with every colour of the rainbow, and a bowtie to match.

The setting only added to my vertiginous dismay. This was my old high school hall all over again, only this time mostly yellow: wooden walls lined with faded banners, high windows you could only open with long metal sticks hooked at the ends, and the wooden stage with dusty (yellow) curtains and a lonely podium in the centre. The banners bore pictures of angels and trumpets and crosses and burning bushes and a giant blonde figure holding out his arms towards us, a spiky halo crowning his head like a silly summer hat. I presumed this to be God.

In front of the stage, on long trestle tables covered with white butcher's paper and dotted with the occasional bottle of tomato sauce or jug of milk, were bowls and platters of food and a couple of industrial toasters; the kind that suck your bread into their gaping fiery maws, then after an interminable period of time spit it out stunned and undercooked.

Heavenly Hosts, all just as yellow and perky as the one who had greeted me at the gates that morning, hovered near the food, occasionally stirring the contents of a bain-marie or fiddling with a toaster knob. My young, sweaty friend grabbed my elbow and steered me towards an almost empty table, plastic and round. As we took our seats, the band twanged and stumbled its way into a breathtakingly discordant version of "The Girl From Ipanema".

The table started to fill up. The elderly couple I had spied earlier took the two seats to my left. The woman, who was clutching a green handbag, said a quiet "Good morning" as she sat down, shrouding me in a dainty wave of lavender perfume. Her husband sat stiffly, staring precisely forward.

More people filed in, a number of them red-faced and freshly showered: the exercisers. With only half an hour to go until breakfast was over, it was clear most people were only arriving now.

The band wound up in a fumble of octogenarian drum rolls as one of the Heavenly Hosts, a man this time, skipped up the steps to the podium, tapped the microphone, and cleared his throat.

"Good morning everybody! What a beautiful day God has given us! And now for our nine am briefing. As you all know, it's not compulsory – " his eyes flicked quickly to the back of the hall " – but it's wonderful to see you all here." He beamed, scanning the 200 or so-strong crowd until his eyes settled on me. "Everybody, I would like to introduce our newest citizen. Mr Maurice Toogood, please stand up!" He started clapping loudly and the band broke into a snippet of "For He's a Jolly Good Fellow".

"Do it. Stand up," my young companion whispered. He poked me so hard in the thigh I jumped, and suddenly I was on my feet and every eye was on me. Not remotely like the days of school group visits to the library, when nearly every student was asleep, staring out the window, doodling, or snogging the student next to them instead of listening to me explain the Dewey Decimal System.

I had never been so riveting.

"We are *delighted* to welcome Maurice Toogood to our little slice of paradise!" trilled the young man. "In fact, it's the whole cake this morning!" He threw his arms wide as if to embrace the entire hall, then brought them together with a slap and pointed the tips of his fingers towards me. "I'm sure Maurice will fit right in. How about you tell us all a bit about yourself, Maurice?" He beamed. I coughed. Everyone was waiting.

"Um, hello." I reached up and coaxed my hair left, then right. "As the, um, young man said, I'm Maurice, and, ah, this is the last place … the last place not on Earth I thought I'd find myself. Ha, ha." The fluorescent lights clicked like tired cicadas. Someone coughed. I felt as out of place as Arthur in *The Hitchhiker's Guide to the Galaxy* (whose dressing gown had suddenly become strangely appealing in the face of Heaven's sartorial limitations). "Er, yes. Well. I'm looking forward to meeting you all." My voice cracked on "all", making me sound like a startled choir boy. "Excellent. Thanks very much." And I sat down.

There was a moment of awkward silence, punctuated by frantic applause from the Heavenly Host on the podium. The old woman on my left touched my arm and offered me a small smile. Then, in a clatter of cutlery and scraping of chairs, people started to rise and file towards the tables at the top of the hall. It was the standard sort of fare you'd expect at a church youth camp – cheap cereals and tinned fruit, messy piles of cold, overdone toast, jugs of sugary juice. The bain-maries held hash browns, baked beans, tomatoes and bacon, and pancakes.

I have no idea what I put on my plate; a slice of toast and a banana, I think. As I was walking back to my table, I noted that seven incredibly good-looking men, each of them dressed in white, were spaced at regular intervals along the back wall, on either side of the door. They stood motionless, their eyes wandering over the crowd. I scanned the line and recognised the dark-haired man from the gatehouse. Peter. His gaze slid over me, giving no indication that he remembered our brief encounter.

Everyone was going out of their way to avoid passing too close to the men. The Hosts scampered around and between the tables, clearing plates and wiping spills, but they kept their distance from the back wall.

I sat, my back to the men once more. Hairs on the back of my neck trilled.

"That was a very nice speech." The old woman on my left tapped my arm. "I couldn't do it when we got here. My husband had to speak for both of us."

I looked at her husband, who nodded once in my direction. Everything about him was buttoned up.

"Never was one for public speaking," I said with a complicated laugh. "Particularly when it's to dead people."

The woman laughed politely in return. "It takes a bit of getting used to." Her husband harrumphed and started to cut up an apple, placing perfectly symmetrical slices on his wife's plate.

"How long have you been here?" I asked him, dentally compromising my way through a slice of toast.

"Two months." His throat cut off the words as if keen to disown them. "Two months too long."

"Don't mind him; he didn't sleep well last night," said the woman, patting her husband on his forearm. "I'm Penelope, by the way. Welcome." She reached out, and we shook hands. Hers was papery and warm.

"I slept perfectly well, thank you," snapped Penelope's husband. "Apart from the kerfuffle next door at four am. And I know exactly what they were doing." He jerked his head towards the back of the room, then looked directly at me for the first time, furrowing a bushy cliff of eyebrow. He pointed his knife at me, stabbing at the air for emphasis. "Let me tell you something about this place. Watch out for…"

Three things happened at once. There was a slick movement at the back of the hall as two of the men in white moved closer to our table. Penelope gripped her husband's arm, her eyes wide. And my young companion poked me in the thigh again, so hard I was beginning to think he had a leg fetish.

"Look straight ahead. Eat," he whispered.

All chatter in the hall had stopped, and the whisper-rip of flesh parting from skin as I peeled my banana was deafening. I chewed and peeled, chewed and peeled, until smatterings of small conversations resumed.

"What wa – " I started to ask, but the word became a dribbly gurgle as two people approached the podium.

The woman had ebony hair to her waist and eyes the colour of violets. Her hips traced an obscene gesture as she walked, and she knew it. The man had a receding hair line, but his bone structure suggested he had once been movie star handsome. He tripped slightly as he approached the microphone and his "Oopsie daisies!" was a magnified shout. He righted himself, gave a guffaw in the woman's direction – she looked studiously the other way – and dropped his notes.

They were both stark naked.

The man turned and bent over to retrieve his papers and the hall recoiled with a collective gasp. As he straightened he banged his head on the edge of the podium, and in a well-practised move the woman grabbed the notes, shunted him aside with one of those hips, and leaned into the microphone.

"Good morning, everyone. Please excuse my husband." She sniffed and shook out her hair. My loins clutched. "Today's activities include egg and spoon races on the front meadow; charades, limbo, and shuffleboard right here in the hall; and a nature walk around the lake." She consulted her notes. "The chef will also be leading a 'Carve Biblical Figurines Out of Fruit and Vegetables' workshop in the kitchen after lunch, and – "

"No apples involved!" guffawed the man. "Badum-tish!" His right hand struck his wife's naked buttock with an audible crack.

There was a smattering of awkward laughter. The woman looked as if she had swallowed a wasp.

"May I remind everyone that Michael's rowing regatta is tomorrow," she continued, straining away from her spouse as he bobbed eagerly from foot to foot. "Those competing will be assigned to a team, and we look forward to seeing everyone there. We hope you have an enjoyable day." She tapped her papers briskly together on the podium. As she crossed the stage she stared for a long second right into my face. I could have stared at those eyes all day, almost as much as the delights beneath them. Her hips disappeared behind the yellow curtains as her husband trotted after her.

"Activity leaders. The man's an idiot. Her, not so much." The young man yanked the flaccid banana peel from my hand – I had been gripping on for dear life – and pulled me up and towards a side door. He had inhaled his breakfast like a whale engulfing plankton.

"Let's go. I need some air."

As we made our way outside, I turned to see Peter staring at me without blinking.

We followed a gravel path down to the lake shore, where canoes were lined up along a small jetty, crude numbers painted on their hulls. My companion loped off to the left, following the path almost halfway around the lake – we glimpsed the far shore periodically through perfectly ornamental tree formations – before stopping at a wooden bench which, strangely, had its back to the water, overlooking an exactly circular clearing littered with cigarette butts.

"The disciples," he sighed. "They came here to play poker every Friday and couldn't be bothered cleaning up afterwards." I helped him haul the bench around until it faced the lake. Then we sat.

"I'm Kit. Cabin two-four-nine." He stuck his hand out in a strangely formal gesture. I grasped it. He had a good handshake, firm and short. And best of all, no sweaty palm, despite the armpits. I was desperate to ask a million questions, but I didn't know where to start.

It seemed too rude at this point to ask him how he had died. He looked like most of Andy's university friends: young men and women who believed it desperately cool to dress in ripped and smelly clothes, live in even smellier flats with mushrooms growing behind the bath, sit and talk ignorantly about literature and philosophy in the Student Union café all day, and regularly consider topping themselves due to the angst of it all.

And then he dropped a bombshell.

"I knew your daughter. Before I died, I mean. I knew Andy."

5

Monday morning

Dear Dad,

I pretended not to hear you when you yelled at me to get up. I knew I would miss my first lecture, but I really didn't give a shit. I had a new short story to work on, and I write best in the mornings, when you're gone and the place is silent, ready and waiting for my muse to come and whisper to me. She didn't, of course. A police officer knocking on our door made her flee so far away I'm not sure if she'll ever come back.

So I'm on my own. My dressing gown is tight around me. I've picked up my pen and I'm at my desk and the birds are singing, and Mrs Hardy from next door is walking along the boundary, sniffing. Lunatic.

I have to write something.

Aunt Fleur is in the kitchen. I can hear the faint clink of objects being picked up and put down and picked up again.

I was in the shower when the doorbell rang, the water raining down on my head, drowning my hair. ("Putting out the fire", as you used to say, as if water could magically remove the red. It never did.) I didn't hear it at first, but the police rang again and again.

I opened the door in two towels: one around my body, barely joining ends, and one around my hair. A man and a woman. Uniformed. For a brief, deluded second, I thought they had found out about all the half-written stories under my bed and had come to tell me to finish them. But I think I knew the truth, which was more rational, and more terrifying.

The man scrolled through the landline contact list for Aunt Fleur's number. When she arrived she sort of whimpered, then put her arm around me and hugged me very tight. Her fingers left bruises on my shoulder. She's going to stay with me for a while at your place. At least until the funeral.

I can't decide whether to wear my jeans or a skirt. Should I wear my jeans or a skirt?

Mum's coming home. I couldn't make out whether she sounded angry or sad when I spoke to her. I don't imagine the ashram gives refunds. She asked me to tell Aunt Fleur to pick up her black kaftan dress from the drycleaners. The drycleaners or the dressmaker, I can't remember which. Why can't I remember which?

Aunt Fleur said there will probably be some people coming over today, when they hear what's happened. Why? Nobody comes over any other time. Nosy bastards. Will they expect coffee? I don't know how to make coffee.

I can't decide if I should wear my jeans, or a skirt.

How does it feel when your father dies? Surreal, like you're suddenly the star of a macabre stage show and you've forgotten all your lines and the spotlights are blinding you and all the makeup on your face is running because you've sweated so much, or cried. And the show must go on, and no one applauds at the end.

Andy

6

I was so stunned by Kit's revelation that the first thing to come out of my mouth was probably not the most appropriate. "Not in the biblical sense, I hope?"

Kit looked at his enormous feet and his ears reddened. My heart was racing. It was bizarre to hear my daughter's name uttered by a stranger sitting by the side of a lake in Heaven.

I tried again. "How did you know her?"

"Last year of high school. We moved to Bressington in the summer holidays, so I was only there for that one year. We moved a lot because of Dad's job; I'd already been to three schools." He scuffed at the dirt, his shoulders hunched. "I sat next to her in English sometimes. She used to write amazing stories. And poems. I used to wish I could write like her. She was incredible." His ears turned a deeper shade of red.

Incredible? At writing? Andy? I had no idea she was good at writing – or anything for that matter, except sleeping and ignoring me. Maybe he had the wrong person.

She and I had argued the previous night, long and hard. Even if we hadn't, she would have still ignored me. Andy was in her first year of a law degree. Perhaps, I thought to myself when I first realised I was dead, shuffling off the mortal coil before having to tell people my daughter was a lawyer wasn't such a bad thing.

She'd been staying with me the week before I died because Robyn had left on an Elizabeth Gilbert-inspired "self-discovery" voyage to an ashram in the industrial estate out by the airport. I joked to my colleagues (as much as one can joke with librarians) that my ex-wife's trip was more *Eat, Eat, Eat* than *Eat, Pray, Love*. A photo Robyn had emailed to Andy (since when did ashrams have email?) showed she had packed on at least five kilos, all around the beam. Made my day.

"Andy?" I asked now. "You're sure? Long hair, a bit chubby..." I made the shape of a beach ball with my hands, then downgraded to a soccer ball.

Kit stole a glance at my stomach. "I didn't notice if she was chubby or not," he said, "but her hair was red. Like fire."

Andy's hair. Thick amber swatches that flowed over her shoulders as she slept, trailing fiery strands that clogged the shower and tested the vacuum cleaner's patience. It was my mother's hair. As soon as Andy had hit puberty she trapped it every day in a low ponytail. I preferred it out. I think I told her so once.

I felt a prickle of irritation. "Were you a bloody law student too?"

Kit balled his fists and stuck them in his pockets. "More into computers, me. Didn't go to university. We moved again, to Australia. Dad said it was our last chance to get ahead." He coughed. "Couldn't really afford uni."

Silence sat tentatively between us. On the far shore of the lake the trees parted and an old man with a beard almost down to his knees strode to the water's edge. He had an intense, feverish look on his face as he flung his arms wide, a stout wooden staff in one hand. He threw his head back, closed his eyes, and waited a few seconds. Then he looked down at the lake and his expression morphed from surprise to frustration, to anger, and then sadness. This behaviour was repeated several times.

"Ignore him," said Kit. "He's always doing it. Can't for the life of him figure out why it doesn't work here." He took a cigarette out of his pocket, lit up with a match, and inhaled. He held the smoke in until I thought he'd swallowed it, then slowly released a lazy cloud that curled above him and out towards the lake.

"How did you know I was here?" I ventured. "And how did you

know I'm … I mean was … Andy's father?"

Kit looked uncomfortable. "Um. I found out you were coming. I recognised your name. And I saw your photo, so I knew what you looked like." He coughed again. "You look a bit like Andy."

I shifted stray strands of hair back and forth; greying strands that had only ever whispered faintly of amber. *He knew I was coming.* My mind tried to wrap itself around that, then sighed and gave up. I tried another question.

"Is this really Heaven?"

Kit took another long drag and released it. "As far as I know. Quite a mind-fuck, right? I expected more angels and singing and God and stuff. And I'm still lactose intolerant. Not exactly paradise." He offered me the cigarette, but I waved it away.

"Are the Heavenly Hosts angels? And what about those guys dressed in white?" I nodded back the way we had come. "The ones standing at the back of the hall."

Kit paused. "I'm not sure yet. I call them the White Guys." He sucked on his cigarette and stared at the lake. "The Heavenly Hosts, I don't think they're in charge exactly, but they get a kick out of telling the citizens what to do."

"Is that what we are? Citizens?"

"That's what they call us." Kit flicked ash on the ground. "And don't ask me why everyone's dressed in yellow. Everything's fucking yellow here." He waved his hand around, despite the fact that mercifully, nothing in the clearing was yellow except for our clothing. "It's nauseating. I refused to wear the trousers."

Now there's a line I would never hear my ex-wife utter, I thought.

"Well, I refused at first," he continued, "but since I arrived in a white paper choir-boy gown I had no choice, so … yeah." He shrugged.

"Same here," I said, "but I still had my slippers on. They're tartan." I looked down at my newly acquired yellow sneakers. I had left the scuffed slippers in my cabin. Much as my feet had protested at the very thought of donning yellow, it was better than falling flat on my face.

"Are all the famous people here?" I ventured. "Ghandi? Elvis? The Gibb brothers?" I asked this last one with real interest. When Andy was born people would joke we only needed Barry to complete the family. Robyn and I hadn't even clicked when we'd named her Andrea. After that I always had a bit of a thing for the Bee Gees.

"Haven't seen any of them. Looked for Kurt Cobain and Jim Morrison and Amy Winehouse but there's no book for … no sign of any of them. And another thing: there's none of my relatives – grandparents, great-grandparents, other dead people I might know. I don't know anyone except you. I've asked some other citizens and they don't know anyone either. I thought you were meant to be reunited with your whole family and stuff when you died." He puffed out a sigh with the smoke. "Tell you what though, lots of people from the Bible are here. And they're all fucking loony. Like Adam and Eve in there." He nodded back towards the Hallelujah Hall. "Joseph in that god-awful jacket; he can't sing for shit." He gazed across the lake. "And old Moses."

The old man was still bobbing up and down, shaking his fist alternately at lake and sky. Kit kicked at an abandoned cigarette butt.

I had a rudimentary knowledge of the Bible, of course. I guess you have to if you're a librarian. I knew about Adam and Eve, and Noah's Ark, and Joseph and the Amazing Technicolor Dreamcoat (I may be mixing genres here), and Jesus and the Devil. But now I was being told by a dead teenager that these biblical figures were real, and they were *here*. In the flesh (an expression more applicable to some than others). I scratched my head. This was becoming more surreal by the minute. Then I asked what I suppose is the most important question to ask if you find yourself in Heaven.

"Where's God? Have you seen him?"

"Nope. Went to Cocktails with God last week, but he wasn't there. On holiday, apparently. Adam stood in for him. Now that's one cocktail party I won't forget in a hurry."

"And Jesus?"

Kit shook his head. "No one's even mentioned him. You'd think he'd at least turn up for cocktails. Father and son solidarity and all that."

I swivelled to watch as he got up and walked to the far end of the clearing. He reached into a tree and pulled out an empty beer bottle. Taking a final drag on his cigarette, he slotted the butt into the bottle's neck.

"Here's another thing," he said, walking back to the bench. "People keep on disappearing. One day they're at breakfast, next they're not. Matthew and Mark went missing after lawn bowls last Friday. Then all the other disciples – except Peter. He's been a White Guy for a while now. Oh, and one other's still here."

"Peter's the one I saw at the gates. When I arrived."

Kit nodded, then sat down close to me and leaned in, lowering his voice. "I think they've escaped. The people who've disappeared. They've found a way out of here."

Across the lake, Moses threw his staff to the ground and jumped up and down, yelling indistinguishably, spittle flying. He made an obscene gesture at the sky and stomped off through the trees.

Kit tossed the bottle into a perfectly symmetrical shrub. It settled with a leafy thump. "We'd better get back too. They'll come looking for us soon." He stood up. "We can talk later if you want."

"What do we do now, then?" My head was aching from the pressure of countless unasked questions.

Kit's face darkened. "Games."

7

Monday, late afternoon

Dear Dad,

All I can think about is that poem by Dylan Thomas about not going gentle into that good night and raging against the dying of the light:

> *And you, my father, there on the sad height,*
> *Curse, bless, me now with your fierce tears, I pray.*
> *Do not go gentle into that good night*
> *Rage, rage against the dying of the light.*

I say this, over and over. And I'm thirsty, like, all the time. I'm drinking glass after glass of water and it's never enough. My feet are cold.

The thing is, I can't imagine you raging about anything.

There have been quite a few visitors already. I'm surprised; I didn't think you had many friends. Turns out most of them were people from the library. Maybe they just wanted a free lunch. That weird boss of yours was even weirder today. That freaky eye of hers kept swivelling, like Mad-Eye Moody's in Harry Potter. She kept saying, right up close to me until I thought I was going to gag, "I can't believe I'll never see his face again."

I can't even picture your face. I try to place you in my mind, to formulate some sort of order, some diagram of death, and there's just a white mask where your face should be.

I told Aunt Fleur this, and she put her arms round me and held on

41

like a drowning person.

The other guy survived. He's in intensive care. Apparently he'd stolen the car and didn't even have a valid licence. One of the cops told me this. I don't think she was supposed to. She held my hand and got my sweatshirt for me from my room when I said I was cold. She held it above my head as I slipped my arms into it. Then she crouched down in front of me and tucked the hair behind my ears, like Mum used to do when I was little. Trying to tuck away the hurt.

And you, my father.

Rage against the dying of the light.

My father. The words feel weird to write, like they're in a foreign language, or a dead one.

Andy

8

In the days leading up to our biannual team-building workshop I would break out in hives and cold sweats, often simultaneously. Interacting with others, in its varied and excruciating daily guises, was an imposition I avoided when I could. That was the one good thing about being a librarian: I could spend most of my day dealing with books instead of with the people who read them.

I didn't have a formal qualification in librarianship, but I'm reasonably confident that twenty-one years, five months, one week, and two days working at the Bressington Heights Community Library entitled me to my laminated name badge:

Maurice Toogood
Ask me, I'm a Librarian!

"First things first," I would kick off the library's summer holiday seminar, *So You Want to Write a Book*. "If you can't get the basics right – good grammar, proper punctuation, ability to string a halfway-decent sentence together – then don't even bother. The world doesn't need umpteen more amateur writers who think they're God's gift." By the time I had finished, attendees would be slumped in their seats, jotter pads abandoned, a haunted glaze in their eyes: terror punctuated by capitulation. No one left with their dreams intact.

My boss didn't even know I could write when she assigned me to that particular seminar. Head Librarian Felicity Bonmot was the same age as me – fifty-two when I died – with a short grey bob, severe halitosis, and an exceptional double chin. When she spoke she had the disconcerting habit of placing emphasis on words that didn't warrant it.

"You'll *be* fine, Maurice," she said with a wave of her hand when I protested. "They don't want *an* expert. Bored housewives *with* too *much time* on their hands and *a* notebook full of adverbs; they *just* want out of the house for *an* hour."

At least I didn't get *So You Want to be a Librarian.* They'd be scraping dead people off the floor.

Speaking of which.

The rest of my first day in Heaven passed in an excruciating blur of egg and spoon races, charades, and team limbo competitions. I wasn't sure how much of what Kit had told me I could trust. Granted, I had always had trust issues, but when a dead teenager tells you that he knew your daughter before he died and, moreover, that he suspects the twelve disciples and others are escaping from Heaven, trust issues are, quite frankly, an asset rather than a liability.

As I lurched, incredulous and sweaty, from game to race, I observed the hierarchies of Heaven. As Kit had indicated, the Heavenly Hosts were loud and chest-puffy but seemed to lack real authority. They outlined the rules of each activity and zealously supervised, but I noticed that when one of the citizens, an old man with a long beard and a limp, refused to join in the sack races, they huffed and puffed and banged pencils on clipboards but could ultimately only watch as the defector limped to the nearest tree and leaned against it, arms crossed.

"That's Jacob," said Kit, as we hopped and stumbled to the start line. "He's always arguing about something. Apparently he and his brother got into a fight in the bar a while ago. Smashed a lot of bottles. Jezebel was furious. They were probably fighting over her; she should have been flattered."

"Who's Jezebel?" I asked, as a Heavenly Host blew her starter's whistle.

"You'll find out," called Kit, as he bounced ahead of me, sack flapping.

The White Guys, as Kit referred to them, were a different story. Even Jacob hobbled back to join in a late afternoon game of Twister when one of them approached, a glorious smile on his perfect face. When the game was over, a number of us left tangled and undignified, noses and elbows in one another's armpits and crotches, he drew aside one of the female Heavenly Hosts, pulling a notebook out of his pocket as he did so. He seemed to ask her a series of questions, which she answered with her eyes to the ground. The White Guy made notes as she spoke. At one stage he turned to look at Jacob, who stared back defiantly.

When the strange sun started its gorgeous descent, yellow shot through with orange and fire, games were declared over. Most of the citizens, Kit included, headed straight back to their cabins, presumably to rest or shower before dinner. But death hadn't removed my dependence on alcohol to obliterate a bad day, and I could feel the saliva pooling in my mouth as I followed a signpost to the Boogie Bar.

The path wound down a steep slope towards the lake then veered off to the right, meandering through a grassy copse towards a low yellow building. The grass was blindingly green. I bent down and looked closer. It was the artificial turf favoured by rich middle-agers the world over. Fake lawns, cosmetic surgery, and in-home gourmet catering: they wanted perfection but they didn't want to work for it.

There had been a patch of this turf outside the Bressington Heights Community Library, in the tiny back yard accessible only through a door by the toilets. The door was regularly left open by Katrina, the part-time book shelver, who could shelve for no longer than five minutes before taking a fifteen-minute cigarette break. No one else ever went out there except for old Mrs Henderson's geriatric chihuahua, which would slip through the door while its owner was checking out her Barbara Cartlands. It would crap in odorous nuggets, leeching patches of turf of its brilliant green until the courtyard looked like it was slowly succumbing to vitiligo.

Straightening up, I looked around me. Every tree was exactly the same: same height, same circumference, same configuration of branches and leaves. There was no moss or lichen on the perfectly straight trunks. There were no twigs or leaves on the ground. I put my nose to a nearby tree and inhaled. Nothing. There was no earthy pungency, no tang of sap and fresh wood.

There were no flowers, anywhere.

The silence was suddenly disconcerting, and with a start I realised that since arriving in Heaven I hadn't heard bird song. I squinted at the trees and stared at the sky. No birds. I felt unbalanced, and curiously bereft. It wasn't as if I had loved the bloody things when I was alive. In fact, a tūī that had learnt to imitate the microwave and did so with astonishing persistence outside my bedroom window most mornings had been the bane of my existence. I threw a paperweight at it once, which missed the tūī but hit Mrs Hardy's car bonnet with a gleeful clang. My neighbour rushed out in her curlers and nightie, puffing and tut-tutting. The tūī flew up into the pōhutukawa (which, with its red flowers relentlessly falling and clogging up my gutters every summer, was another bane of my existence), and eyed me primly. From then on it imitated the sound of Mrs Hardy tut-tutting.

I did a slow 360-degree turn. Heaven was a panorama of blandness. There were no signs of life other than the bleeding, plummeting sun and me – and I was dead. Feeling queasy, I stepped off the artificial grass back onto the main path and continued walking towards the promise of alcohol and temporary memory loss.

Despite the disconcerting landscape, I was optimistic. I was imagining a place much like my local Irish pub: dark, enfolding, "Whisky in the Jar" setting the scene, the stale but not unpleasant smell of spilt beer ushering you in towards a warm welcome and a cold pint. There might even be bar snacks.

Thinking fondly of peanuts and the bouncy few hours I had spent with an Irish barmaid a few years previously, I opened one of the double doors and stepped inside. The door clicked shut behind me. I adjusted the front of my trousers.

I should have realised that my being the only person winding down the hill towards the bar had been a sign. For a start, it wasn't dark. It was so *not* dark that my retinas screeched. Before me was a room the size of a tennis court, and every inch of it was yellow. Not just the stock-standard yellow dotted throughout Heaven. This yellow had an attitude. It shouted. Every inch sparkled.

Round tables were spaced evenly, each covered with a plastic tablecloth. Yellow chairs surrounded the tables, none of them occupied. In the centre of each table was a shimmering gold statue about a foot high. A table close to the door held a beaming cherub playing a harp, its genitals discretely covered by a swathe of gold lamé. Another boasted a cross, mercifully empty. As my eyes became accustomed to the glare, I spotted a pair of wings, a winged chariot, the Ark of the Covenant (I was a huge Indiana Jones fan), a crown of thorns, and a Christmas tree with random decorations sticking out in every direction. There was also a happy little chap that looked suspiciously like a Buddha.

In the back left-hand corner, on a small semi-circular platform, stood a karaoke machine, complete with yellow microphones. Behind it was a sign:

Sing Your Praise to the Lord! (Limit TWO songs per person)

Three of the walls were striped with fairy light curtains that winked on and off at a dizzying speed. In a blank space someone had painted in giant gold lettering, outlined in black to make it stand out from the yellow wall:

Wine Was Water Until Jesus Got His Hands On It!

I looked down. The carpet was a dizzy swirl of paisley clouds. I looked up. The roof was painted with a bad imitation of Michelangelo's *The Creation of Adam.*

Along the fourth wall, facing the door, ran a long bar with shelves on the wall behind it, holding glasses, bottles, cocktail shakers, and jars of sliced lemon and yellow glacé cherries. Above the bar flashed an enormous golden neon sign suspended by gold chain, five of its letters cracked and light-less:

Welc me to th Boogie Bar! Th nk God for the Holy Sp it!

Bryan Adams's "Heaven" whined thinly through discount-store speakers.

A door in the wall behind the bar thwacked open, and a woman with a tea towel over her shoulder wrestled a large cardboard box through the doorway. She wore a red strapless dress. She looked like the singer who had been married to Kurt Cobain. Earthy, but at the compost end of the scale. Her lipstick was slightly smeared, and a tangle of wild hair was caught up in an old rubber band.

She dropped the box behind the bar with a grunt. As she straightened up she saw me.

"Can I help you?" She made little attempt to sound welcoming.

"Um. I'd like a drink, perhaps?"

"No shit, Sherlock. That's usually why people come to a bar. Beer?" She started towards a glass-doored fridge, grabbing the tea towel off her shoulder and flinging it on the bar. It landed on a bowl of nuts.

I weaved my way between the cherub, the cross, and Noah's Ark.

"A Southern Comfort, if you have it."

She stopped abruptly and turned towards me, eyeing me in a slow upwards sweep. "Southern Comfort? I wouldn't have picked it." She reached up to a high shelf, one breast nearly popping out of her dress. She made no effort to adjust it as she placed a bottle on the bar and reached for a glass. She poured, spilling a little on her hand. "Do you want a cherry with that?" She stuck her index finger in her mouth and slowly sucked.

I blinked. "No thanks. Just the Southern Comfort, straight up. No ice."

"You new? I haven't seen you in here before."

"Just got here," I said. It sounded like I had just caught the shuttle from the airport.

The woman gestured around her. "It didn't used to be like this. It used to look like a real bar should. Smoky, an edge of mystery. Lots of dark corners. I had nothing to do with the new décor."

"Who did?" I asked.

She shrugged. "Who knows? No one ever tells me anything. Wanted me to dress in yellow, too. Fuck that, I said. Not to God, clearly, but I said it to Adam. It'll be a cold day in Hell when you get me out of this red dress, I said." She roared with laughter, tipping her head back. I could see her uvula trembling in the back of her throat.

She placed the glass in front of me, still chuckling. "There you are, Mr Southern Comfort. I hope it gives you some. Actually," she said, with the fake spontaneity of someone who always knew she would, "I might just join you." She poured herself a large shot, hers with ice, and we clinked glasses. Led Zeppelin's "Stairway to Heaven" took over from Bryan Adams. The woman groaned. "Oh, for Christ's sake. I told him to put another compilation together. Listen to this enough times it'll drive you to drink." She roared again. Her breasts bobbed alarmingly.

I sipped and perched awkwardly on a golden bar stool. "Do you run this place?" I ventured.

"Run the bar? Ha! Not fucking likely. I take my orders, just like everyone else." She came round to my side of the bar and pulled up a stool. As she climbed onto it the split in her dress parted, revealing an alarming amount of thigh. I got the impression she didn't mind in the slightest.

"We're all under the thumb now," she continued, mimicking the words with her hand. "Well and truly. Put a foot wrong, they're down on you like a tonne of bricks." Her face darkened a little. "It didn't used to be like this," she said again.

I frowned. "What do you mean?"

She crossed her legs and the split widened. "You'll find out soon enough. Just do what you're told, and you'll be OK. It's what I do." She smiled. "Most of the time." She stood up again and walked to the table with the cherub. "This one's new." She ripped the lamé cloth off to reveal moulded plastic. "Sure enough," she sighed. "Invariably disappointing."

I looked round at the other statues. "Isn't a Christmas tree a little out of place? Not exactly biblical, is it?"

The woman raised an arched eyebrow. "That's the burning bush. Did you not notice the 'Christmas tree' was on fire?"

"Ah," I said, embarrassed. Flames, then. Not cheap tinsel. "Well, what's with the Buddha? Isn't he a little blasphemous, given the setting?"

The woman downed her drink in one gulp and started to pour herself another. "Come one, come all, I say." She belched. "It's not like Buddha was an atheist. Anyway, God's not here, so who cares?"

"Where's he gone?"

A naked man appeared in the doorway behind the bar. Adam was rubbing his wet hair with a towel, partly obscuring his face. "Can't keep away from the drink for one minute, you naughty little minx. Come on, we've got time for…" He pulled the towel away from his face, and, seeing me, stopped abruptly.

This time, I stared for as long as I wanted. He had the most perfectly smooth skin I had ever seen, fiercely black hair, and eyes like emeralds. He looked – and this is the only way I can describe it – newly minted. I glanced up at the painting on the ceiling. He bore more than a passing resemblance to the naked man stretching out a lazy hand to meet God's. (Is it just me, or when you see that painting do you just itch to scribble a speech bubble above God, saying, "Pull my finger"?)

I raised my glass. "Afternoon."

Adam recovered quickly. "Afternoon, yes. Yes. I was just coming to check if Jezebel here had time to …" his eyes lighted on the box Jezebel had carried though earlier "… help me carry another box of chips. Yes, that's it, another box. Jezebel? A box?"

Jezebel leaned on the bar, swaying slightly. She took another sip. "I'm through with physical exertion for one day. Perhaps if you're still keen you could … do it yourself?" She winked at me.

I stood up. "I can help. Where's your box?"

Jezebel snorted. Adam held his hands up in front of his chest, palms outward. "Oh, no no no no no, you sit back down and enjoy your drink. No hurry, no hurry. I'll fetch it myself, not a problem." He cast a pointed look at Jezebel. "I'll see you later?"

"Maybe," she said. She put out a hand to touch my shoulder. "Now, where were we?"

The naked man backed out, looking furious, and the door closed firmly.

Jezebel roared once more, then gulped her second drink and banged the empty glass smartly on the bar. She stood and adjusted her cleavage. "Treat 'em mean, keep 'em keen. That's one to live by. Unfortunately, I'm not the only one who does." She suddenly looked serious. "Watch your step. Do what you're told. And don't trust anyone. Back in a tick." Jezebel kissed me juicily on the lips and disappeared behind the bar and out the door.

"Knocking on Heaven's Door" came on the stereo. I stared at the cherub's exposed plastic moulding, then poured myself another drink and ate a cherry.

9

Monday night

Dear Dad,

When the policeman told me you had died, I didn't feel anything much; I was numb. Aunt Fleur said this was a "perfectly normal" response. Then she suggested that I write stuff down to help me "sort out my thoughts". She said I should write what I remember about you – the good stuff as well as the bad stuff. I don't think I have much of the former, to be honest. I told her I had already written two letters to you. This made her cry. Then she said that writing letters was a good thing, a brave thing, and that if I wrote just like I was talking to you, it could be "very healing".

Whatever.

I remember sitting in the shrink's office after the divorce (Mum made me go every week for a month, remember? It made her feel better about my suffering) and him telling me that divorce was like death, and me replying, "How come they're not dead, then?" and you sort of laughing when I told you about it. I didn't want you to laugh.

The shrink also told me that the one thing divorce had over death was that it wasn't too late to say how you really felt.

I remember telling you that. You grunted and said, "Believe me, your mother hasn't stopped telling me how she really feels about me for years. She'll probably carry on telling me after I'm dead. She'll write me bloody letters and post them: Maurice Toogood, C/- The Afterlife."

I remember thinking that I didn't really blame her.

I remember one night when I must have been about six. I remember the pony duvet on my bed and Gerda the rag doll. I was crying and crying, and Mum came into my room to comfort me. I remember pushing her away and yelling that all I wanted was "my Daddy". But I bet you wouldn't remember that.

I can't remember anything else. I keep telling myself you died this morning. This Morning, like the title of a movie. It feels like I'm in a movie. Everything has a haze around it, indistinct and edgeless. I feel like I'm hovering by the ceiling, watching people come and go, watching myself write this. My hand is shaking. I feel panicky and I'm breathing really fast, like I'm running and running. A guy from your work – the one with the weird name – cracked a bad joke, but it was good as well, and I laughed until my stomach hurt and I had to vomit.

I'm going to put this in an envelope and post it. Maurice Toogood, C/- The Afterlife. Why the hell not.

Andy

10

Books were my mother's love affair. She spent money on them as soon as my father, who was a practical and unscholarly man, could earn it. The house groaned with books. My father tried to cull them from time to time when my mother was out, but she could sniff the deception of relocated words as soon as she walked in the door. I would go on mini missions with her to "find the lost books" while my father seethed in the front room. On our searches my mother would cling to me like a woman drowning, urgently whispering how much she needed me, how clever I was, how I must show her where he had hidden them. For her, I would have searched forever, for all the books in the universe.

You would have thought, then, that being a librarian was the perfect career for me. You would have thought wrong. Librarianship, I discovered, was simply cataloguing and tidying dressed up in a fancy name, with a few books thrown in.

Tuesday mornings had been "Safer Workplaces Together" mornings at the Bressington Heights Community Library. Felicity insisted that we set aside an hour every Tuesday to ensure the library was "fit for purpose".

"*Now* come on people. We *simply* must tape down *the* section *of* carpet next to *the* men's toilet. One *of* these days some child is going *to* trip and cut open *their* chin."

In her office she kept a large metal container on which she had taped a laminated sign bearing the instruction:

HEALTH and SAFETY: DO not TOUCH without THE express permission OF head LIBRARIAN FELICITY Bonmot

Every Tuesday she would bring it to the front desk and place it in front of her as she lectured on the risks inherent in librarianship. Occasionally she would tap it briskly with her pen to emphasise a point. I had no idea what was in there. I'm betting no breath freshener.

One Tuesday morning when I was feeling particularly pissed off – perhaps Andy had eaten the last slice of bread – I made the mistake of suggesting that it wasn't actually all that dangerous to read and check out books, and that perhaps our time would be better spent sorting and shelving. Felicity's chin shook alarmingly as she turned and pinned her gaze on me. This was always a little disconcerting, as she had one eye that looked straight ahead and one that swivelled off to the right like an errant schoolboy. An inattentive pupil, one might say. Hardacre, fresh out of university and not yet worn down by the reality of fulltime librarianship, used to refer to her as Bung-Eyed Boss Lady when she was out of earshot. (Yes, Hardacre. His parents clearly hated him.)

"Since you are *of* that opinion, Maurice, I *am* sure you won't mind using *the* stepladder *to* ensure that all the files on the *highest shelves* are safely arranged and *do* not threaten to tumble down on *an* unsuspecting patron." Felicity sniffed. "Please ensure *the* rungs are wiped down with disinfectant after *you* have finished. As *we* both well know, slippery *rungs* lead *to* ruin."

Hardacre sniggered. One eye swivelled in his direction. It was 9:10 am.

This was my life.

Whether Tuesday in Heaven was turning out any better was debatable. I had skipped dinner the night before (that's if you don't count around fifty glacé cherries and two slices of lemon in the company of an increasingly drunk Jezebel, who eventually slapped me hard on the backside and stuck her wet tongue briefly but comprehensively down my throat before tottering behind the bar and collapsing on a pallet of tea towels. The woman can snore), making my gently tipsy way back to my cabin just as the last rays of light loosened their grip. After a quick shower I went to bed early, stomach lurching, and woke to a sunny morning, precisely identical to the previous one.

During breakfast, which was once again accompanied by Heaven's hellish house band, I wondered what Andy might be doing. A small, secret part of me questioned if she cared at all that I was dead. I smothered the thought immediately by getting worked up over Robyn's selfishness. I hoped that she had caught the first bus back from her money-sucking incense pit. I didn't want proof of her grief (believe me, there would be precious little), but rather of her ability to put her daughter's feelings before her own for once. I hoped that Fleur would stay with Andy to act as an antidote to Robyn's histrionics. I also hoped she would give the house a bloody good clean, because apart from the driveway, I had left it looking like a tip.

Kit shovelled in his breakfast at our table near the set of double doors that opened onto the sorry excuse for a deck and the lake beyond. He was a smelly teenager and not my idea of the perfect restaurant companion, but he was the only person I had really talked to in Heaven (besides Jezebel, but endless sexual innuendo does not necessarily a conversation make), and he had known my daughter. For now, I would eat with him. Through the trees I glimpsed two Heavenly Hosts in yellow motorboats, towing large canoes to the far end of the lake. Anxiety hovered, making me lose my appetite. Given the appearance of the porridge, that wasn't necessarily a bad thing, but I couldn't shake the feeling that I was destined for one of those canoes, and that nothing good would come of it.

After we had scraped our plates and stacked them on the table next to the kitchen, Kit and I made our way outside. There was a covered porch just outside the front door, one wall of which was dominated by a large blackboard. The heading, permanently etched across the top, said **Daily Notices**. There was no chalk on the lip just below the board. Perhaps the threat of graffiti attacks was deemed too great to leave it there. (I woz here. God wozn't.) Today the board bore only one notice, written in shouty yellow capitals:

PLEASE JOIN US AT THE LAKE FOR MICHAEL'S "ROW THE BOAT ASHORE" ROWING REGATTA! (Attendance Compulsory)

Kit and I made our reluctant way to the far end of the lake. On the way I filled him in on what had happened in the Boogie Bar.

"Jezebel and Adam?" said Kit. "I suppose it's not surprising. He's naked all the time, his wife's a ball-breaker, Jezebel's up for it with anyone."

Jezebel. I recalled a song my father used to sing in a low voice on hot summer nights after my mother had left, about the Devil and a wicked woman and a fallen angel.

I shrugged off the uncomfortable memory. "What did she mean, watch your step? What was she warning me about?"

Kit scowled. "Only this entire place and everyone in it." We arrived at a large clearing crowned with a banner crudely suspended between two trees:

Row the Boat Ashore! HALLELUJAH!

The canoes were now spaced out along the waterfront, with eager Heavenly Hosts ticking off names on clipboards and shepherding people towards each boat. Citizens were emerging out of the bush and into clearings all around the lake, and a large crowd was gathered at the finish line, near the Hallelujah Hall. Many of the citizens were carrying yellow flags.

"Ah, Maurice! Wonderful to see you! Fantastic! Come right this way! Boy, do we need *you* today, mister!" A male Heavenly Host, eager and awkward in equal measure, appeared beside me, waving a yellow flag and wearing a giant foam hat shaped like a pair of oars. Kit wished me luck as he headed to the side of the lake to watch. The Heavenly Host ushered me towards the boats. I found it both amusing and alarming that anyone would "need" me for a rowing race. My idea of exercise was peeling my daily banana at breakfast. If I was really energetic I did it with three fingers instead of two.

We passed teams in various stages of preparation, some already in their boats, some limbering up on the grass, others being given a pep talk by their leader, each one a White Guy.

We reached Lane Five and there was Peter, rallying his team around him, speaking in a low voice and making earnest notations on a handheld whiteboard. His team members looked variously bored, terrified, and excited. An older man with a beard to rival that of Moses stood just behind Peter, tapping his shoulder repeatedly and postulating loudly about the probability of an imminent downpour.

I had been assigned to the team just beyond, in Lane Six. My team leader was wearing a white muscle shirt with "Gabriel" embroidered on the chest in gold glitter. The dot on the "i" was a halo. A leather strap ran from one slim hip over the opposite shoulder, and I glimpsed a flash of gold behind his head. He was holding something in his hand and peering earnestly at it while his team stood waiting. It wasn't until I was right next to him that I saw it was a small mirror, embellished with tiny gilt leaves and swirls, a plump cherub perched on top.

He quickly licked his finger and smoothed his perfect eyebrows, then put the mirror away in a sequinned fanny pack. He turned and smiled at me like a department store perfume demonstrator, almost blinding me with the whiteness of his teeth.

"Maurice, is it? Come along, come along, we've been waiting for you! Tsk tsk, second day in Heaven and already late, eh? Ha, ha!" He didn't sound remotely amused.

I looked around at my fellow team members. There were eight of us. Jacob, puffing through jerky push-ups on the grass, was one of them. A younger man tapped me on the shoulder. He reminded me of the Jehovah's Witnesses who used to come to my door in a misguided attempt to convert me. They gave up after five minutes, usually. Perhaps it was my tendency to hum "Highway to Hell" very loudly as they fetched into their man-bags for their tracts.

This man had the same keen but slightly defeated expression; one that said, *Come on, then. Tell me to piss off. I know you're going to, so we might as well get it over with.*

"I'm John. You ever been baptised?"

The non sequitur made me blink. "Maurice. No. Why?"

"No reason, no reason." He looked glumly from me, to the water, then back again.

Teams were climbing into their boats, taking up their oars, and arguing over seating arrangements. Gabriel reached behind his head and pulled a golden trumpet from its harness like an arrow from a quiver. He pursed his glossed lips and gave the trumpet, which glistened like fire in the sun, one short blast. "All right, team! On we go!"

We climbed into our boat, bent over and hobbling like tipsy grandfathers. Gabriel punctuated orders with short blasts from his trumpet as he directed us to our places. "That's right! On we go! Take your seats! That's right! On the boat you go! Whoopsie-daisy!" He beamed and nodded and parped. I was at the front on the left, with John to my right. When we were all more or less seated, Gabriel clambered into the bow and gestured for us all to lean forward. His face was extraordinarily handsome – beautiful, even. He smelt divine. I'm not gay, by the way. I like women (except my ex-wife).

People used to think I was gay when I was younger. It wasn't just because I wore paisley shirts and listened to Barbara Streisand and liked quiche. I think it was because I did an English degree for the love of literature, not because I wanted to go to one lecture a week and work at McDonalds after I graduated. I also read a lot and never had a girlfriend before Robyn. My parents used to worry about that.

"Don't you *want* to meet a nice young female?" my father would bark, when I was as young as sixteen.

"They're not exactly falling out of trees in their eagerness to get with me, Father," I would reply, embarrassed. I think he thought finding a girlfriend was something you simply *decided to do*, much like going to the shops or mowing the lawns. You just woke up one morning and, partly aided by a pre-dawn adolescent erection, resolved to pop out (as it were) and get laid, and boom! As soon as you jumped on the school bus, there she was waiting for you, all legs and burgeoning bosom.

"Now listen up, you lazy fuckers," Gabriel growled out of the side of his mouth, beatific beam still intact. I almost dropped my oar. "We've lost this *sodding* regatta three times in a row to Peter's team. There is *no way in Hell* I am going to lose today, or he'll be lording it over me all week." He hurled a glance at the neighbouring boat, where Peter looked to be giving his team a similar lecture. "So I suggest you put your pathetic excuses for muscles to work and get our arses down to that finish line before anyone else, or I will personally ensure that you are *all* on latrine detail for the rest of eternity. Got it?" He stood up, flicked his hair, and flashed his radiant beam once more. "Marvellous! Lovely! Good luck team, try your best, have fun, let's remember our Hippy Happy team motto … all together now … *Michael Row the Boat Ashore*!" He put his trumpet to his lips and blasted a jaunty flourish.

We eyed one another grimly and gripped our oars. Gabriel slung the trumpet over his back and cracked each of his perfect knuckles in turn while eyeballing Peter.

"And a three! Aaaaand a two! Aaaaand … a one!" A starter's gun cracked and in a spat of uncoordinated, over-excited oar clashes we were off.

The next three or so minutes were a blur. I'm sure the cheers from the spectators were loud, but all I could hear was the slap and swallow of the oars in the water and my own rasping breath. Gabriel was shouting and gesturing, almost foaming at the mouth. Around the halfway point I glanced over at the shore to see Kit glumly waving his flag. He was standing next to Moses, who seemed to have calmed down somewhat from the previous day but was now carrying what appeared to be two giant concrete blocks and looking earnest.

Our boat announced its arrival at the finish line with a jerky bump on the shore, and it was over. Peter's boat had arrived fractionally ahead of ours. Peter leapt out and fist-pumped the air with a whoop of triumph. He then shouted an obscenity at Gabriel, whose face and ears turned bright red (but he still looked impossibly handsome, the unnatural bastard). He jumped out of our boat so violently it abruptly overturned, depositing us all into the water.

The eight of us thrashed around for a bit, trying to gain traction on the muddy lake bottom. We puffed and sputtered and swallowed grubby water. John was the first to find his feet, and he reached out his hand to help me up. I clutched it, grabbing the hand of the old man next to me, who grabbed the hand of the woman next to him and so on (it was all very *The Enormous Turnip*), and together we steadied ourselves.

Panting, John looked thoughtfully around our soggy semi-circle. "Actually, while we're all in the water, folks…" But his next words were obscured by an urgent call from the shore.

"Fight!"

Gone in an instant were the fixed smiles and polite flag waving. There was a moment of incredulous suspension, then in one unorchestrated surge dozens of citizens started pushing and shoving towards a small stage that had been set up as a podium for the race winners. As I emerged from the water, my dripping trousers fetchingly bunched around my knees, I saw Peter and Gabriel whip off their hats and shirts (and trumpet) and commence an edgy exchange of air punches and misdirected slaps.

Citizens pushed and elbowed their way forward with increasing urgency, and a few people were pushed to the ground or into the shallows of the lake. No one stopped to help them up. The two White Guys started throwing real punches at each other (at least, Peter punched and Gabriel slapped), missing most at first. Then Peter got a few powerful ones in at stomach level. Gabriel slumped over, moaning. When he straightened up again his eyes were wild and his perfect teeth were set together in an exquisite leer. He started hissing and slowly circling Peter. The crowd pressed in closer. It was all very *Lord of the Flies.*

A frantic whistle sounded. Adam was running from the Hallelujah Hall towards the fight. I was careful to keep my eyes on his face. The whistle parped in time with his feet. He drew up by the crowd and continued parping, to little effect. The fight continued, the two men's blows accelerating.

Then Adam stared up the lake, his perfect face draining of colour. He spoke one word.

"Michael."

It wasn't loud – barely loud enough for me, standing four to five deep in the crowd, to hear it – but the effect was immediate. The citizens of Heaven melted away from the podium like treacle from a hot spoon. Peter and Gabriel stopped fighting. They retreated to their corners and stared up the lake towards the start line. I craned my neck to see what had caused the monumental shift in atmosphere.

Walking slowly from the far end of the lake towards us was another man dressed all in white; one I hadn't seen before. As he came closer, I gasped an astounded shock of air.

My first thought was: *He is the male version of Botticelli's Venus.* He was so handsome, so extraordinarily beautiful, I immediately wanted to frame him and hang him on my wall (and not just to replace the woman with bananas on her head). His eyes were the colour of blue flame, his aquiline nose perfectly positioned between cheekbones divinely planed to perfection. Blond hair luxuriated down his back, catching the light as he moved. He was tall and lean, but I could see muscles shifting and flexing under this shirt. If I could have stared at him all day, I would have – until he came closer, and I looked into his eyes. They had something in them; something dancing and twisting and floating, just out of reach. I thought of the insane, dancing deadlights in Stephen King's *It*. And I thought to myself: *That, my friends, is the gaze of a madman.*

He had taken at least five minutes to reach our end of the lake, and during those minutes Heaven had remained utterly silent. With one graceful leap he was on the podium. He turned to face the crowd and smiled. When he spoke, his voice was as gentle as an intimate dinner companion's.

"Citizens of Heaven. Thank you for your participation. The regatta is now over. Return at once to your cabins. Stay there until further notice." He nodded to the Heavenly Hosts who had been standing aside, helpless to stop the fight and the breathless appreciation of it. They snapped back into action and started to roughly push citizens towards the path back to the cabins. Everyone complied in complete silence.

"Who the hell is that?" I whispered to Kit, who had been herded in my direction.

"Michael. They call him The Burning One. It's his eyes." I felt something flip over in my stomach. Then Kit was shoved and told to hurry up.

As we left the shoreline, I stole a last look at the podium. Gabriel and Peter were putting their shirts on, Gabriel complaining loudly about his damaged trumpet. Michael said something to the two men that I didn't catch, and they kneeled slowly at his feet and held out their arms, their upturned wrists exposed. I gasped as Michael suddenly looked directly at me and winked. And then I reached the trees, and the podium was hidden from view.

11

Tuesday morning

Dear Dad,

I never used to believe in Heaven and Hell. I wanted to believe in an afterlife, but I couldn't get my head around the sort of God who would show mercy to some and damn others to eternal oblivion, much in the way I extract all the black jellybeans from the packet and throw them in the bin.

I've been trying to imagine where you are. I can't believe you've suddenly just disappeared and there is no "you" anywhere, like in cartoons where someone just disappears and there's a pop *as the air rushes to fill the vacuum they've left behind.*

But if there really is more to it than just nothingness, where are you? Are you all in one piece? Can you see me? Can you hear me?

Do you want to know if I'm OK?

Mum arrived home last night, late. She came straight over to your place and tip-toed into my room and sat on my bed, but I pretended to be asleep. I have a feeling she wanted to have a dramatic "mother and daughter bonding in their grief" moment, but there was no way I was giving that to her. When I got up this morning she was sitting at the breakfast table in a purple kaftan, smoking and reading the paper. As soon as she saw me she leapt up, spread her arms wide – Jesus above Rio – and burst into tears. "Baby! Oh, my baby! My poor baaaaby!" I went along with it for a few minutes, allowing myself to be enfolded by purple hessian and karma oil, because I knew from experience that if you denied Mum her performance often enough, the emotional tension would eventually escalate and explode like soup in a lidless blender.

I heard Aunt Fleur say quietly, "All right, Robyn, let the poor girl breathe." Mum pulled back, sniffing, and sat down again with a Norma Desmond-esque flourish. "Toast, darling?"

I grabbed a glass and went to the sink. "Just water, thanks. I'm not hungry."

"You have to eat, darling. Keep your strength up. Shall I make you some cereal? Weet-Bix?" She wanted to make me something – anything – to make herself feel better.

"I said no, thank you."

Mum's face dropped. There they were: the calling cards of my childhood. The hurt expression. The small, wounded voice. The dewy threat at the eye brims. My daughter, my daughter, why hast thou forsaken me?

The Mistress of Manipulation: Coming Soon to a Kitchen Near You.

It's Tuesday. I hate Tuesday mornings. You know that old song by The Mockers? Of course you don't. You hate music, particularly music I like. (To be fair, nobody likes the music I like. Everyone I know thinks Kate Bush is weird, but she's my favourite singer ever. Even Carolyn says she's weird and old-fashioned. I don't care.)

We have Law 131, Legal Method, every Tuesday at 10 am. Obviously I'm not going today, but I skip it most other Tuesdays as well. It's enough to fry the brain with boredom. I still ask myself sometimes why I decided to do a law degree. Going to lectures every day feels like I'm wearing someone else's ill-fitting clothes.

You never knew I wanted to be a writer. I started when I was tiny, writing poems about kittens and elephants and baking and trees. At some point I graduated to short stories, and I even wrote a few half-decent songs when I was fifteen (mostly due to the fact I was in love with Shane Anderson for precisely seven weeks, three days, and eleven hours, and the amateur fumbling behind the science lab lent itself to lyrics). I now have six or seven half-written novel drafts in the drawer under my bed. I can't seem to finish any of them. I'm not sure why.

I never told you I wanted to be a writer because I don't think you would have been the slightest bit interested. For someone who spent the majority of his life surrounded by books, you didn't actually read them. You just criticised them. Maybe your career (if you can even call it that) was a result of horrified laziness (and fear, perhaps) at the prospect of engaging with the real world outside the musty walls of librarianship. The easiest position was the one of least resistance. So you cloistered yourself in your little word womb and built a life there, swaddled in safety and cynicism. Funny how a life turns out. And ends.

When I was nearly eighteen, I decided I simply couldn't bear to become like you, scathing in the face of brilliance, a mocker of mastery. So I chose what I believed to be the antithesis of creativity, the murderer of free thought, the killer of artistic impulse. I needed something to fight against, to resist, to fuel my revolutionary hunger. I chose law school.

OK, so I'm not like most teenagers.

I remember how aghast you were. The only thing worse than having a lawyer for a daughter would have been having a lawyer for a son. Since I was your only child, I saved you from that fate at least.

* * *

I just walked down to the post box at the end of the street with the letter I wrote yesterday. Mrs Hardy was lying in wait as I passed. She leaned out her window, barely able to suppress her excitement, and rasped, "Terrible news, Andrea, terrible news. Goodness me. Is there anything I can do, dear?"

Yes, I thought. Piss off and die. I shook my head.

"You off to post a letter, dear?"

I stopped. "No, I'm milking a goat," I answered. Being possibly the most stupid person on Earth, the sarcasm didn't so much elude her as stampede past her. She blinked. "No, I can clearly see it's a letter, dear. Who to?"

"My father," I said. "And it's 'to whom', not 'who to'. By the way, your shitty garden stinks like rotten eggs."

You should have seen her face.

Andy

12

If I had thought Heaven was a strange place before the regatta, it was nothing compared to what happened afterwards. As Robyn used to say, you wouldn't read about it.

I detest that expression, by the way. I'm not sure if I always hated it, or if it was Robyn's ability to trundle it out like a squeaky tea trolley at the faintest whiff of surprise that bred the hatred. Vacuum cleaner's on the blink? You wouldn't read about it. Motorway traffic's backed up to Coveton at midday? You wouldn't read about it. Husband's a failed writer who now wastes his pathetic little life in a suburban library that smells like wet mushrooms from May to September? You wouldn't read about it.

I always wanted to say to her: Actually, Robyn, you *would* read about it. Somewhere in the world someone has written a book on recalcitrant domestic vacuum cleaners. Someone else has written one on midday motorway traffic jams and how to avoid them. And hundreds of bright-eyed, wanky bachelors have rubbed their hands together before churning out chapter after chapter of best-selling drivel on how to save a doomed marriage.

I wanted to say it, but I never did.

Lunch was silent and oppressive. The White Guys were clearly ramping up their surveillance. Instead of standing along the back wall they were spread out amongst the citizens, a stunning but disturbing diaspora. The Heavenly Hosts were all seated along the sides of the Hallelujah Hall, their expressions blank.

After we had finished eating, the Hosts cleared the tables of food and utensils and brought out the board games. We were split into teams and spent a maddening afternoon going from game to game, a shrill whistle indicating when it was time to move to the next station. We never had time to finish a single drawing in Pictionary, or to build more than a single cross of letters on the Scrabble board. There was very little talking, and everyone was careful not to do anything to make themselves conspicuous.

At about three o'clock Adam dropped all his Pick-Up Sticks, and as he bent over to get them everyone looked studiously the other way. I slipped out the front door and made my way back through the tree tunnel and up the path towards the main concourse, desperate for fresh air and solitude. I wasn't ready to go back to my cabin. I felt restless and headachy, and I needed to walk.

Directly opposite the path I had just walked up was the path that apparently led to God (500 metres). I wasn't in the mood to encounter a deity I didn't really believe in, but it was either that or the Boogie Bar again, and the thought of another tipsy fumble with Jezebel held no appeal. I decided it was unlikely that God would try to stick his tongue down my throat, so I crossed the concourse and headed down the path towards him. The sun was lowering in the sky directly in front of me with less furious beauty than the previous day. Perhaps it, too, was on its best behaviour.

The path was blanketed in white pebbles that gently ceded underfoot. I bent down and scooped some into my hand. They were exactly uniform in colour and size, as if they'd been ordered from a catalogue. The path was lined with bushes in enormous terracotta pots. The bushes had been expertly trimmed and clipped into leafy shapes: crowns and crosses and harps and cherubs and giant pairs of wings. It was like a green-fingered version of the Boogie Bar. The jerky sinking sun cast the sculptures' shadows hugely around and behind me. For a brief moment I was an enormous angel in flight.

Further along the path I passed three or four pots that held nothing but charred and twiggy skeletons. The bushes had been burnt so badly that only their frail frames had been left to participate in this vaguely disturbing introduction to the art of topiary.

A cough. I paused, my ears twitching as they tried to determine where the sound was coming from. I was sure it had come from behind. My heart hammered a little more than necessary. Ahead of me, Moses stepped out from behind a bush shaped like a giant trumpet. He was circling the pot, muttering softly to himself. He hadn't seen me.

"Now, let's see … let's just see what happens this time if I just…" He was suddenly out of sight again. I heard shuffling and a scratchy fizz, and after a few seconds a thin plume of smoke started to curl upwards. A small flame shot out sideways from the bush, then another.

"Hey!" I exclaimed. "Hey! What are you doing?"

A startled face appeared, partly obscured by smoke plumes. "I beg your pardon?"

I waved a hand towards the bush. "I said, what the hell's going on?" Flames were starting to shoot wider and higher.

Moses stepped out into the path, shaking his head. "No, no, you don't understand. God's OK with it. He gave me his lighter." He frowned, patting himself around his hips and stomach. "Now if I could just … can't for the life of me remember where I put it. So I'm just trying these matches." He held up a small red and black box.

"God has a lighter?"

"We all have our vices," shrugged Moses. The bush was well alight by now, the fire shooting up to meet the yellow-tinted sky, the branches reaching through the flames as if in supplication. Moses moved back as the skeleton started to collapse, the branches and leaves folding in on themselves. Twisted twigs flittered, flaming, to the pebbled ground. I felt myself shiver. After a few more minutes the trumpet was destroyed, a black and charred knot left gently fuming.

Moses gave a grunt and kicked the pot. Then he yelled and hopped around a bit. *He seems to spend a lot of the time being angry*, I thought.

I waited until he had stopped hopping and was sitting on the ground, rubbing his toes. I approached with some caution. "What exactly were you doing?"

Moses looked sideways at me, rubbing his foot. "Haven't you read your Bible? What do you think I was bloody doing?"

I dredged through my mind for memories of my childhood Sunday School lessons. (What I remembered most, to my dismay, was my teacher. Mrs Fransham had an enormous shelf of breast, a beehive hairdo that looked like lemon candy floss and a large ring of sweat under each armpit in the summer. Once I went back to fetch something after my lesson – everyone else had left – and was mortified to find her in a sweaty embrace with the church organist. I remember watching, revolted and fascinated in equal measure, as his purple tongue pistoned in and out of her ear.) After a few moments I recalled a play we did one Sunday, of Moses parting the Red Sea. I was one of the Israelites and Tommy Harding was Moses, which I felt was very unfair because he was fat with pimples and I was pretty sure Moses was not fat, having been in the desert for rather a long time, nor pimply, having long since passed adolescence. At the beginning of the play Tommy was required to kneel before a pot plant that Mrs Fransham had decorated crudely with red cellophane.

If you'll pardon the pun, I twigged. "The burning bush."

Moses stood up and looked again at the trumpet. He shrugged his shoulders and sighed. "I'm just trying to talk to him," he said. "That's what he did last time. He talked to me from out of the bush." He cleared his throat and looked down at the pebbles. "I haven't talked to him for so long." He sniffed. I hoped he wouldn't start to cry. I shuffled from foot to foot, punctuating his sniffs and gulps with the crunch of pebbles, desperate to diffuse the awkwardness. I was just about to tell him the one about the first mention of medicine in the Bible (When God gives Moses two tablets, badum-tish), when the old man saved me from my discomfort. He wiped his face, the gesture replacing vulnerability with exasperation. "Anyway. No luck. They all bloody burn." He gestured at the bare bushes lining the path.

"It's no great loss, really," I jollied. "Topiary's an eyesore at the best of times."

Moses fixed me with a steely gaze. "I did them," he said. "Took me ages." He started to limp past me down the path in the direction of the concourse.

"Why did God give you his lighter?"

Moses turned and stood still for a moment. "I presume it was God. I woke up one morning and the lighter was by the side of my bed with a note: 'And behold, the bush burned with fire, and the bush was not consumed.' That's Exodus chapter three, verse two, by the way. I thought it was a sign. That he wanted me to talk to him." He sniffed and turned to go again. "Anyway, what's the use. I've lost it, and God's not talking. I'm off back to the lake." He half-turned once more. "It's Maurice, isn't it?"

"Yes." I was surprised he knew my name.

"Have a nice walk. Don't expect to find God, because he's not there." He jerked his chin in the direction I was headed. "Apparently he's gone into hiding." He walked away, shellsuit swishing.

I continued. Topiary pots gave way to tall hedges, exactly uniform on both sides. I touched them, and just like all the trees I had seen and touched in Heaven, they were falsely perfect. The path rounded a corner and started to rise, and the hedges seemed to rise along with it, enclosing me in a dark tunnel along which I stumbled and puffed. Overhead the sky retracted, pulling back from the darkness, leaving me to find my own way.

And then, just as my armpits started to prickle and my thighs were considering an official protest, the path levelled out and the hedges gave way to an enormous walled clearing.

A huge sign announced:

God's Glory Glade. HALLELUJAH! Please form a queue.

The glade was a large semi-circle, and I was standing in the centre of the straight edge. The ground was paved with bricks, spray-painted golden, and – as if in an over-enthusiastic effort to make up for the lack of flowers elsewhere in Heaven – every skerrick of wall was slathered with enormous artificial yellow roses. Glittered.

On the other side of the glade, at the apex of the semicircle's curve, was an enormous throne on a raised platform. The throne was golden with a crimson seat, and extravagant curves and swirls smothered its frame from top to bottom. The headrest was fashioned in the shape of a crown with the word GOD emblazoned on it in sequinned lettering. It was hard to tell, I reflected, if this was a helpful hint for those who had forgotten to whom the throne belonged, or a pithy curse one might utter upon seeing so many artificial flowers in one place.

Between me and the throne snaked a system of ropes and poles such as one might find in the customs hall at the airport. A sign where I was standing barked:

Wait time from here: 15 minutes. Silence, please.

So not only did you have to queue to see the Almighty, you couldn't even complain about it to the person in front of you.

I made my way across the glade, illicitly ducking under ropes and around poles as I went, then climbed the three stairs to the raised platform. I hesitated for a moment before remembering that I didn't necessarily believe in God, so fearing divine retribution wasn't necessary either. Then I sat down on the throne of the great Jehovah. Now all I needed was my crown and sceptre and Jesus at my right hand. There was an umbrella stand just to the side of the throne, though, so he wouldn't have fitted on the platform.

I shifted around, trying to get comfortable. It was a lumpy, unyielding seat for anyone to sit in, let alone God. I was just imagining being him, and having Robyn bow down to me and trying to decide whether or not to show her any mercy, when I heard voices. I leapt off the throne so fast I almost catapulted myself into a freestanding trellis. It was adorned with more roses and silk butterflies and topped with a procession of bobble-headed cherub statuettes. I regained my balance then scrambled behind it. Little harps and bellies bounced.

In the gaps between the cacophony of roses I saw two men enter the glade. One was Peter. The other was a man I hadn't seen before. He was dressed like a White Guy, but there was something that set him apart; the way he walked, perhaps, as if he had pebbles in his shoes, making every step a punishment. Or it could have been the fact that he sported dusky dreadlocks piled in enormous, grubby coils.

The two men stopped by the steps to the throne. "You won't let me down, will you?" Peter said. "I'm going out on a limb here. The others don't trust you. Why do you think you're permanently relegated to office duty?"

The man with the dreadlocks looked steadily at Peter. "You have no choice *but* to trust me. There's no one else." He took an object out of his pocket and gave it to Peter. As Peter put out his hand to take it, his sleeve rode up a bit. Even from where I was hiding, I could see a large red welt branded across his wrist like an angry bracelet. I watched him wince as the muscles flexed.

"Don't worry, I'm on your side," said the man with dreadlocks, as he, too, looked at Peter's wrist.

Peter pulled at his sleeve and nodded. "I'll take this down now." As he slipped the object into his pocket, the sun glinted momentarily on its metallic edge. It was a key.

The man with the snake-coil hair started to weave and duck his way back through the ropes towards the topiary path. He stopped before he reached the sign directing people to queue. "I'm just trying to redeem myself here. But don't forget I'm not the only one who did the betraying, Peter. When it came to the crunch." He turned and walked out of the glade.

Peter stood still for a long moment, his fists clenched. For a few horrifying seconds he looked straight towards the trellis. I ducked my head and held my breath. The thing was choked front and back with fake flowers; surely I was impossible to spot. I felt a weird and desperate urge to pee.

Foot falls, coming closer. A small trickle of urine whimpered into my underpants. I closed my eyes.

A few moments of nothing. Then, very close by, a muffled swish, a click, and after a delay of a few seconds, a hollow *thunk*. Then silence.

I waited a few more moments before daring to peek. Peter wasn't there. I was so surprised I stepped out immediately from my hiding place despite the possibility that one or both men could reappear at any moment. I turned in a circle, looking for a door through which Peter could have gone. Nothing. The only entrance to the Glory Glade was the one through which we had all come.

Peter had disappeared.

13

Tuesday, 2 pm

Dear Dad,

Your funeral is on Friday afternoon at that funeral home on East Road. Mum wanted a Buddhist blessing but Aunt Fleur won that one, thank God. "Maurice would have wanted something normal, Robyn. Middle of the road. Not a bald orange hippie convention with tofu and chanting and incense."

"They don't all eat tofu, you know," muttered Mum.

But a funeral home it is. Apparently Aunt Fleur asked for a Christian service. Which is ironic because you always said God was for weaklings. Well, there you go. It doesn't get much weaker than dead.

We just met with the funeral director at your place. Her name is Gwyneth, and she's brittle and unbearable. She was dressed all in red and had dyed blonde hair and emerald green-framed glasses, and she smelt of cigarette smoke. When she drummed her nails on the table (which she did for a few seconds each time before she spoke, like a manicured drumroll) they sounded like scrabbling beetles.

She wanted to know all about you. Aunt Fleur covered your childhood and student days. Mum talked about what a wonderful father you were and how much you had loved me (cue dewy eyes and frequent dramatic pauses). Gwyneth seemed very taken by her. Perhaps the poor dried-up woman was thirsty. Drowned by a deluge of drama: what a way to go. I then covered the divorce and the fact that you were a shitty small-time librarian and that you had never wanted me to become a lawyer.

Gwyneth laughed a little too loudly. Scrabble, scrabble. Tap tap tap. She helped herself to a piece of shortbread and asked who would be writing the eulogy. Silence. Aunt Fleur looked at me and said, "Andy's a good writer. Andy, would you like to give it a go, or would that be a bit much?"

Immediately Mum switched into performance mode. She rose dramatically to tower above us, both hands clutched to her chest. Gwyneth nearly swallowed her shortbread whole.

"Are you serious? My daughter has just lost her father, and you're asking her to write his eulogy? Can't you see she's heartbroken? What she needs right now is to be left alone to grieve." She sat. "Besides, she's a law student, not an English major. She couldn't possibly write the bloody eulogy."

That clinched it. "I'll give it a go," I said. "But don't expect very much," I said to Gwyneth, who looked like she was about to bolt for the door. "As I'm sure you've figured out, Dad and I didn't get on well."

"Your father didn't get on well with anyone, Andy." Mum sniffed. "It's a wonder he and I …"

"That's enough, Robyn," said Aunt Fleur loudly. Then again, more quietly: "That's enough."

"Right then, that's sorted!" tinkled Gwyneth. She scooped up her handbag, ring binder, and cigarettes and scuttled her way out of the lounge towards the front door. Mum followed her. I heard low murmurs and then Gwyneth saying, "I know, I know. It's a difficult time," in a low voice. They murmured some more, then I heard Mum's low laughter and a single answering bleat from Gwyneth.

"I can hear you laughing, you know," I called. "I'm not deaf."

There was a hurried scrabble for the door and the click of the latch, and Mum came back. "I'm sorry, dear." She sniffed. "It's just that sometimes, at times like these, a little laughter relieves the tension."

"Yes, Mum, I'm sure your grief must be incredibly fucking hard to

bear," I said. I got up and walked towards the hall. Aunt Fleur put out her hand to me as I passed but I ignored it. When I got to my room I slammed the door behind me, hard. I hadn't done that since I was about twelve, and for a second I felt silly and juvenile. Then I just felt sick.

Mum went home soon afterwards. She said to Aunt Fleur that her heart felt weak and she needed to go somewhere quiet to meditate and check her emails. I don't think I can stand being around her over the next few days. Already your death has become just the latest scene in the soap opera that is her life.

Aunt Fleur said to be patient and that Mum was hurting too, but just didn't know how to show it. "She's never really known how to be vulnerable, sweetheart. She puts up walls. We all do. Hers just happen to be dramatic cliffs with crashing waves."

It's pissing down. You used to hate it when it rained. I quite like it. It reminds me of when I was little and I would run outside and jump in puddles. Mum was appalled when I came back inside covered in mud. I think that's why I did it; because I knew it would get her all worked up. You just laughed, I think. I can't really remember.

I have no idea what I'm going to write.

Andy

14

Kit was at a loss to explain Peter's disappearance, but he was able to tell me about the man with the dreadlocks. "That's Judas. He keeps to himself a lot, but you see him occasionally, meditating by the lake or doing the odd bit of yoga."

I coughed out an incredulous laugh. "Judas? As in, the guy who betrayed Jesus?" I thought back to what Peter had said. "No wonder people don't trust him."

"Which explains why he keeps his head down," said Kit. "I don't think many people know who he is."

"How do *you* know?" I asked.

"Found his book," muttered Kit, glancing around to make sure no one was nearby. "Right next to mine. Irwin, Iscariot."

"What book? What do you mean, next to yours?"

"Tell you later. Not discussing it now."

It was just before six o'clock, and we were on our way to Cocktails with God. After leaving the Glory Glade I had found Kit skulking near my cabin. He was in a foul temper, having been roped into a game of strip poker by Adam (who played the game backwards). He seemed to blame my absence for this, though I wasn't sure why. Maybe he was annoyed that I had gone off to explore by myself without suggesting he come along. I didn't waste time worrying about it. He was a teenager. They got in sulks all the time, and when they were like that it wasn't worth giving them the time of day. That was one lesson I had learnt living with Andy. Ignore her sulking. In fact, ignore her entire adolescence. It was safer, and more peaceful.

We followed a path around to the back of the reception building to a paved courtyard, partly shaded by a yellow pergola. The courtyard gave onto a large, perfectly coiffed lawn surrounded on three sides by tall hedges. Several trestle tables had been set out and twenty or so citizens were standing around holding plastic cups decorated with small paper umbrellas and curly straws, looking awkward. (The citizens. And the cups.) Heavenly Hosts were circulating with plastic trays of spring rolls. No one seemed be eating. I was starving, so I beelined for a table holding tooth-picked cheese and pineapple cubes. Kit loped to a cluster of plastic chairs and sat down without looking at me. *Let him sulk,* I decided. *I'm going to eat.*

"Toad in the Hole?"

I turned to see Adam holding a tray of pastries. He beamed and offered me a paper serviette. Around his neck hung a large silver medallion with "She's the Boss!" written in jaunty font above an arrow pointing to his right. As he held out his tray I noticed a tiny tattoo on the inside of his right wrist. An emerald snake wrapped around a ripe red apple was thrown into gentle relief by the tendons beneath his skin.

"Welcome to Cocktails with God! Maurice, wasn't it?" The snake rippled as he transferred the tray to his other hand. "This is your first time, I think? Cocktail virgin? Haha!"

I kept my eyes fixed on his face. "That's right. Just thought I'd come to meet God, given that he's the main attraction." I took a pastry.

Adam smiled apologetically. "I'm so sorry, but God is unavailable today. I'm standing in for him. I don't think I introduced myself properly the last time we met? Adam's the name. First man ever on earth, one half of the genetic blueprint for all of humankind." He thrust out his hand.

"Maurice Toogood." We shook. "Your distant descendant, but with clothes on."

Adam threw his head back and laughed like I had just cracked the most hilarious joke ever. He then clapped me on the back repeatedly.

"Brilliant! Funny guy! Hahaha! Hey, Eve!" he called over his shoulder. "Come meet Maurice! We've got a comedian here!"

I turned and saw Adam's naked wife standing with Moses and the old man who had been chewing Peter's ear about the weather at the rowing regatta. He was holding a large mallet and looking agitated. Despite his age, which must have been around eighty, and the fact that he was about five foot one and lean, he looked strong, his sinewy arms lifting and lowering the mallet with ease as he spoke intensely to Moses.

Eve excused herself from the conversation and sashayed over to us, hips swaying. As she drew closer I could smell her: violets and vanilla and something else I couldn't quite put my finger on; something wild and musky. She had skin like alabaster and lips so red they could have been drawn on with a Vivid marker. Her hair was an obsidian river. *She looks like a freshly sketched cartoon Snow White, only less innocent,* I thought. My gaze left her lovely breasts with some difficulty and moved to her stomach, which was soft and gently rounded; the kind you could rest your head on for hours, blow gentle raspberries into, be enfolded by. Not like Robyn's, which for years had been flat and arid; a slakeless plain. Here was a woman who ate. *I bet when she eats steak she has it rare and she lets the juices trickle down her chin,* I thought. *I bet her kisses are magnificent.* A tattooed snake curved around her bellybutton, its forked tongue pointing downwards. I felt the giddy, dragging tingle in the pit of my stomach that usually signalled the start of an erection. I clenched my buttocks and thought about rugby scores and Camilla Parker Bowles and ISBN numbers. I couldn't get an erection in Heaven; that would just be wrong, like masturbating on a Sunday.

"Who invited Noah?" Eve snapped at Adam. "He's banging on again about his bloody 'Let's build a boat' campaign. I saw him tying up canoes in pairs this morning. I mean, for fuck's sake. The man's obsessed." A red bloom was starting to flush across her neck and cleavage.

"Ignore him, darling. The regatta just set him off. All those boats, putting ideas in his head. And he can't hold his drink. How many cocktails has he had? Five?" Adam slapped me on the back again and I nearly dropped my pastry. "Eve, darling, this is Maurice. A new citizen. He's as funny as all-get-out! Hilarious! And this is the first time we've met! Absolutely the first time! Yessirree! It's our *virgin* meeting! Hahaha!"

Adam was looking at me, his smile wide and desperate. He was silently begging me not to mention our earlier meeting in the Boogie Bar. I complied; his choice of bed partner had nothing to do with me, although I couldn't understand why he would choose Jezebel over his wife.

"Please ignore my husband," Eve withered. "I call him Mr Inappropriate." Adam adopted the expression of a slapped puppy. Eve rolled her eyes. "Now if you'll excuse me, I'm meeting Jezebel for a game of Snakes and Ladders." She turned and sashayed off, taking a side path through a gap in the hedge that presumably led towards the Boogie Bar.

"Damn fine woman, that," boomed Adam, gazing after her. "Holy crap, I'm one lucky man." He popped a pastry in his mouth and chewed loudly. I ventured a question.

"Can I ask why God isn't here?"

Citizens continued to eat and conduct low conversations, but they all turned almost imperceptibly towards us. The Heavenly Hosts closest to me appeared to falter, as if thrown off balance by my question. One of them tripped and dropped his tray, and asparagus rolls scattered like tiny felled logs.

Adam cleared his throat and coughed, spitting pastry flakes onto my collar. "God? Oh, well, he doesn't often make it to these cocktail thingies. Got far more important things to do, what with saving the world and smiting down sinners and so on and so forth, you know. Anyway, I'm here! The world's first man! Pretty good, yes? Can't sniff at that!"

"But it's advertised as Cocktails with God, every Tuesday at five," I insisted.

Kit got up from his chair and came to stand beside me. "He wasn't here last time either," he glowered, putting his grumpiness to good use. "Or the time before that. I don't think he's ever been here, and I've been coming every Tuesday for two months."

Adam spluttered a bit more. "Well now, look, what can we do if the Almighty has more important things to do? Can't argue with the Big Guy, now can we?"

"I'd quite happily argue with him if he'd only show himself," said a firm voice.

We all turned to see who had spoken. Noah was standing by the drinks table with his mallet. "In my day, you could count on God making an appearance sooner or later, even if it was to obliterate the entire planet in one watery swoop." He put down his tool and picked up a drink, lifting out the cocktail umbrella and holding it above his head. A Heavenly Host giggled, and Noah turned slowly towards her.

"You think you're safe, deary? You think your tiny umbrellas and stupidity will save you from what's about to come for all of us?" The Heavenly Host turned red and looked at her feet. Noah stared up at the perfectly blue sky. "Looks like rain," he said loudly. "Definitely looks like rain." Then he looked directly at me.

"You watch yourself." He was suddenly close to my ear, whispering. "You take care. It's not safe." He scowled at Adam then swept past us and disappeared around the side of the reception building.

We stood in silence. After a moment Adam clapped his hands, making me jump. "OK folks, show's over. We all know Noah has a … special take on things, now don't we? Bless him." He smiled as one might when regarding a toddler's first attempt at art. "Now then, that's it for Cocktails with God for today. Thank you all for coming! See you next week! Lovely, lovely!" He flapped his arms a bit, hoping to wave us all off. Then, with an awkward bow, he hurried up the stairs and through the back door of the reception building, trailing crumbs and cocktail umbrellas behind him.

The Heavenly Hosts started clearing the tables as the citizens dispersed.

"Come on," said Kit. "I've had enough of his bullshit. I want some answers." He started after Adam. I followed only because I had no desire to go back to my cabin and stare at the banana lady all evening. We pushed through the door and nearly collided with a trembling Adam, who was standing hunched before a figure in white.

Michael.

"No citizens in the reception building. Go back to your cabins." He spoke without looking at us.

I was turning to comply when I heard Kit speak. "Since when are we not allowed in here? We used to be."

There was silence for a moment. Then Michael walked around Adam towards Kit and put a hand on his shoulder, like a father congratulating a son. The fire in his eyes pranced. Kit winced, his knees buckling. His fists clenched and unclenched as he fought to remain upright. Michael smiled, showing his perfect teeth. With a movement as gentle as a caress, his fingers embraced Kit's neck and Kit crumbled to the ground, moaning.

"Daniel three, verse six, my young rebel. Take heed." He turned to me. "And for you, my friend, Revelation twenty-one, verse eight." He stepped over Kit and walked towards me. I backed up until I hit a wall. He leaned close and whispered, "Don't think I don't know you, Maurice. Don't think I don't know what happened." He kissed me gently on the forehead, then turned, nodding at Adam to follow him, and disappeared down a hallway to the left.

I touched my forehead, which had started to burn. Kit was slowly standing up, clenching his shoulder. I went to help him but was halted by a wallop of nausea. My forehead throbbed and pulsed.

"Are you OK?" asked Kit.

I nodded, only vaguely aware of him. *Don't think I don't know you, Maurice.*

"What did he do? Your forehead is bright red." Kit leaned closer, then gave a low whistle. "The fucking bastard burned you, with his lips. When he kissed you. Fucking crazy bastard."

Don't think I don't know what happened.

* * *

He watches as the flames leap higher, licking and slurping. Fahrenheit 451, Ray Bradbury, Fahrenheit 451, Ray Bradbury. He repeats it in his head, over and over like an incantation as the smoke blurs the outline of the fence in front of him and his wife behind him, running. He is hot, so hot, but he doesn't move further away from the flames.

Maurice, watch out! Oh my God, Maurice no no no no!

* * *

15

Tuesday, 5 pm

Dear Dad,

I just woke up from a nap. I had a dream that I was in a huge lecture hall, and you were the lecturer. You started talking about what it was like in Heaven, quoting from the Bible. I was trying to take notes, but you were talking too fast, and all of a sudden my note paper started scattering and flying round the room in a mini hurricane. I was leaping from desk to desk trying to gather it up, but my legs felt like they were stuck in mud and I couldn't move without a mammoth struggle. Meanwhile you just kept talking, seemingly unaware of the pandemonium around you. I was calling and calling for your help but no sound would come out, and you just kept on talking, even though all the other students had disappeared and there was just me and you and an empty lecture theatre and the insane storm of paper.

I've had a look on the internet. (I don't make a habit of it. Caroline laughs at me because I don't have a smartphone. Dumbphone, if you ask me.) In this case, though, reaching out to cyberspace seemed easier and less frightening than going inside my own head. I Googled "How to Write a Eulogy advice Bressington" (always best to start close to home) and got a hell of a fright when Gwyneth's bespectacled face slammed onto my screen. Turns out she writes a column in her funeral home's monthly e-newsletter, 'Over the Rainbow' (OMG you would have BARFED), and one was about how to write the perfect eulogy. Guess what? She

*can't write for shit. I counted five comma splices and three greengrocers'
apostrophes. Like fingernail's down a blackboard, as you used to say.*

Then I looked at WikiHow:

*A eulogy is a speech given at a memorial service in memory of the
deceased. [No, really?] You don't have to be a great writer or orator to
deliver a heartfelt and meaningful eulogy that captures the essence of
the deceased. [That sounds vaguely horrific, like I'm about to drain his
essence into a little bottle, like Harry Potter does to Professor Snape
after he dies.] The best eulogies are brief while being specific, as well as
thoughtful and not without the occasional touch of humor. [Great. No
pressure.] If you want to know how to write a eulogy in spite of being in
grief [thank you for the token acknowledgement], just follow these steps.*

1. *Decide on the tone. [Not sure. Grumpy, maybe.]*
2. *Consider the audience. [Mum, wailing with false grief; Aunt
   Fleur, silent with the real deal; the weirdos from the library.]*
3. *Briefly introduce yourself. [That's easy. The daughter he
   hardly knew.]*
4. *State the basic information about the deceased. [Divorced
   father-of-one. Librarian. Average. Agnostic.]*
5. *Use specific examples to describe the deceased. [Well, let's see.
   He hated books so he worked in a library. He ate toast with
   lemon honey and a banana every single morning for breakfast,
   which goes to show how fascinating and adventurous he was.
   He never told me he loved me, which I guess means he didn't
   or maybe he did. I don't care. He never seemed to care about
   anything much, so I guess it doesn't really matter what I say
   about him.]*
6. *Be concise and well-organised. [Concise isn't a problem – I
   don't have much to say. Well-organised? How disorganised
   can you be, stepping sparsely through the life of someone you
   barely knew?]*

7. *Get feedback. [There is no way in hell I'm asking Mum or Aunt Fleur to give me feedback unless I want to be deafened by gnashing of teeth (Mum) and gentle admonishments like "You can't possibly read that in public, dear." (Aunt Fleur)]*

So, there you go. So much for WikiHow telling you everything you need to know. It doesn't. It tells you only what some computer geek inputted years ago in order to make vast sums of cash.

I searched up one more thing: your first name. An image came up of that Bee Gee with the beard and receding hair line and little round glasses. He always used to wear a hat. He's dead, too. You look a bit like him.

Remember how much you used to love the Bee Gees? Remember how you and Mum used to joke about that when you weren't fighting? Maurice, Robyn, and Andy. All we needed was the other one with the high voice and the tight trousers.

You never told me how you and Mum met. Was it love at first sight? Did you ever really love each other?

Andy

16

I skipped dinner. My head was burning. The banana lady glowered as I paced my cabin. "Fuck off," I said. Just like my ex-wife, she ignored me.

The yellow bed creaked as I sat and opened the top drawer in the bedside cabinet. Sure enough, there it was. A Gideon Bible. The God-fearing Gideons had made it as far as Heaven. I was grateful to them, if slightly perplexed. Why would one need the Bible in Heaven? It seemed to me that if you were going to read the holy book up here in an effort to garner God's favour, you were A. too late, because obviously your presence proved that you had already done so, and B. a poor schmuck (going by my impression of the place so far).

I wasn't a church goer. As I saw it, God and church were for weaklings or people with no social life. Although, as previously mentioned, this didn't prevent me from believing with the vague, cushiony confidence of the hopeful agnostic that if there *was* a glorious afterlife, I would be entitled to it.

Robyn and I didn't marry in a church. I was on the fence and Robyn was stridently atheist. She (and later Andy) used to say I didn't have the courage to be an atheist; it would have meant being convinced about something. Robyn wanted a huge garden party with a circus theme, complete with men on stilts, somersaulting clowns, and a merry-go-round. It fitted with the kind of person she was when we first met. We sat next to each other in the Tuesday tutorial for Critical Thinking 101. I majored in English; Robyn (rather incongruously, I used to think) in accounting.

We both took Critical Thinking as an easy elective to make up course requirements. She got an A for every assignment. (She was, even back then, an expert in criticism.) She wore bright pink and purples and greens, carried a basket instead of a book bag, and had luxurious waves of dark hair that curled down to her bottom, which in those days was the shape and colour of a ripe peach. She laughed like a hyena and dramatically jabbed a bejewelled index finger at the ceiling every time she expressed a critical thought. I adored her from afar, too shy to speak to her, too entranced not to stare.

One day, dressed in jade green overalls and a pink waistcoat, she asked to borrow my notes. She had been off sick and probably thought I was a soft touch (she couldn't have helped but notice the staring). By that afternoon we were lovers. We deflowered each other in my small flat on Crane Street, in my tiny bedroom with pictures of famous authors and literary quotes papering the walls and books occupying every spare inch of space. It was a bedroom full of longing, and full of my first love: words. She usurped them. I remember trembling as I removed her bright plumage to reveal something even more wonderful underneath. As we made love, me clumsy and desperate, she delightful and brave, I remember thinking that she was exactly what I needed. She would set me free; wake me up. Be everything I wasn't.

She used to say that it was my burning desire to write, to commit myself to something, that made her fall in love with me.

It was also what made her hate me, in the end.

Our wedding, just eight months after that first afternoon of literary passion, was devoid of God. Much like Heaven. If you've read the Bible, you'll know that God is pretty much central to everything. He's just ever so slightly necessary. And yet he was nowhere.

I opened the red cover of the Gideon Bible and turned to Genesis chapter one, verse one. In the beginning. *If I can't meet the author, I figured, I'll just have to read what he's written.*

As I've already mentioned, the Bible wasn't completely foreign to me. I had consulted it numerous times as a student (try reading

Paradise Lost without one), and I could advise library users on the virtues of the King James as opposed to the NIV, but I had never read the thing right through. I winced as the welt on my forehead twitched and pulled. I flicked to Daniel 3:16.

… and whoever does not fall down and worship shall be cast immediately into the midst of a burning fiery furnace.

Then I turned to Revelation 21:8.

But the cowardly, unbelieving, abominable, murderers, sexually immoral, sorcerers, idolaters, and all liars shall have their part in the lake which burns with fire and brimstone, which is the second death.

The cowardly. The sexually immoral. All liars. I remembered Michael leaning close like a lover. *Don't think I don't know you.*

I shook myself a little, shrugging off an unpleasant twist of emotion. Then I turned back to the beginning, to Genesis, and skimmed through the Garden of Eden, the fall of Adam and Eve (*Not ashamed of being naked now, are you?* I thought), Cain and Abel, Noah's Ark, Sodom and Gomorrah, Lot and Abraham and Sarah. I flicked over to Exodus and read about Moses with great interest. He had had a bastard of a time in the wilderness, wandering about for more than 40 years with a bunch of whining Israelites. I would have let them all drown in the Red Sea along with the Egyptians.

I flicked to Psalms and read 23 in a very different light, now that I was dead. I had read it at my mother's funeral, at her request.

Yea, though I walk through the valley of the shadow of death, I will fear no evil; For You are with me; Your rod and Your staff, they comfort me.

Next, I took a quick trip through the gospels: Matthew, Mark, Luke, and John. I remembered Kit telling me that all the disciples except Peter (and one other – Judas) had disappeared. That was a shame; I would have loved to have met James, son of Zebedee. (I was a huge *Magic Roundabout* fan.) They seemed a nice enough bunch of young men, if a bit wet and clearly misguided. I read about Judas and Peter with particular interest. Who would have picked that Judas had dreadlocks? And how did he make it to Heaven after what he did?

As for Peter, apart from denying Jesus three times, he came across as a decent chap, and just ever so slightly vital to the entire history of Christianity. Jesus identified him as the rock on which he would build his church, giving him "the keys of the kingdom". I thought of the message on my cabin keyring and wondered if Peter ever got pissed off at this misappropriation of an eternal promise that was originally made exclusively to him. Was it this that had turned him so sour that he had become one of the White Guys?

I flipped to the back again. Revelation had always struck me as the Bible's miscalculated final descent into literary madness, with its lambs and seals and fire and blood and earthquakes and beasts with multiple heads and drunken prostitutes. I could never take the fall of Satan and Armageddon and the Second Coming seriously; it felt to me like God was just planting a few red herrings to keep the Pentecostals busy.

I was up to the bit where God (or Jesus; I'm never sure which) says "Behold, I stand at the door and knock" when there was a tap on the door. I jumped so high my head practically dented the ceiling. My heart was still hammering as I opened the door.

Kit pushed past me, reaching the bedside radio in two giant strides and flicking it on. Eric Clapton was limping his way through "Tears in Heaven". Kit turned the volume up, then came towards me and leaned in close. For a minute I thought he was going to kiss me (had he read my mind as I watched a half-naked Gabriel wrestling at the regatta?), but then he started to whisper in my ear.

"Our talk, yesterday. By the lake. You haven't told anyone about it, have you?"

I shook my head. Kit pointed at the bed, and we sat down.

"Want to know how I knew you were coming?" he asked, his voice still low.

I nodded.

"I sneaked into the library and read the books."

My stomach gave one dull, sickly thud. "Heaven has a library?" I managed to half whisper, half hiss. "Where? And what books? Books about what?"

"Under the reception building. And … us. The books are about us. Every single person in Heaven. Well, the citizens, at least. And there's an office right next door with filing cabinets full of stuff. There's an 'Imminent Arrivals' file. And a 'Just Arrived' file. That's how I found out about you."

I digested this, recalling what he had said during our first talk by the lake, about there being no books for dead rock stars. I hadn't really registered it back then.

"So what's in them? The books, I mean. What did yours say?" Eric Clapton's dirge had segued into "There Must Be an Angel" by Eurythmics.

"Everything," hissed Kit. "Not just my death, my whole life – my family, my friends, where I went to school, exam results, what I did on the weekends, how many times I took a piss – well, not really, but you get the idea. Everything. And there was all the stuff from my funeral. All the things they said about me, and the hymns and readings and all." He paused. "Man, I didn't realise my parents loved me that much. They said really nice things about me." Kit tucked his hair behind his ears then looked at the floor and blinked.

I didn't know if I wanted the answer to my next question. "Did you read mine?"

Kit shook his head. "You were still in the 'Just Arrived' file. Crap photo, by the way."

I frowned. I couldn't remember having my picture taken.

"You know the weirdest thing about my book?" continued Kit, still whispering. "This is going to sound crazy, but…" He paused. "It's like it's carrying on, even though I'm, you know, dead."

"What do you mean, carrying on? Carrying on how?"

I must have barked a bit – as much as one can bark and whisper at the same time – because Kit went red in the face again. He picked at a loose thread on the duvet. I had to lean in close to catch his next words.

"It's hard to explain, but … I've been in there three times now, right? And each time there are more pages. It grows. Like someone's still writing it."

Neither of us said anything for a good minute. If I had been alive I would have laughed and made a flippant remark about Kit losing his marbles. Given, however, I was in the afterlife and had just chatted over vol-au-vents with Adam and Eve after having observed Moses trying to set a bush on fire, I was a little less inclined to deem anything ridiculous.

"Writing what? What's in the extra pages?"

Kit stood up suddenly and started pacing around the bed.

"Um. Well." He stopped pacing and leaned in again. "Don't laugh." His breath was warm on my cheek. He swallowed and his eyes glinted, and I realised that he had started pacing in the hope that it would make tears less likely. I coughed and looked hard at my fingernails.

"My mother's been writing letters to me," started Kit. "Every day since I died. Telling me about what she does and stuff. Mr Tinkles isn't eating and I think he misses you. I went to the movies by myself when your father was at work and someone spilled lemonade all over the seat next to me. Broccoli was three dollars fifty at the supermarket today. You should have seen the sunset tonight. The cards have stopped coming. I miss you so much my heart hurts."

He turned and faced the wardrobe, stabbing at an edge of carpet with a massive foot. I could see the desperate muscle work in his jaw as he fought back tears. *Oh God*, I thought. *Another awkward emotional moment.* I was unsure what to do. Should I hug him? Slap his back? Bark at him to pull himself together?

"Who's Mr Tinkles?" I asked finally.

"Goldfish." The word was strangled and soggy.

"Good name."

"Thanks."

He kicked for a little longer then sat next to me, his fists balled on his knees. "Anyway, all the letters are there. In my book. All dated and in her handwriting."

"Christ," I said.

"Exactly," said Kit. He huffed out a shadow of a laugh, and I breathed an internal sigh of relief. I wouldn't have to put my arm round him or see him crying after all. Sympathy was so bloody awkward.

On the radio, Carrie Underwood was imploring Jesus to take the wheel. *I hear you sister*, I thought. *Bit late, though.*

When Kit spoke again, I knew it was the thing he had wanted to tell me from the moment he had walked in the door. He whispered so close to my ear it tickled. "There's another file. It's labelled 'Departures'."

I frowned. "Did you look in it?" I whispered back.

Kit shook his head. "I thought I heard someone coming so I stuffed it back in the drawer and ran." He whispered more urgently. "But this just confirms what I said by the lake. There's a way out of here. And if other people really have escaped, then maybe we can too. Maybe there's another Heaven, a better one, maybe one where God is. Where everything isn't so, you know, fucked up. Where…" The next words came in a low, almost inaudible rush, and I had to strain to catch them. "Where I don't have to miss my mum so much."

I thought of the Hallelujah Hall house band and of the endless sea of yellow shellsuits and group activities. I thought of Adam playing Pick Up Sticks, and I thought of Michael's eyes.

I touched a finger to the welt on my forehead and winced. "I think perhaps you should go back and check out that file," I suggested.

"Only if you come with me," said Kit. "You're the librarian, aren't you? You could come in handy. Finding stuff."

The demented fiddle intro of "The Devil Went Down to Georgia" kicked off. For about the millionth time, I passed a brief but bitter moment detesting my career.

17

Dear Dad,

I heard Aunt Fleur crying through the wall as I was brushing my teeth tonight. She's sleeping in your room. I don't know how she can sleep in her dead brother's bed. I knocked on the door and she invited me in, her voice thick. I sat next to her, and she just took my hand and held it for a long time. After a bit she blew her nose, then she got up and opened the top drawer of your dresser. She came back to the bed holding a photo frame.

"I've been looking through some of his belongings," she said. "I don't really know where to begin. How do you pack a life into boxes?" She cleared her throat, then straightened her shoulders.

"This photo was taken when your dad was born. I was three years old," she said, handing the frame to me.

A solemn little girl with auburn curls stared out of it. The years had made her eyes indistinct and her skin swirled, like a watermark. She was sitting on a hard-backed chair and held a white bundle in her arms. The white fell in snowy swoops to the ground. One tiny fist, blurry, waved above the white sea. Help. I'm here. Rescue me.

"That's Dad?" I was having trouble reconciling the picture I had in my mind of you, my cynical, shabby father, with this little smudge.

"It was taken the day after he was born, at the hospital. Apparently straight after this I dropped him. Mum said it was on purpose. It might have been, I don't know. Apparently I was pretty unhappy for a while

after he came along."

That explains a lot, I thought. Dad was dropped on his head as a baby. I felt a prickling behind my eyes, and I gripped the photo frame tightly.

Aunt Fleur got up again and reached into the same dresser drawer. This time she brought out an old child's exercise book, stained and dog-eared. The edges were black and charred.

She handed it to me without saying anything. The name on the front was written with a child's painstaking neatness. Maurice Toogood. I looked up questioningly at Aunt Fleur, but she just gestured at the door. "I'm going to make a hot chocolate. Would you like one?"

I nodded, and as soon as Aunt Fleur had left the room I opened the book. The first page had a picture of a skull and crossbones at the top. How appropriate, I thought, then felt a bit sick. The words on the page read, "My Poems and Stories. Do Not Read. Maurice Toogood."

I disobeyed my father and thumbed my way through the book, reading bits here and there, taking in the small pictures that accompanied many of the stories, marvelling at the words and rhymes that had originated in my father's head and been placed deftly on the paper. He was good. How old had he been? Ten? Twelve?

"He wrote all the time when he was younger." Aunt Fleur was standing in the doorway with two steaming mugs. "He used to write poems for me. He would create little bound books and plant them all round the garden, telling me they were from the fairies." She placed the mugs on the bedside table and went to stand by the window. It's a full moon tonight, and the beams were sneaking through gaps and thinned-out patches, milky and determined.

"Oh, Maurice had a marvellous way with words. I used to wish I could write like him. My clumsy attempts at stories and poems were a great disappointment to our mother, I'm sure. She adored Maurice. Treasured every word he wrote. She had drawers bursting with his essays and poems and stories and reports. I used to sneak in and read

them. The writing becoming neater but no less magical as he progressed through school." Aunt Fleur turned away from the window and came to pick up her mug, gesturing for me to do the same. "He even entered some competitions when he was in high school. I don't think he ever won anything, but he was highly commended a couple of times, if I remember rightly." She sat down next to me again. "For a long time his dream was to be a writer. Just like you."

I felt a punch of shock. "Why didn't he tell me?" I asked.

"Maybe he wanted to, but he never had the opportunity." Aunt Fleur hesitated. "Or maybe it was a time in his life he didn't want to remember." She paused. "He went on to university. He kept writing. You should have seen his flat: you could hardly move because of the books. 'All the lost books in the world have come here,' he used to say. 'They know I'll take care of them.'"

Aunt Fleur put her mug down on the bedside table and took my free hand. Hers was papery and warm. "I know you think he was a dreadful father, sweetheart. To be honest I did too, sometimes. But he did love you. I know he did."

I looked down at the book with its fragile, charred edges. "Why is it burnt?"

Aunt Fleur looked strange for a moment, and somehow precariously balanced, as if she were debating which way to jump. Then she simply said, "I don't know dear. It's very old."

She kissed me on the cheek. "Try to remember, and write the good stuff, sweetheart. Trust me. Try."

I've been sitting here in my bed for ages, staring at the photo of her holding a newborn you in her arms. I can't believe you wanted to be a writer, too. Why didn't you ever tell me?

Can you remember holding me in your arms, Dad?

And what else did you never tell me?

Andy

18

It was obvious that in the wake of the rowing regatta fiasco – and perhaps the unexpected ending to Tuesday's Cocktails without God – the Heavenly Hosts had been instructed to tighten their grip. On Wednesday they scheduled a morning so full of compulsory games and structured activities that Kit and I didn't have a moment to discuss our planned illicit trip to the library. It wasn't until Kit pointed out that everyone was joining in the sack races without objection that I noticed Jacob's absence. I realised that I hadn't seen him since the regatta. Had he, too, found a way out?

Luck intervened at lunch. Just as I was helping myself to tapioca and tinned fruit salad, there was an almighty crash from the kitchen. Hundreds of spoons on their way to mouths were suspended, *Matrix*-like, for a split second before the curious buzz of whispers began.

From where I was standing at the dessert buffet I only had to lean a bit to the left to see into the kitchen. Jezebel was lying on the floor, a tray of broken dinner plates strewn about her, a Greek goddess in her shattered kingdom. She was wearing the same red dress she had been wearing in the Boogie Bar, but the split was now open to above her waist, and, interestingly, she was wearing no underwear. Before I could crane my neck further, a Heavenly Host appeared, waving his arms like a manic policeman. "OK! All right! Nothing to see here! Move along, move along please! Nothing to see!"

Jezebel chose that moment to stand up and start hurling profanities at the chef behind her. She screamed and swayed and stabbed at the ceiling with random fingers.

"Jezebel, you're drunk, you stupid slag," opined the chef loudly. The entire Hallelujah Hall drew a collective scandalised breath. Jezebel strode over to the chef (not a small feat considering the pile of broken plates and her level of inebriation) and slapped him hard on the cheek, the force of which almost caused her to fall over again. I was willing her to do just that so I could get another glimpse up her dress when the chef threw off his hat, yelled "I quit!" in the general direction of the roof, strode out of the kitchen, through the tables of ogling citizens, and out of the hall, slamming the door behind him. Three seconds later the door opened.

"By the way, she's shagging Adam. Heard them in the pantry yesterday. That slut'll bed anything with a dick and a pulse." The door slammed again.

There was a stretch of shocked silence. Jezebel swayed and hiccupped. Then the hall erupted into hushed, scandalised chatter. I saw Adam and Eve at a table near the back. Their lunch companions melted away. Adam was talking hard at Eve, hands gesticulating, ears red, presumably trying to dismiss the cook's outburst as the ravings of a madman. Eve was staring straight ahead, the sky's entire store of thunder rolling behind her eyes. That red rash was spreading over her chest and neck at lightning speed. "I'd get out of there if I were you, mate," I whispered, more to myself than to Adam. I had seen that look before, on Robyn's face.

Heavenly Hosts were circulating, ordering citizens to sit down, calling for silence, looking more and more harried as everyone ignored them. One of them led Jezebel to a chair and started fanning her and adjusting her dress, the top of which had slid down almost to her waist. Another one of the hosts whacked his clipboard on one of the tables, the sound echoing like a gunshot, and shouted, "Silence, I said! Be quiet!"

The last titters and whispers died down. And then Penelope's husband slapped his hands onto the table, pushed himself to his feet, and spoke.

"Why should we be quiet? Why should we? Is this Heaven, or jail? We're not prisoners. We are citizens of Heaven!" He waved his fork at the nearest Heavenly Host. "I'm sick of you young people telling me what to do all day long. I'm old enough to be your grandfather, goddamnit, and I will *not* be treated like a child any longer!"

"Hear, hear," rejoined Penelope as she stood to join her husband, her handbag still stowed neatly on her wrist. All around the Hall there were murmurs of "Hear, hear," and "Quite right". Then, unbelievably, citizens started to rise to face the Heavenly Hosts, until three quarters of them were standing in defiance. Those left sitting stared hard at their plates.

There was a stretch of silence as Heavenly Hosts and citizens stared at each other. The Hosts looked puzzled, and nervous. They clutched their clipboards like life rings. They had no idea what to do. No one had prepared them for dissidence.

The old man rapped his fork smartly on the table. "I want to speak to God. I want to speak to God right now. I'm not happy, and I want to tell God."

Adam sprang to his feet, obviously grateful for the distraction. "God isn't available at present. You can talk to me if you want though. He's left me in charge. I'm the first man! First man on…"

"Top!" roared Jezebel, then collapsed into tipsy, giggling mumbles.

Eve rose to her feet, hands on her lovely hips, and addressed Jezebel in a low voice rich with fury. "I trusted you. We were friends. I let you win Snakes and Ladders every time, and not just because I'm scared of snakes." She drew a breath. "I confided in you. I told you my husband had a tiny penis!"

Adam turned to her, eyes wide and face flushed, and for a moment I sensed the man he really was: original, significant. In love and foolish. "Tiny? It's perfectly in proportion! And I've never heard you complain…"

"What do you mean, he's unavailable?" bellowed Penelope's

husband. "He's *always* unavailable! He's never at his own cocktail party. He's never around. We never see him. Where is he? *What in the blazes is going on?*" The old man slapped the table hard and took a step back to steady himself. His chair toppled over, and Kit rose to pick it up.

Murmurs of agreement sparked like stars coming out at night: first one, then two, then a rush of determined appearances. They grew louder. Adam went to speak again, his hands raised as if to ward off the growing unrest, but was stopped by Eve. "Shut up, you good for nothing, cheating wanker. Who's tasting the *fucking* forbidden fruit now? Just shut up and tell them the truth." She turned to the Heavenly Hosts, most of whom had huddled together against the left wall, confused and afraid. "Come on! Come on then, you cowardly morons. We've heard some of the truth tonight, so we might as well carry on the way we've started. So let's tell them where God is. Go on, *tell them*!" Eve's chest was scarlet and heaving, her eyes wild and defiant. A clearly terrified Adam had sidled into the kitchen, leaving his wife marooned. Penelope's husband left his table, beelined for the Heavenly Hosts, and stopped in front of a clearly terrified young woman with pigtails. His eyebrows formed a bushy arrow.

"Well? We're waiting! *Where is he?*"

At that moment the front door slammed open. Every head turned as Michael and the White Guys strode into the hall. Michael's eyes danced. He and his companions made their way towards Eve and Jezebel, snaking between tables with authority and grace.

Eve stood defiant, even when they reached her and Michael pinned her hands behind her back. He started to march her towards the kitchen. Jezebel was as compliant as a child, still giggling weakly as another White Guy led her away.

"Wait a minute! Where are you taking them?" shouted Penelope's husband, leader of the short-lived revolution. "Leave them alone!" He started towards Eve.

I was close enough to hear Michael's whispered, vicious reply.

"Hold your tongue old man, or you'll be next."

Every head was turned towards the kitchen when I heard Kit's voice at my ear.

"Come on. Now's our chance."

19

Dear Dad,

Mum took me out for coffee this morning. Not that either of us drink coffee. It's one of those weird phrases that doesn't mean what it says. "Let's go out for coffee" means "We need to talk", or "I'm leaving you", or "Let's pretend".

We met in a new café at the end of Carisbrook Street. Oh God, you would have hated it. It's called "Time for Tea". There are clocks everywhere, and I mean everywhere. Not just on the walls, but suspended from the ceiling, painted on the floors and furniture, embedded in the toilet seats (ewwww), on every shelf and in every nook. There's a green rug in the entrance that says in enormous black lettering:

Time Waits for No One. Coffee's all round!

I stamped on the apostrophe.

We ordered and sat down. I felt like Bridget Jones. Tick-tock, tick-tock. Mum looked around brightly. "Well, this is certainly different!"

"Not very zen-like, is it?" I said.

Mum pshawed into her handbag as she drew out her patchouli hand sanitiser. "Oh, Andy. Most Buddhists like to be on time, you know." She squeezed out a noisette of gel and set the bottle down on the glass table, which was etched with a clock face. She rubbed her hands together more vigorously than necessary. I could tell she was nervous. I tried to bear in mind what Aunt Fleur had said. Cliffs and waves. I took a breath. Give her a chance.

A perky young woman arrived with our drinks and melting moments. She wore a giant Mickey Mouse watch. His white-gloved hands jabbed at the numbers and the little lines in between. Now! Now! Now! Funeral! Eulogy! Hurry!

I waited until we had both started eating. I was nervous too. Scared, in fact. I was sitting across from my own mother, and I was scared. Mothers can be terrifying, I thought. It's the power, and the love, and the violent struggle between them.

"Aunt Fleur was crying last night," I said.

Mum made a small tone of pity, complicated by biscuit crumbs.

"I went in to comfort her, and she showed me a book that belonged to Dad. An exercise book that Dad wrote in when he was a boy."

Mum stopped chewing. The grandfather clock in the corner chimed, providing timely exclamation marks. In that moment I realised that she knew about the book, and what had happened to it.

"Really?" Mum picked up her green tea bowl and hid her face behind it. "Fancy that. What was in it?"

"Stories. Dad's stories, and poems. He wrote them when he was young. Younger than me. Didn't he ever show it to you?"

I swear, even during a nuclear apocalypse, as all the fires of Hell are burning around you and you're bidding adieu to the dying loved one cradled in your arms, a beaming waitperson will appear to ask if everything is OK with your meal. Sure enough, right at that moment Ms Mickey Mouse materialised at my elbow.

"How are we going here, ladies? Everything all right?"

"Fine," I said, hoping I was emitting fuck-off vibes.

"Can I get you ladies anything else today?"

"No, thanks, we won't have time."

The pun escaped her. She left the bill on a little dish with a picture of the white rabbit from Alice in Wonderland looking at his fob watch.

I sipped my diet coke. "They were good," I said.

"The melting moments?"

"The stories."

Mum poked at the last crumbs. "Oh. Mmmn?" She licked her fingers.

"Dad wanted to be a writer. Aunt Fleur told me. Why didn't you?"

"Want to be a writer?"

"Mum. Just tell me." I had very little patience left.

"I … well, I don't know. It wasn't really relevant, was it?" She laughed awkwardly, reaching again for the hand sanitiser, squeezing too much into her palm, making a show of reaching for a napkin to wipe off the excess.

I was starting to get angry. "Why couldn't you have let me be the judge of that?"

Mum shifted awkwardly in her seat and redundantly consulted her watch. "Well, I mean, it's not what happened, is it? In his life. He became a librarian. And that was that."

The door of the café opened and a group of middle-aged women with brown shoes and hessian shoulder bags came in, chattering. Book club, I thought. Probably reading The Time Traveler's Wife. "You and Aunt Fleur aren't telling me something," I insisted. "Something important about Dad. Are you going to tell me, or not?" I felt the sting behind my nose that signalled imminent tears. I bit my lip, hard. I didn't want to be like my mother.

Mum whipped up the bill. "There's nothing to tell," she said as she rooted again in her bag, this time for her wallet. "I don't know what book you're talking about. He used to tinker, that's all. Tinker. He was never going to make a living from it, was he? Maybe it was just … school stuff."

"It was burnt, Mum. Around the edges."

Mum went pale, and for a few seconds the bill was forgotten. And then, for longer than a few seconds, I watched her wilt. We sat in silence until, with a jolt of surprise, I saw one tear slipping from my mother's eye, down her nose, and onto the table. I don't know why I did it, but I reached for her hand. She grasped it for a few seconds and held on. We hadn't touched each other for such a long time. She squeezed my fingers and looked at me as if she wanted to say something, something significant, and I thought to myself that this wasn't one of her performances, this was real, and I squeezed back, but of course the bloody waitress arrived again to collect the bill and clear the table.

"Okkkeeeey dokey, ladies! We all set?"

"Time to go," said my mother in a strange kind of voice as she drew back her hand and prepared to leave. We didn't speak on the way home. Neither of us knew what to say, or how to cradle the brief intimacy we had shared.

I wish you were still alive, Dad. Then you could tell me what happened.

Andy

20

Kit grabbed my arm and we backed up in what I hoped was nonchalant unison towards the front door. No one was looking at us. The Heavenly Hosts had forgotten to be guards, their attention stolen by the angelic arrest. In a minute we were out and heading towards the reception building.

My legs were no match for Kit's enormous stride. I had to do a strange little dance-jog to keep up. "Where will they take them?" I asked, panting.

"Dunno," said Kit grimly, glancing behind. "But I'm starting to wonder if all those missing people really did escape." He strode even faster. "Don't you think it's weird that Jacob causes trouble, then suddenly he isn't there anymore?"

I was really jogging now, my throat tight and hot.

Kit spoke faster, his words racing his feet. "Come to think of it, about a week before you arrived, Abraham started raving on at lunch about being the 'goddamn father of every nation' and demanding an audience with God. I remember the White Guys trying to hustle him out of the hall. Then he didn't turn up for dinner, and we haven't seen *him* since." He barked out a bitter laugh. "Another coincidence? To disappear just after displaying dissent?"

I huffed in reply, but he was already metres ahead.

The reception building looked deserted – everyone was at lunch – but Kit didn't even bother trying the front door. Instead he disappeared round the right side of the building. I panted after him, following a concrete path lined on the right by an immaculate box hedge, over which I glimpsed the Hallelujah Hall roof and a sparkle of lake. Just before reaching the end and emerging onto the cocktail lawn, Kit stopped, reached up one gangly arm, and pulled down a fire escape ladder in a rusty clatter. He must have seen the look on my face because as he put his foot on the lowest rung and started to haul himself up, he threw over this shoulder, "It's held me every other time. Come on." It was too late to point out to him the obvious flaw in his logic: that I weighed at least a third more than him. I redundantly adjusted my waistband and followed him.

The ladder gave onto a narrow metal platform that ran around the second storey. Kit nimbly made his way to the back of the building as I followed, grasping the railing. He reached a sash window just above the back door overlooking the cocktail lawn and stopped.

"Right," he whispered as I caught up. "Let's hope it's still open. It was last time." He wiggled his fingers about in a tiny gap at the bottom then heaved with a grunt. The window slid silently upward. He winked and stood aside. "Wait till you see who this office belongs to. He obviously forgot to lock it properly. Now, when I pull it all the way up, climb in as quickly as you can; it tends to slam back down after a bit."

A few undignified seconds of middle-aged gymnastics and I was in, crouching on the heavy-duty office carpet and watching as Kit leapt through, agile as a cat. He grabbed the window before it fell and closed it quietly, latching it behind him. Then he pulled down white plastic venetian blinds and flipped them closed. "Don't want any unexpected company," he whispered.

We were in the kind of office you'd find in any large corporate: oversized grey formica table, black chair, whiteboard, filing cabinet with cheap ornament on top – in this case what looked like Noah's Ark made entirely out of matches – and a bookcase, almost empty apart from a smattering of manila folders, a couple of ring binders, a thesaurus, and a yellow thermos. There was a laminated fire escape plan on the back of the door. **Do YOU Know Your Escape Route? If**

Not, Your In DANGER, it scolded. *No idea,* I thought, *but at least I know the difference between your and you're.*

I shifted my gaze to the desk, which held an hourglass paperweight, a closed laptop with a mouse in the shape of a racing car, and half a dozen coffee mugs. Inside them, dregs of coffee were sporting patches of green and yellow mould. In the rubbish bin by the side of the desk several banana skins, brown and shrivelled with age, nestled between balled-up paper, pencil shavings, and an empty Coke can.

A small metal sign sat by itself in the middle of the front edge of the desk, facing the door. It said:

GOD

I gaped at Kit.

"Yup," he nodded. "I snooped around a bit last time, didn't find anything bizarre apart from the bidet." He nodded towards a sliding panel in the right wall that I hadn't noticed. Then he moved towards the office door and turned the handle. "Bit slack on security. Maybe God doesn't need any. Come on."

"Wait." I grabbed Kit's arm. "How do we know it's safe? What if we've been followed? What … what makes you think it's safe to bring me here and expect me to just … just follow along?"

"We don't have time for this, Maurice," Kit hissed, opening the door. "Michael will be back soon. That's his office just across the hall."

A white door with a pair of painted wings above it stood ajar.

I gripped Kit tighter. "We're not moving until you tell me you're not nuts. And not leading me into some sort of death trap." I harrumphed a bit, trying to look threatening.

Kit sighed and turned back to me. "When I first arrived, a couple of months back, I worked in the gatehouse for a bit with Peter, OK? They needed someone good at computers; something about their 'arrival algorithms' going on the blink. I just tinkered in the back end a bit;

not sure I was any help. Peter hardly talked to me, just watched. One day he had to go and do something urgently for Michael, and he left a screen open by mistake with a locked file just sitting there."

I loosened my grip on Kit's arm.

"If there's one thing I can't resist, it's cracking a code," he continued. "Got in easily. The file showed plans of the reception building and notes on security weaknesses and codes and 'Top Secret' documents." He started pulling me through the doorway. "First time, I got into God's office. Second time, right down to the library. Third time: who knows?"

He grinned. I scowled and held on to the doorjamb, refusing to budge.

Kit's voice softened. "Look. I played computer games a lot. Sometimes I broke into places online. I was a nerd and lactose-intolerant and I didn't have many friends and I had a weird thing for pens and pocket protectors, but I never was, nor am I now, crazy. Come on!"

I glanced once more around God's office. "One tick," I said, crossing the office to pluck a magnetic marker pen from the whiteboard. Then I added an apostrophe and an "e" to the fire escape sign on the back of the door. "I may be dead, but grammatically correct English isn't," I said.

"And he thinks *I'm* nuts," muttered Kit as we hurried out, shutting the door quietly behind us.

We turned left. A short distance and a side table sporting a bonsai arrangement of a cross later, we turned right, then past several unmarked doors and a giant framed cross stitch of *The Last Supper* before turning right once more. The dim lighting and faint smell of carpet and day-old sandwiches made me think of the staffroom at the Bressington Heights Community Library. I never used to eat there: I couldn't stand the amateur attempts at small talk and the chewing noises. A green elevator sign at the midpoint of this stretch of corridor blinked. Kit pressed the down button and the doors opened immediately. There was an enormous mirror on the back wall. I looked terrified and plump; Kit looked tall and excited. The fearlessness of youth, I thought. Why had I never had access to that? I coaxed my sparse hair from one sweaty side to the other. My hands were shaking. I clasped them together, hard.

There were three buttons inside the lift:

Ground Floor
Library
Conference Room

Kit pressed the one I dreaded the most. The doors closed and elevator muzak meandered. There was no sensation of movement. I was just about to tap the button again, in the irritating way that people redundantly jiggle the button at pedestrian crossings, when a "ping" and an almost imperceptible jolt reassured me that we had at least gone somewhere. There was a long pause, a suspension of breath, then a gentle exhale as the doors slid open to darkness.

"We're underground now," Kit whispered, fumbling with his trousers. "Best to be discreet until we know if we're alone." I experienced a brief moment of alarm before he drew a small torch out of his trouser pocket. "Had this with me when I died," he said.

"What were you doing?" I asked, tentatively. "When you … when you died?" Even in Heaven, death was one of those tiptoe-on-eggshells topics.

"Sending a letter," said Kit, busily fiddling with the torch. "Damn batteries."

"To whom?"

"Someone important," said Kit, not looking at me. "Didn't send it, in the end." He slapped the torch violently against his palm, and a weak beam flickered, then intensified. "Finally."

We were in a tiled vestibule. On our right was a fire escape door with a laminated sign of a stick person running down stairs with spindly flames pursuing him. There was a single door directly in front of us. It was yellow and bore a silver name plate identifying it as the **Library**, and warning people like Kit and me to **Keep Out.** A silver padlock hung from a sliding bolt. It was very obviously locked. I felt my stomach drop with relief. Then Kit reached into his other pocket and pulled out a small silver key.

"Borrowed this from the gatehouse. Turns out Peter leaves a few things lying about." He winked.

A few seconds later the door clicked open and we were in a small administration office housing a desk, a black swivel office chair, and a single filing cabinet. Perched on the front of the desk was a triangular cardboard sign: **Quiet Please.** Below the words a tiny cartoon angel held a finger against its lips.

There were three doors in addition to the one we had just entered: one each to our right and left and one directly in front of us. The sign on the left-hand door read: **Non-fiction. Autobiographies. Encyclopaedias. Dictionaries.** On the right: **Fiction. Bibles. Religion in General.** The one facing us was either a description of what was inside or a strongly worded warning: **Citizens. KEEP OUT.**

Kit handed the torch to me then strode over to the filing cabinet and pulled out the top drawer. He took out a manila folder labelled **Just Arrived** and opened it. I directed the beam over his shoulder. There were six or seven sheets of paper, each with a photo in the top right-hand corner. The photos had obviously been taken at the gatehouse near the entrance of Heaven. The arrivals looked variously shocked, non-plussed, and politely curious. Names were printed at the top of each page, with a few short snippets of information, including one that was subtitled "Method of Death". Two car crashes, one operating table misadventure, three cancers, and one "undetermined".

"Still no one I know," said Kit, quickly scanning pages. "You?"

I realised I was really only interested in one name. "Where am I?" I whispered. The existential ambiguity wasn't lost on me.

"You'll be in there now," he said, nodding at the middle door. "Come on."

Kit replaced the **Just Arrived** file and closed the drawer. "We'll have to make it quick," he warned, as he headed to the door. He looked back and motioned for me to join him as he opened it.

We walked into darkness. Immediately, I could smell books. Kit shut the door, and we stood shoulder to shoulder in inky blackness. "We can probably risk the lights in here," he said after an anxious moment.

In the seconds after Kit flicked the switch and a dozen fluorescent bars blipped and jolted awake, I felt like I was going to faint. The room before me was so like the Bressington Heights Community Library that I swayed and had to clutch the wall to steady myself. It was about the size of a tennis court, with rows of bookshelves running like dominoes down the left-hand side, across the back wall and back up the right-hand side to form a giant, rather awkward letter U. There were the laminated signs on the end of each shelf, indicating the filing system. A – C. D – F. There were the grey chairs and tables in the middle, set out in such a way that you were forced to read your selections uncomfortably close to strangers; there, just to the left of the entrance, was the checkout desk with its computer and coffee cup rings on the fading faux wood. Even the carpet was the same dizzy swirl of sickening colour. I half expected Felicity to stride out from behind a stack, coffee flask in one hand and unfortunate pre-schooler in the other, and bark: "There you *are* Maurice. Now for *God's sake* can you clear *the* trolleys and find this child's mother. *And* the toilet *roll* needs replacing."

Kit's voice tickled at my ear. "You OK, Maurice? You've gone all pale." He was looking at me with concern. "Do you need to sit down? Only, we haven't got much time."

I blinked. "Right. Yes. I thought I'd seen my workplace for the last time before I died, is all."

Before Kit could ask me to explain I was heading to my right across the swirly floor towards "T". In a practised movement I ran my finger along the edges of the books, narrowing down my search. Taylor, Suzanne. Templar, Penelope. Thomas, Doubting. Todd, Matthew.

Toogood, Maurice.

I picked myself up.

21

Wednesday, 1 pm

Dear Dad,

I'm in the university library. I had to get out when Mum turned up with her mad-as-fuck friend Barbara. They asked me if I wanted to come out for lunch at the Hare Krishna restaurant in town – the one just across from McDonalds. I said I couldn't go because I had study to do.

"Oh, Robyn," breathed Barbara, her First Nation necklaces and Trade Aid earrings jangling as she shook her head. "Isn't that the bravest thing you've ever heard? Father not dead three days and she's already back to thinking about her studies. Grief is so transitory for the young, is it not? Look, I got a new tattoo." She pulled down her kaftan to reveal the top of one stupendously saggy breast. "It's the Native American symbol for sexual love. See the two wolves? Do you think they'll have samosas?"

Told you she was mad as fuck.

This is one of the places I feel most at peace. It's weird, sitting here surrounded by books, thinking of you at work every day, surrounded by books. The difference is, I love them and you hated them. I wonder if you miss them now that you're dead.

A friend told me once that as she approached the end of a book she would start rushing, tumbling towards the end, clumsily tripping over letters and words, racing the pages to see who would get there first, her or the story. I could never understand that. When I'm reading a book I love, I start to slow down near the end, delaying the inevitable, reluctant

118

to let the story finish. I can never rush through the last few pages. I'm afraid of missing out on the savouring; the delicate picking over of each and every word. Also, when I get down to the last few pages, I need to get away to be on my own, so I can feel what has to be felt in the quiet. I say my farewells in solitude.

I think if I was reading a book about you I would rush. I would rush right to the very end and I would read it in crowded train stations and at school assemblies and in swimming pool cafeterias heaving with small children.

There's a boy looking at me from the periodicals photocopier. Every time I look up he looks away, back to the shelf. He's probably thinking, there's the girl whose father just died. He's probably wondering what the hell I'm doing in the library when I should be at home, broken with grief.

I was never very interested in boys. Messy, stupid, and smelly was my pre-adolescent summation of them. (Particularly their feet. What is it about boys' feet? They're like giant smelly paddles. Even in shoes they look grotesque.)

When I was about 12, Caroline told me that if you liked a boy you had to let him stick his tongue in your mouth and "rub your titties". From that moment on I was determined to never let a boy within an arm's length of me. The "titties" thing didn't bother me so much (perhaps aided by the fact that I had not even a hint of them until I was nearly fifteen), but the thought of a slimy testosterone-driven tongue swilling around in my mouth, remnants of breakfast jostling in gobby whirlpools, made me want to vomit.

Do you remember when Caroline and I became friends? I'll bet not. Sometimes you couldn't even remember her name. We were ten, and we were both the weird kids. Caroline had developed "titties" early and was already in a bra. At ten! All the other kids at school would tease her, the boys pinging the plastic clasp at her back, the mean girls running their fingers down her back and chanting, "Caroline, Caroline, I can feel your braaaaa line."

One lunchtime I found her in tears down the bottom of the field. I went there to write most days. Being with other kids didn't really interest me. All they talked about was who liked whom and who had the latest accessory/pencil case/clothing range. Or they made fun of my hair, or my stomach. But I didn't really care about that.

I sat down beside Caroline and put my arm around her shoulders. When she had stopped sobbing she told me that someone had scribbled a picture of a stick person with enormous breasts and stuffed it in her lunchbox. I offered her some of my chocolate, and we ripped up the picture and buried it under dirt still wet with her tears.

As we grew up and all the other girls grew breasts, Caroline became "normal" again. I never did. She was accepted back into the fold, but I preferred to stay out of it. She gained a whole new group of friends and over the years we had less and less in common. I'm surprised we're still in contact, to be honest, especially since Caroline works in an accountant's office now and I'm at uni. I guess those early humiliations forged a bond. We see each other once a month or so. I haven't heard from her yet. Maybe she doesn't know that you died, although the notice went in the newspaper this morning.

I don't really have any friends at law school. I don't want them, to be honest. I'd rather just go to class then come home and write. They all dress and walk and talk like bloody lawyers already, anyway.

I can't ever remember you having friends. Did you even know how to make them?

Andy

22

My book was about as large as the Gideon Bible in my cabin, and perhaps half as thick. Just as Kit had said, it was a proper hardback. The cover was dark blue, the slightly textured surface cool under my fingertips. My name was embossed on the front in gold lettering. I recognised the font immediately as Book Antiqua, the same one I had favoured many years ago when I was writing my novel.

I opened the cover. There was no index page, no frontispiece, no papery throat clearing. Instead, my face stared out at me, as if to challenge its reflection. It was, I realised, the photo taken of my arrival at the gates of Heaven. I looked like I had just woken up with a thumping hangover. I could see the arm of the Heavenly Host who had greeted me elbowing its yellow way into the bottom left-hand corner.

Was my hair really that thin on top? That stringy? There was no distinguishable part. Greyish strands darted this way and that, unable to make up their minds. I reached up again and smoothed them right, then left.

Kit appeared at my shoulder as I turned the page. Brief information about my death followed, and a record of my arrival. The third page contained basic information about my family.

Wife (divorced): Robyn. Daughter: Andy (complicated).
Sister: Fleur (no longer close).
Parents deceased.

There are moments in life (and death) when it feels as if time is suspended and you are outside your body, floating, grasping at clouds, flying at a million miles an hour yet desperately still. Page three brought with it possibly the strangest moment of my afterlife thus far, as I began to read about myself:

Maurice Brian Toogood was born on the 25th of June, 1965. His parents, Barry and Adeline, were a factory manager and schoolteacher respectively. Adeline suffered from severe anxiety, no doubt exacerbated by the verbal and emotional abuse suffered at the hand…

I flicked quickly from my childhood to the next page, which was filled with a neat and clinical summary of my youth. Page five recounted my university years, my whirlwind courtship, my wedding. My heart clapper faster. I knew what was coming. I sensed myself slamming back into my body, the stench of books exploding freshly in my nostrils, and I stumbled suddenly backwards.

"Watch it!" hissed Kit, awkwardly catching my fall as my book tumbled from my hands and slapped shut on the floor. He helped to set me straight on my feet before scooping it up. I ripped it from him with a loud "Don't!" before he could find my lost place.

Kit knit his eyebrows. "Christ, calm down. I'm not going to read it, if that's what you're worried about. What did you do, rob a bank or something?"

I gripped my book tighter. "Of course not. A bank, Jesus Christ. What the hell? Just … just go and read your own fucking book. I didn't do anything, OK?"

Kit raised his eyebrows and his hands to his chest, palms facing me, and started walking backwards. After a few steps he pivoted on one foot and made his way to a stack on the other side of the room.

Still flustered, I stomped about a bit then looked down at my book. I had flicked forward several pages, and waiting for me were a few short, hand-written paragraphs, capped by two words in the top right-hand corner, like a daydreaming title that had wandered to the edge of the page: Monday morning.

It was a letter. *Dear Dad,* it began.

The letter was in her handwriting; that round, unpredictable scrawl that annoyed me so much every time she wrote "eggs" at the top of a shopping list I had written, deliberately looping the tails of the g's down to obliterate the item below. I took a breath. I knew my daughter thought I was a pile of excrement, but I wasn't sure I was ready to see it in print.

Dear Dad,

I pretended not to hear you when you yelled at me to get up. I knew I would miss my first lecture, but I really didn't give a shit.

Thank God for a lazy daughter, I thought. I read to the end and felt a spasm of relief. Nothing nasty – apart from the fact that she was apparently trying to convince herself she was a writer. Actually, I thought, it sounds like she's in shock. I turned the page. Another letter, written later the same day.

Dear Dad,

All I can think about is that poem by Dylan Thomas about not going gentle into that good night and raging against the dying of the light.

> *And you, my father, there on the sad height,*
> *Curse, bless, me now with your fierce tears, I pray.*
> *Do not go gentle into that good night.*
> *Rage, rage against the dying of the light.*

I say this, over and over. And I'm thirsty, like, all the time. I'm drinking glass after glass of water and it's never enough. My feet are cold.

The thing is, I can't imagine you raging about anything.

I felt a little indignant. I used to rage about a lot of things. Andy always being late, for example. The way she would hog the bathroom. The way she wrote "g". The time she borrowed my razor to shave her legs and rendered it so blunt I practically cut my throat the next morning. I did plenty of raging.

I vaguely registered a door opening behind me. I glanced up to see Kit disappearing out to the foyer. He could just wait a few more minutes. I turned the page.

Monday night

When the policeman told me you had died I didn't feel anything much; I was numb. Aunt Fleur said this was a "perfectly normal" response. Then she suggested that I write stuff down to help me "sort out my thoughts". She said I should write what I remember about you – the good stuff as well as the bad stuff. I don't think I have much of the former, to be honest.

Still in shock, obviously. I read on.

The psychiatrist. Now there was a memory I promptly turned my back on. Ridiculous.

But then Andy reminded me of one particular incident when she was young, when she'd cried out in the night and wanted me instead of her mother. We'd been arguing a lot, Robyn and I, and Robyn had said some pretty horrible things that day. I think even Andy knew it was a bit over the top. I felt chuffed that she had chosen me instead of her mother, hoping that perhaps, in her childish way, she was coming to my defence. One: Nil. I stroked her hair as she fell back to sleep, and I was struck by how soft it was, like silk flames against her pillow. My Fire Princess, I used to call her.

Or did I? Maybe I just thought it sometimes.

I looked up from my book and blinked. I remembered holding Andy when she was little. When she was a newborn, my arms nearly fell off from carrying her around all day. She just would not sleep, and Robyn would insist faintly that she couldn't handle it and retire to her bed. All the night feedings were left to me, too. Another punishment. Funny how it didn't seem like a punishment, though. I quite liked those secret hours in the half-light, just me and my daughter, the only ones awake, sharing something. We would smile at each other, and she would be asleep before finishing her bottle.

Anyway, I thought. *Pity she turned into such a ghastly teenager.*

Kit called my name and I turned to see his head jutting around the door.

"Come and take a look at this!" I glimpsed wild eyes before his head disappeared again. I hesitated for a nanosecond before lifting the back of my jersey and stuffing my book down the back of my trousers. Then I hurried over to the door, flicked the light switch, and went out into the foyer.

Kit was standing in front of the filing cabinet, the top drawer pulled out. He held an open manila folder loosely in his hands. His eyes were huge as he looked from me to the file and back to me, saying nothing. I crossed the little room, knocking over the **Quiet Please** sign in my haste.

Kit flipped the file closed for a moment to show me the single word printed on the front. Departures. He then flipped it open again.

We had both hoped to find a list of the all the people who had disappeared, and, more importantly, some sort of clue as to how we could follow them. But there was only one piece of paper. And this is what it said:

Departed: GOD
Date of Departure: NOT SURE
Reason: UNSPECIFIED
Action to be taken: ABSOLUTELY NO IDEA. ADAM TO STAND IN FOR THE MEANTIME. CITIZENS TO BE TOLD NOTHING.

Kit and I looked at each other. "Holy fuck," whispered Kit.

I took the file from Kit's hands, dropped it back in the filing cabinet, closed the drawer, and then picked up the sign I had knocked to the floor. I fired it into the rubbish bin. "Couldn't have said it better myself. Let's get out of here."

23

Wednesday, 6 pm

Dear Dad,

Just about to leave the library. I haven't studied much; I can't stop reading your book. I can't help thinking how little resemblance your poems bear to the memories I have of you. You wrote a lot of poems. Some of them were quite good. They were about simple things – spending a rainy Saturday at home, the colour green (Green is a freshness, Green is a tang, A pasture, a vineyard, Green grapes in there hang), your dog. But I see you also tried your hand at limericks and haiku and even a Kipling-esque account of how the elephant got its trunk. (It's actually pretty clever. If you had been famous I could publish it; a posthumous tribute.) That dreadful stab at an epic poem all in clumsy rhyming couplets, though. I see it was scratchily attempted at age fourteen, which perhaps excuses it a bit. The thing that strikes me most is that there was an innocence, a simple joy to the poems that I never saw in you. Was it Mum who knocked it out of you? Or was it me?

The stories are mostly about battles and astronauts and epic journeys. But there's one that really gets to me, for some reason. It's right at the end of the book and it's very short. I can't stop reading it aloud, over and over, like an incantation.

Once upon a time there was a strong and handsome soldier. He liked fighting and he was very good at killing all the bad people. One day the soldier met a beautiful queen. She was really a witch in disguise but he didn't know that, he thought she was really nice and kind. One day the queen told the soldier she didn't want him to fight anymore because she was afraid he would die. But what she really meant was she didn't like him fighting because it was boring and he went away a lot. But the soldier said he wanted to fight. So the queen turned into the witch and put a spell on him so his sword broke and then she cut off his head (with a different sword that wasn't broken) and he died and went to Heaven. And then he got to fight with all the angels and he fell in love with a beautiful little star princess (who really was a princess and not a witch) so he was pretty happy.

You had drawn a picture on the inside back cover of a little soldier on a horse with lots of angels flying around his head. The soldier is smiling but all the angels look angry. In the background, through a set of gates, you can just make out a little figure with long red hair, just like mine, and a crown and stars all around her. You can't see God anywhere.

I hate having red hair. It's almost as bad as being overweight. I still get "ginga" comments, often in jest, but sometimes not – even from Caroline when she's pissed off at me. And it's not like she's Bressington's Next Top Model. Her hair's all stringy and looks dirty all the time. I flung that at her once, in an argument. "Boys like dirty blondes," she said. I used to tell Mum about the teasing when I was younger, and she always used to say things like ignore them, they're just jealous, sticks and stones, etc. I think I'd rather have had the sticks and stones.

You didn't like my hair either. You always used to say how silly it looked up in a ponytail.

Anyway, I don't really care. I never wanted to be pretty. I just wanted to be brave, and brilliant.

There was one boy I liked, I guess. It was last year, at school. He arrived halfway through, so there were only two terms to go.

You would have hated this boy. Particularly his hair. He wore it long and he slouched and mumbled and he was a bit smelly, if I'm perfectly honest. But he made clever jokes and his handwriting was neat and he was amazing with computers and he always carried a copy of Khalil Gibran's 'The Prophet' around with him. (Pretentious but had potential.) When I spoke or asked a question in class he always looked at me intently like he was trying to record everything I said so he could take it away and pore over it afterwards. And I got the feeling he didn't really notice that I was overweight.

One day in science I dropped my briefcase right in front of everyone as I walked in. Pens and pencils and mints and – oh, horror – a lone tampon tumbled out and rolled gently across the floor. People coming in had to dodge and step over them.

Everything decelerated to slow motion. I felt my neck and face burning as I picked up the briefcase and started to retrieve my pens. I saw the tampon disappear under the teacher's bench. I left it. Someone stepped on a pen and nearly fell over, cursing. Someone at the front bench laughed.

Then I noticed this boy ducking up and down, picking up pens, saying "Excuse me, sorry, excuse me" as he weaved in and out of people. When he had them all he brought them over, and we both sat down in the last two seats at a bench by the window.

"Why so many pens?" he asked as he handed them to me.

I looked straight ahead as I answered. "I like having loads of them. I'm against minimalism."

The teacher entered and closed the door. She walked to the bench and started fiddling with her bunsen burner as the place hushed down.

"Me too," he whispered, and he turned out his pockets to reveal around a dozen pens and pencils. We looked at each other and smiled. I glanced at his feet. Huge, but I didn't mind.

I didn't speak to him much after that. I would see him occasionally in the quad at lunchtime, by himself, his head in a textbook, or just staring at nothing in particular. Sometimes I would catch him staring at me, but he always looked away like he was embarrassed. I think he was in the computer lab, mostly. Lots of the other kids thought he was weird. I thought he was sort of cool. I should have tried to make friends with him, I guess, but I think I was a little afraid. I think I was afraid that I would like him a whole lot. Sometimes it's safer to dream about things than to have them.

And then the year was over and that was that. I have no idea what happened to him. I think his family moved overseas. I guess I'll never know.

I remember that his fingers were long and slender. Piano player hands. Sometimes I wondered what it would feel like to put my own hand in one of his. Sometimes I even imagined him touching my hair, or my face, or other parts of me. Not my thighs, obviously; they're too fat.

That's the only boy I was ever interested in. Oh my God, I would've rather died than tell you this stuff when you were alive.

Two more days until the funeral. Still haven't started the eulogy but writing these letters has got me thinking an awful lot about you.

Andy

24

I lay awake for hours the night of our illicit library visit. The image of God on the run, silver beard and streams of glory stretching out in his wake, played over and over in my mind. What was so dreadful about Heaven that its monarch would abandon it?

At 1 am I got up for a pee. As I stumbled past the window I could see hundreds and thousands of stars, brighter than I had ever seen on Earth. They were all spaced equidistantly, as if someone had precisely measured out a giant grid and placed a star at each intersection. They winked and fizzed on their inky backdrop. *They look alive,* I thought. *They look like they're whispering secrets to each other.* I couldn't see the moon. Perhaps there wasn't one, or perhaps God had run away with it.

If I ever get out of here, I mused as I peed, *I'm going to write another book. I'm going to call it: Are you there God? It's me, Maurice.* Librarian jokes. I chuckled as I flushed. Then I remembered the book I had stuffed under my mattress for safekeeping.

It was too risky to read it, I decided. It wasn't that I was scared to read what my daughter had written about me. It wasn't that. Not at all. I was simply being careful. Who knew what sort of surveillance equipment they might have in Heaven? How did I know the White Guys weren't watching me pee and dress and cry and sleep? I had spent an interesting few minutes squinting closely at light fixtures before bedtime. I had brushed my teeth in the dark.

Finally, at 3 am, perhaps due to the disorientation of sleep deprivation, I took the bedside lamp, stuck it under the duvet, then retrieved my book and started to read it under the covers like the young boy I had once been; the boy who had tried to hide his nocturnal reading from his angry and heartbroken father.

More letters from Andy had appeared since we had been in the library. Did they appear as soon as she had written them, or did she have to post them first? I had to shake my head at the preposterousness, the ridiculous improbability of it.

I started reading. It was like spying on a stranger. She hated me: that, I knew. But I didn't know she had gone to law school as a rebellious gesture against everything she thought I stood for. Fleur had given her the book I wrote in when I was young. She had read it. She was trying to find out what had happened, and Robyn was scared. I felt a moment of jubilation at that thought, but it faded quickly. If Andy found out what really happened, the whole sorry business, she would hate me even more: for my weakness, my half-fulfilled ambition, my failure to fight back.

I felt a flash of anger at my sister. Why had she told Andy about my writing? Why had she given her my notebook?

I had made her swear she wouldn't tell. Any of it.

When I was a boy, I saw Fleur only as a big sister; not a person in her own right. I remember sitting with her at the top of the stairs once, late at night, both of us in our pyjamas, listening to the spikes and troughs of adult voices at war in the living room below. I was around seven, Fleur three years older.

I was desperately afraid that my parents' unhappiness was my fault. I was too quiet; too shy. I stayed in my room too much. I read too many books. I didn't find the lost ones. I found the lost ones. I had failed in my perceived duty to tightly bind the two parental strands. When they separated permanently two years later, I was so used to the fighting that peace was a novelty. Normal conversation held hidden daggers, and I was endlessly on guard.

We both went to live with our mother. I wanted unequivocally to be with her, to search for lost books together forever. We were inseparable. "I'll never let you go," she would whisper to me, pulling me close. Fleur, on the other hand, insisted on splitting her time between our mother and father equally. She showed no rancour to either, and no preferentiality.

As the years passed, she and her friends drifted in and out of our mother's house, segueing from tweens to teens to young adults as I observed from behind my books. Mother sat and read with me, but Fleur flitted freely between her two universes with the aplomb of someone who knows much more about life than their age should entitle them to.

One day – I was about fourteen, Fleur seventeen – I asked her why she bothered spending so much time with our father when he had been so cruel to our mother.

"Because there are always two sides to every story, Maurice," she had said, not unkindly. "You're a reader; you should know that better than most."

As far as I could tell, Andy was only getting one side of this particular story; the one in which I was the main protagonist. I hoped, despite Fleur's indiscretion, that it would stay that way.

They were planning my funeral. Who had chosen the funeral director? I wanted to slap her. By the sound of it, Andy did too.

I didn't know she had liked a boy. (She was right; he sounded like a tosser.) I couldn't quite get my head around the idea of my daughter being attracted to someone. Was it only yesterday I had stamped in muddy puddles with her?

Most significantly, I never knew that Andy genuinely wanted to be a writer. She had never told me, and I had assumed she didn't have a literary bone in her body. She was studying to be a lawyer, for God's sake. Surely that was as far from creative writing as you could possibly get. Was she any good, or was this just a teenage phase? Didn't all teenagers think their tortured recordings of angst had the makings of the next Pulitzer? Now she was supposed to be writing my eulogy. I hoped, for my sake and hers, that she had a modicum of talent.

As I read and re-read her letters, these one-way conversations from so far away, I was surprised to find myself growing increasingly angry. At Fleur, yes, but mostly at Andy. I was angry at her for not letting me know her. For hating me. I was furious at her for reading my private notebook. I was even more furious at her for wanting to write. And there was another feeling, one I could not name, something that gripped my heart so tightly that I gasped and had to run, blindly crashing into the bedside table and then the bathroom door before retching and retching again into the toilet, eyes watering, head pounding.

When I was calmer I paced the room for a while, then sat down on the bed. No longer giving a shit about hidden cameras, I returned the lamp to its place on the bedside table and flicked it on. I re-read the last letter, written at 6 pm the previous evening.

Once upon a time there was a strong and handsome soldier. He liked fighting and he was very good at killing all the bad people.

My heart clutched, then released.

I suddenly felt dull and limp and papery around the edges, like a pot plant wilting after a brittle summer afternoon. Exhausted, I lay down, clutching my book to my heart. I thought of Andy's red hair, hair that burned like embers in the sun, streaks of hot anger and passion and longing tumbling together in a glorious waterfall of fire, and eventually I tumbled with it into a troubled sleep.

25

Thursday, 3 am

Dear Dad,

I can't sleep. It's three in the morning but I don't feel remotely tired. I read some of your stories under the duvet with a torch, like I used to do when I was younger.

After leaving the library I dropped by home to pick up some clean clothes. When I walked in I could hear Mum talking in the way one might talk with a lover: purring, conspiratorial. (Not that I have vast experience to call upon.) I stood in the half-light just outside the kitchen and listened. Between her words lay long pauses that I could only guess at. She was on the phone.

"No, I told you, I can't. Not before the funeral, anyway. Mmmm-hmmm. Well, I am in mourning, after all. Uh-huh. For her sake, really, but I did once … yes … Well, he was her father, so … yes, me too. Uh-huh. Mmmm. So perhaps we could do that when things have settled down a bit and we can … uh-huh …" I moved into the doorway and the phone clattered to the countertop as Mum did an awkward kind of leap and pirouette.

"Darling! You're here! How lovely! How was the library? Profiterole?" She grabbed an empty plate from the bench and shoved it under my nose.

"The plate is empty, Mother," I said. "You've obviously eaten them all." I looked pointedly at her hips then back to her face.

The abandoned phone lay on the bench between us. I could hear a faint, tinny voice calling from it, as if from another dimension, or the afterlife. "Hello? Hello? Robyn? Are you th – "

Mum lunged for the phone, but I got there first. "Hello, this is Robyn's daughter, Andy. Mum can't talk to you right now because she's overcome with grief. So perhaps you could go and fuck yourself until such time she is ready to talk to you. Which may be never!" I shouted that last bit as loud as I could, then jabbed at the end call button and threw the phone on the bench. It skittered across the surface and clattered onto the floor. I was rivalling Mum for the title of Drama Queen of the Year, but it felt good. Mum just stood there with her mouth hanging open, and I think I may have even seen her eyes filling up with tears. I didn't care. "I'm only here to pick up some clothes, Mum. Don't let me disturb you." I brushed past her and jolted down the short hallway that led to my room.

I loved my room when I was a little girl. You had to go through the kitchen to get to it; I guess it had once been a pantry or an out-house or something. It was now a tiny afterthought, all weird angles and redundant pockets of space.

There was just enough room for a bed, a little chest of drawers, and a tiny desk that I had to move every time I wanted to get into the wardrobe. I had to be careful not to bang my head on a sloping beam when I got into bed. It used to fit me perfectly, this room. Now I had outgrown it, but not the idea of it: a secret, magical haven where I could dream and write and hide.

I closed the door, shutting Mum out. Through the little window I could see out to the garden that no one tended anymore. It was dark, but I could just make out the shape of Mum's Buddha that she had bought on sale from the garden centre about a year ago. I was with her at the time, and although I actually quite liked it, I wasn't about to tell her. She would have had me in a kaftan and off to the Hare Krishna vegetarian restaurant on Odessa Street before I could say "samosa". The fact that she claimed to be a Buddhist didn't prevent her from worshipping at the edible altar of another religion. I challenged her on this apparent heresy once, and she looked at me like I was stupid. "I don't believe in their god, silly, I just happen to like their onion bhajis," she said.

I didn't know Mum was seeing someone. It doesn't bother me, actually. I couldn't care less. But she could at least have put it on hold for a bit. At least until after the funeral.

I got down on my knees as if about to say my bedtime prayers (Now I lay me down to sleep, I pray the Lord my father to keep) and pulled out a box from under the bed. Although most of my writing is currently at your place, some of my earliest attempts – snippets of poems, tiny child stories penned in this room – are here. I don't worry about Mum finding them. She's too wrapped up in herself to wonder what might lie under my bed. Obviously too wrapped up in someone else too. But I don't care.

I opened the box. On top lay two photographs. One was of me in my school uniform. I was about six, my smile revealing three little gaps top and bottom where baby teeth had been spirited away by fairies. There was a faint smattering of freckles on my nose. Was it Mum or you who had told me that freckles were where angels kissed you in your sleep? I could just make out a little pocket of crumbs at one edge of my mouth.

The other photo was taken when I was ten. I know this because the foreground was dominated by our old dining table holding an enormous cake with ten candles. You and Mum had split up by then but had obviously managed to call a truce long enough to come together in the same room and sing me Happy Birthday. I'm leaning forward, my hands flat on the table and my elbows poked out to the sides. My lips are pursed, my eyes wide. All the candles are still lit, so I'm obviously just about to blow. The tiny flames are slightly fuzzy, faraway stars seen through the warp of years and distance. Mum is just behind my chair, her right hand over her heart, her round mouth mimicking mine. You are behind her and off to the left, your hands by your sides. You look bored, or annoyed, or a bit of both.

I felt a sudden, soggy urge to cry. I fought back. I hadn't cried for years. I blinked hard and the picture of me became a watercolour, the edges blurred and my face half rubbed out. I stuffed the photo into my jeans pocket then threw some clothes into my backpack. As I crept through the kitchen I could hear the faint click and tap of a computer keyboard from the living room, and I left without saying goodbye.

Caroline called when I got back to your place. It was awkward. We were no longer just friends; she was now a spectator, observing my grief but unsure how to meet it. She asked how I felt. I said I still felt numb, and detached, and like I wasn't sure I had ever loved you, and if I had it was impossible to isolate that feeling because it was so tangled up with others.

She was aghast. "Of course you loved him! He was your dad! You're just in shock."

In that moment I felt myself disconnect from our friendship. Click. I don't need another person in my life telling me that I'm not actually feeling what I'm feeling. It's like I've gone through a door into another room and Caroline can't follow me. She's never known anyone who died. I feel like we're universes apart, just like me and you.

Andy

26

There was no sign of Adam or Eve at breakfast. Someone must have stood in for the chef; the hotcakes and eggs and bacon tasted pretty much the same. My eyes were bleary from lack of sleep and my stomach danced with nausea, but I felt jumpy and wired, as if I had drunk a vat of coffee.

The White Guys were positioned around the Hall, scanning the citizens as they served themselves and scurried back to the relative safety of their tables. Kit and I had arrived separately and were sitting apart in the hope that no one would sniff out our shared secret. I saw Peter staring hard at me as I buttered a roll. Perhaps he and his colleagues were already aware of our nocturnal sojourn and were just waiting for the right moment to pounce. I choked on a gob of dough and hacked and coughed, sucking in desperate jags of breath as citizens at neighbouring tables stared with momentary interest. No one asked if I was OK or pounded me on the back. Everyone was wary. It was safer to remain unnoticed, adrift and invisible in a safe sea of yellow.

Eyes streaming, I clumsily poured myself a glass of water. God stared at me from his giant banner above the buffet. The weird sun trembled in the high windows and cut shards through the dust. I noticed for the first time that God was holding something in his outstretched hand. I leaned forward and squinted. It looked like a banana.

I scanned the hall, taking in the shabby paintwork, the tinned raspberries, the gentle burping, the dandruff and the morning breath and the fear and the cheap coffee; the vulgar vulnerability of all of us. Arriving in Heaven had been like checking in to a luxury resort that you had dreamt about forever and saved up for years to afford, only to be greeted by plastic furniture, deep fried everything, and a blackboard sign by the pool that read: **Closed for Repair's**. The thought of staying here for the rest of eternity was terrifying.

God had escaped, but he was God, after all. He had probably just floated out the gates one day, regally invisible, smiting all unsuspecting obstacles before him. I, on the other hand, had no fucking clue where to start. Perhaps it wasn't even worth trying. I probably wouldn't get very far. I wouldn't know how to plan it. I would be caught. And even if I did manage to get out, how would I know where to go? Better the devil you know, and all that. Perhaps, I mused, it would be better to wait until someone else figured all this out and then I could just … tag along for the ride, if it seemed safe enough, and if things here grew intolerable.

By the time the Heavenly Hosts had started to scrape plates and roll up sticky and crumbed paper table covers, I had convinced myself that the best thing to do was to stay put for now and wait. Wait for salvation.

Citizens started to file out past the White Guys. I was nearly over the threshold when I was stopped by a muscly arm.

"Wait a minute. What do you have in your pocket?" I looked to see who the arm belonged to. It was Peter. He ordered me out of the line and pushed me, stomach first, against a wall. *Oh God*, I thought. *Oh God oh God oh God he knows I was in the Glory Glade and the library. I'm dead.*

Peter didn't take his eyes off mine as he frisked me up and down, patting my pockets. Then he roughly shoved me back into line.

"OK. He can pass. My mistake," he said to his colleagues. And I was out.

Kit caught up and pulled me aside. "What the hell was that all about? What did you have in your pocket?"

"No idea, and nothing," I said, patting my thigh as if to reassure myself I was telling the truth. I could feel a small bump in my right-hand pocket. I reached in and fetched out a small piece of paper, folded. I opened it. It said:

They are watching you. Be careful. Read the signs. Mark 1:17.

I showed the note to Kit. Eyes wide, he quickly refolded it and gave it back to me. "He must have slipped the note into your pocket when he was frisking you," he said, raking a giant hand through his hair. His fingers were extraordinarily long. "Is he on our side, then? What signs do you think he means? And who's Mark?"

I rubbed my forehead. I was getting a headache. This was all too *The Da Vinci Code* for my liking. Since when was Heaven a hotbed of intrigue, menace, and secret agents? I just wanted angels and hymn singing and God on his throne and cherubs and everlasting peace. Was that too much to ask?

"It's from the Bible," I said eventually. "Mark chapter one, verse seventeen. I'll have to look it up later."

Kit frowned, then pointed at the sign outside the Hallelujah Hall.

**Athletics on the front field with David and Goliath!
And for those who would prefer something a little less
strenuous, join our Heavenly Hosts in the kitchen for a
Cooking Master Class. Ever wanted to feed the five thousand?
Try our take on Loaves and Fishes!**
(Gluten-free option available)

Kit and I looked at each other. "That sounds like you," I said, gesturing at the accompanying chalk drawing of a packet of rice crackers and a sardine.

"It's lactose, not gluten," sighed Kit. "Why does everyone get them mixed up?"

Most people had made their choice and were either on the way to the field or the kitchen. Kit and I, however, decided to duck away and find a quiet spot. We had much to discuss, not least Heaven's runaway God and the extraordinary possibility that Peter might be one of "us". We made our way to the lake and this time took the path around to the far side, to the clearing where Moses had stood only two days previously as he tried in vain to part the non-existent waves.

"But it all makes sense, then!" Kit gesticulated wildly as we walked. "He didn't leave the screen open by mistake that day in the gatehouse, he did it on purpose! He wanted me to break into reception, find the library! But what do we do next? What if he …"

Someone was sitting on a log by the edge of the water. She had her back to us, and from where we stood we could hear small, dignified sobs. It was Penelope. I signalled to Kit, and we tried to back away quietly, but before we could fade into the trees I stepped on an empty beer can. "Fucking disciples," whispered Kit as Penelope turned around with a start.

I was never very good with crying women. In my experience, anything you said was inevitably going to be wrong, labelling you an insensitive bastard, so it was best to say nothing and be accused of being an unfeeling bastard. I stared out at the lake, absently scratching my hair from one side to the other. Kit looked at his feet. In the distance we could hear the faint clattering of cutlery and plates. Cooking class had started.

After a few awkward seconds Penelope saved us both. "He's gone," she said, her voice gravelly with tears.

For a moment I thought she knew that God had escaped. Then she said the same words again, this time picking with anxious fingers at her wedding ring, and I realised she meant her husband.

"We woke up this morning at five-fifty and chatted a bit, like we always do." Penelope looked back out over the lake, speaking like she was reading from a script. "It was still dark outside. He made me a cup of tea. Then he said I should have the first shower because I wanted to wash my hair and I needed most of the hot water. When I came out he was gone. Just … gone."

Kit and I looked at each other. It was more than obvious now. People weren't escaping; God had the monopoly on that one. Citizens of Heaven were being taken away.

"I called and I called and I called but he didn't come," continued Penelope. "He always comes when I call. He says he's my boomerang. He always comes back. But he hasn't. So I came here."

I sniffed. The oily aroma of fish was making its way across the water.

"They've taken him, haven't they?" said Penelope, her back to us still.

I shrugged, preferring to stay silent. Kit shook his head at me. *Thanks a lot*, he mouthed. Then he started towards Penelope.

"Umm, we think so," he said. "But I'm sure he'll be OK." He sat down next to the old woman and rubbed his hands together briskly. "I'm sure they've just taken him somewhere to give him a little talk. About not causing trouble, I mean. I'm sure he'll come back soon."

"We met at university," said Penelope, as if she hadn't heard him. "We were set up on a blind date. I thought he was handsome. He calls me his Poppet. Never Penelope, or Penny. It's always Poppet."

I took a couple of steps forward. I thought I had better say something. "What do you call him?"

Penelope looked round at me, and her face crumpled like a used tissue. "John. That's his name, so that's what I call him. Never love, or darling. Always John." Her eyes filled again.

Kit pulled an enormous handkerchief from his pocket and handed it to her. It looked reasonably clean. "Keep it," he said.

Penelope guided the handkerchief around her face, then folded it carefully and placed it on her knee. We sat in silence for a few minutes, gazing over the lake and wrinkling our noses as the fishy smell grew bitter.

"Honestly, they have no idea," said Penelope, reaching for her handbag. "I could have told them you never fry sardines in oil. Always butter. Salted, at that. None of this unsalted rubbish." She rummaged for a few seconds before drawing out a small lolly packet. "Mint Imperial? I died with these in my bag. I never go anywhere without them."

I took a mint. "If you don't mind me asking, how did you and your husband…"

Penelope took a long moment to fold the top of the lolly packet down and down and down in horizontal increments before replacing it carefully in her handbag. "We were flying to see our son," she said finally. "He had just had his first baby. Well, not him. His wife."

We all smiled a little.

"We hadn't seen him in over a year. He and John had had a disagreement the previous March and they hadn't spoken a word to each other. I *said* to him, I said, you must ring Jack – that's our son's name – John, please ring him. You can't go on like this. But he wouldn't be told. He would set that intractable jaw of his and say that it was up to Jack to apologise first. I spoke to Jack and Jill – that's Jack's wife, I know, like the nursery rhyme, I know, they always got teased about it – I spoke to them sometimes but I always felt torn; disloyal to John when I picked up the phone and a bad mother to Jack when I didn't."

She paused, and Kit asked, "What did they fight about?"

"I can't remember now. Neither can John. That's the silly thing. We can't even remember what the jolly fight was about." She picked up the handkerchief and dabbed at her eyes.

"Anyway," she continued, "Jill got pregnant, and as she grew she started emailing us photos, taken by Jack obviously, of her stomach getting bigger and bigger. The last one she sent was of her and Jack together. I think he'd set the timer and run to get in the shot. They were both smiling and pointing at Jill's stomach, which had black writing on it. See You Soon Poppa and Nan. Poppa first, then Nan. And that was it."

We waited for a long moment. "That was what?" asked Kit eventually.

"That was it. John booked a flight that same day, and then the next day Jill went into labour and had the baby. Our first grandchild." Penelope swallowed and her eyes filled with tears again. "A boy. Jill rang to tell us just before we boarded our flight. We didn't speak to Jack. John said to me, I'd rather say my first words to him in person. And I said, all right then. And two hours later our plane had engine failure and crashed in a vineyard. No survivors. Can't believe I still had my handbag when I got here."

She coughed a bit. "And we don't even know his name. We never got to see him and we don't know his name and John and Jack never spoke and now they never will and I'll never speak to John again either, and I just … I…" These last words tumbled out along with several Mint Imperials as Penelope lost her grip on her handbag and it dropped to the dirt.

Kit and I leapt up and scrambled for her belongings: lipstick, comb, small black diary held closed with a purple elastic band, a pen, a pensioner's bus pass, two airline tickets and boarding passes, a small crocheted rabbit with pink crosses for eyes, the lolly packet, and a smattering of lint-dusted mints, tiny white stepping stones from the log to the edge of the water.

As we brushed things off and handed them to Penelope ("Leave the mints," she sighed, "it's mainly John who eats them"), Kit looked thoughtful, and I knew what he was going to say even before he opened his mouth. My heart sank.

"You may be able to find out. His name, I mean. Your grandson. We might be able to help you."

27

Thursday morning, 9 am

Dear Dad,

One more day until the funeral and I haven't written a thing. Aunt Fleur just asked me how the eulogy was going. We were sharing the bathroom this morning, both doing our teeth. It was a squeeze, but lately we've found comfort in being very close together.

"So, how are you feeling about tomorrow?" She lay her toothbrush down and reached for a plastic tumbler to rinse with. "Is the eulogy coming on OK?"

She looked at me carefully, and I could swear she knew I hadn't written a single word. Sometimes I think she knows me better than anyone else in the world. I didn't want to let her down.

"Fine. Nearly done, I think." I picked up the dental floss and ripped off a section.

We looked at each other in the tiny mirrored cabinet above the sink. Aunt Fleur looked so very old.

"Let me know if you need any help, won't you, dear?" She wiped her mouth with the flowered hand towel and turned to leave.

I do need help, please, I thought. With a lot more than just the eulogy. I swallowed. "I will." I sent the assurance over my shoulder and out the door with her. I didn't believe it.

Why can't I just write something? Why am I so afraid to put pen to paper? No one's going to give a shit, really. But every time I try to start something the words clog up in my mind like porridge and I get no further than "Dad was born..."

I think when you write a eulogy for someone, you're meant to have known them pretty well. Their history, their back story. The important events of their life, lined up like sentinels to guard against the meaninglessness. What they loved, what they didn't love. What they achieved, what they wished for.

I think the problem is, Dad, I didn't really know you at all. All my life we've been missing each other, just passing but failing to catch a glimpse, or perhaps sensing a presence close by but not pausing to let that presence take shape. What do I know of you? What did you know of me?

Maybe fathers aren't meant to figure too prominently in their daughters' narratives. Maybe they are the fringe character: the one you meet in Chapter One, who resurfaces briefly in Chapter Six, and who turns up, slightly bemused, right before the denouement.

Maybe I was expecting too much. Do all daughters expect too much? Mum used to say, just after the divorce, that I should be careful never to expect anything. "Expect him to let you down," I remember her saying once as she dropped me off at your place for the weekend. "That way you won't be blindsided when it happens."

I remember thinking it was a cruel thing to say to a daughter about her father. It set us up for a compendium of failures – not that there hadn't been sufficient before the divorce. It's just that the ones after were more distilled, and I was less resilient.

I'm biting my nails again. Three of them are right down to the quick, ripped sliver by excruciating sliver. I woke this morning with my fingertips throbbing and pink streaks on my sheets, so I'm obviously doing it in my sleep. What would the shrink think about that?

Oh God, the shrink.

Do you remember the first time you took me there, after the divorce? It was Mum's idea. She found me with my head down the toilet, coaxing up with mechanical efficiency the six slices of chocolate cake I had just eaten. Hand up, bite, hand down, chew, swallow. Repeat. I had meant to lock the door, but in my haste to get the sugary, sticky mess out of me, out of my self, I forgot. She stood in the doorway for a minute, watching as rivulets of saliva hung from my fingers like soggy spiders' webs, crumbs stuck in them, struggling.

It wasn't the first time I had made myself throw up. Caroline and I tried it once, together, when we were about thirteen, just to see what the fuss was about. It wasn't about shame or sadness then; just curiosity and the first inkling that female bodies should never be replete. After that it was something I did occasionally, sometimes when I was too full, sometimes because I wanted to be utterly empty. I did it more when the fighting became fierce, and nearly every day after you left. I don't do it so much anymore. I seem to have lost the knack; no matter how far back I push my fingers or how much I gag, nothing comes up. Maybe it was just something I needed to do for a while. Maybe sometimes things just need to get out, and sometimes you can bear holding on to them.

"Jesus Judas!" Mum breathed, even though she was Buddhist by then. Her face was white. She didn't scream or yell or make a fuss. Funny how the slightest annoyance could see her flinging drama and chaos like a messy baby in a highchair, but when faced with real drama she had nothing to give. The next day she made an appointment with Dr S. Weerasinghe, your friendly family psychiatrist specialising in youth issues and family dynamics.

My first appointment got off to a shaky start when I laughed as soon as he opened his office door. He was so short he came up to my shoulder and so skinny my laughter could have knocked him over. When I got home I wrote down as much as I could remember, thinking that even if it did me absolutely no good, at least it might be good material for a future novel.

You never asked how that first appointment went. Or maybe you did, and I didn't want to tell you. Anyway, here are the highlights:

Dr W (in the interest of brevity, I've shortened his name): Hello Andrea. (Looks at file).

Me: It's Andy.

Dr W: You prefer Andy. OK. (Pause. Pen scratching. Paper rustling.) So, Andy, why have you come here today?

Me: Because my mother made me.

Dr W: And why did she do that, do you think?

Me: Because she feels guilty about the divorce, and she thinks if she can cure me of everything that's wrong with me she won't feel guilty anymore.

Dr W: (More pen scratching.) And how do you feel about being here?

Me: I don't know.

Dr W: You don't know.

Me: No.

Dr W: No.

Me: No. (Testing to see if I can make Dr W say it again.)

Dr W: OK.

Me: OK.

Dr W: Tell me about your father.

Me: What do you want to know?

Dr W: Anything you want to tell me. Anything at all.

Me: There's not much to tell.

Dr W: That's OK. Tell me the first thing that comes into your mind.

Me: He's in the reception area reading an old back copy of 'Cosmopolitan'.

Dr W: And how do you feel about that?

Me: It's crap.

Dr W: The fact that your father brought you here today?

Me: No, 'Cosmopolitan'.

(Long pause. Scribbling.)

Me: Well, this was worth $250.

Dr W: Why do you say that?

Me: Because that's how much my mother paid for this appointment.

Dr W: Your mother paid?
Me: I guess so. Dad wouldn't be able to afford it.
Dr W: And how do you feel about that?
Me: I don't know.
Dr W: You don't know.
Me: No. (Testing to see … etc.)
Dr W: I'm going to ask you some questions, and I want you to respond immediately, without thinking, saying the first word that comes to mind. Would that be OK?
Me: Bullfrog.
Dr W: I beg your pardon?
Me: It's the first word that came to mind.
(Pause)
Dr W: How do frogs make you feel?

At that point I tuned out. I knew he only wanted to diagnose me according to a Troubled Youth Checklist, then medicate me. He didn't really want to talk to me; he wanted to talk to a patient he could fix. But I didn't want to be fixed. I wanted to be broken.

I went a few more times but I refused to take any medication, and I could sense Dr W was frustrated with me. He made lots of notes but nothing really changed except that my weekly appointments seemed to make Mum feel better. One day I refused to go, and you walked in to find Mum in tears. I wasn't crying; I always greeted Mum's tantrums with silence. I haven't cried for so long, sometimes I wonder if my tear ducts have shrivelled up. I remember your exact words as you caught the tail end of the conversation: "For Christ's sake, Robyn, leave her alone. She's got enough to deal with without fending off an incompetent shrink with a ridiculous name." Then you smiled at me; a hesitant, stolen smile. I thought Mum would explode from anger. Me too, but from a very different emotion.

Andy

28

Kit told Penelope about the underground library, and about the books that were continuing to write themselves. I sat silent, sulking. I wasn't ready to let anyone else in on our secret; at least not until we had figured out what it all meant. In hindsight, perhaps I was afraid that if we told someone else it would make it more real, and we would have to actually do something about it.

At first Penelope was incredulous, but as Kit went on and I reluctantly started to nod and add a few comments here and there, she allowed herself to hope. At one point Kit and I exchanged a silent glance, confirming our mutual agreement not to tell her about the Departures file. Even he wasn't ready to share that one, perhaps realising that the news that God was a runaway may well tip her over the edge. Eventually Penelope stood, smoothed her shellsuit, and hung her bag over her balled fist. She bent her elbow so her forearm lay parallel to her chest, her bag protecting her heart like a shield. Her tears had dried and her chin was resolutely firm. "Take me there. I want to go."

Kit explained the risks involved. Again Penelope insisted on coming with us, but after a few minutes of gentle steering on Kit's part and proud face-saving on hers, she agreed to let us go back to the library to find her book on her behalf. Kit also promised to try to find out what had happened to her husband.

I looked sideways at him. Since when had we become self-appointed detectives?

Penelope kissed us both on the cheek then left the clearing, saying she had some washing to do back at her cabin. As soon as she had gone I let out an impatient clasp of air. "What are you doing? You're going all superhero on me when we don't even know what the fuck is going on!"

Kit stared. "What, so I'm not allowed to help a grieving old lady?"

I snorted. "Yes, I'm sure it's all very charitable, and she probably reminds you of your Nan and all that, but in case you hadn't noticed, we're in mortal danger here! We're being watched like hawks by white militia, God's on the run, people are being taken away to have God knows what done to them – or not, actually, since he's not bloody here – they're probably being anally probed as we speak, and you want to, quote, help a grieving old lady." I took a breath. Kit looked stunned. I was on a roll.

"Forgive me, Kit, if I don't join you on your crusade to become the next Mother Theresa, but I have something just a tad more important to do, and that's – " at this point I started to meander a little " – that's, well, to just lie low, you know, sit tight until someone – until someone can, you know, figure out how to get us out of this fucking place. Someone's bound to figure it out, sooner or later. I hope." I wrinkled my forehead and the welt, which was gradually healing, rebelled. It started to ache. I felt all the punch go out of me and I sat down heavily on the log.

There was a silence for a few awkward seconds. When Kit spoke he sounded like something had left a bad taste in his mouth.

"That's all you care about, isn't it Maurice? Saving your own skin. You don't care about anyone else here. Only yourself." He breathed his next words into his armpit as he turned away from me to face the lake. "Christ, Andy was right."

"What did you say?" I stood and shifted awkwardly on my feet, confused by Andy's sudden introduction into the conversation. Kit turned back to face me, clenching and unclenching his fists.

"Andy dropped a whole lot of stuff once, in class. I helped her pick it all up, but I put an envelope of hers back in my own bag by mistake.

I know I shouldn't have read what was inside, but I opened it that night without thinking and once I'd started I couldn't stop." He paused, breathing heavily through his nose. "It was a bunch of poems, and stories, some in draft, some nearly finished. The poems were amazing. I've never read anything so beautiful, and incredible, and ... well, that's what made me…" He caught himself. "I returned it the next day. I lied, said I hadn't even seen it in my bag until the morning, and that I hadn't opened it. But…" He paused, and his next words sped up, terse and urgent. "There was also a letter to a friend of hers, can't remember her name, Karyn or Carly or something, but in it she talked about you."

"You read her private letter? What gave you the right to do that?" I attempted indignation to cover up the fact that I was feeling distinctly uncomfortable.

Kit looked suddenly defiant. "Andy wrote that you were a bitter, ineffectual fence-sitter who couldn't stand up for anything. She joked that you must have a sore arse from sitting on the fence for so long over everything. Except she wasn't really joking." He was breathing hard now. "And she said you were pathetic, and an avoider, and that you always used sarcasm to deflect emotion, and that if you were any more distant you'd have to use a carrier pigeon just to ask her to pass the salt." Kit's pitch ramped up with each accusation. The words wobbled in their ascension and his eyes started to scrunch, and I sensed that tears were not far away. I stood still and silent. This was beyond uncomfortable. My stomach twitched and clenched in a way that was horribly familiar. I had been yelled at like this before, by my ex-wife. When she had found out.

Kit started to cry and didn't even try to hide it. Sobs came in breathy hitches. "And that you were a sad, cynical little librarian who never amounted to much and who thought everyone and everything was below you." He paused. I didn't speak. He pulled his cigarettes out of his pocket and lit one with a trembling hand.

"I loved my Dad, Maurice," he said, taking a shaky drag. "He was a bit shit at most things and he dragged me and Mum around too much and he lost about ten jobs in as many years and he passed on his fucking lactose intolerance to me, but I loved him. And now I can't see him ever again. And he'll never get to hug *me*, ever again. But at least I told him I loved him. Did you ever tell Andy you loved her? Did you? *Did you*?" He walked off a few paces, stubbed out his barely smoked cigarette with one enormous foot, then turned again and walked towards me, fists and jaw clenched. For a second I thought he was going to hit me, and I stumbled backwards, raising my arms in defence. But he didn't. He stopped just in front of me.

"You have to tell people that you love them, Maurice. Right then, when you know you do, you have to tell them. Because I wanted to, and then some bastard in a park stole my wallet and stabbed me and I died and then I couldn't, and I just wish…" He put his balled fists to his eyes for a moment and clenched his whole body, hard. "I wish I had told…" His fists and jaw slackened and his shoulders slumped. "I wish…"

"You wish what?"

He looked at me, his outrage spent, his limbs no longer angular, and seemed to make his mind up about something.

"Never mind. You wouldn't understand, anyway. Tell you what, Maurice, how about you go back to your cabin and stare at the walls and wait for a miracle to happen. I'm going for a walk. Might blow out the cobwebs a bit. I might even figure out what the hell I'm going to do while I'm at it."

I made a half-hearted gesture, wanting to say something but not sure what; wanting to reach out to Kit but not knowing how. I stood, arm at half-mast, paralysed in the familiar in-between of ambivalence, as he turned and strode out of the clearing.

29

Thursday, 12 pm

Dear Dad,

Aunt Fleur and I are on the front porch. We both have tea and a sandwich, but she's hardly touched hers. We're both exhausted. We wear our sleep on our clothes, crumpled circles framing our eyes.

She hasn't worked since you died. I haven't seen her boot up her computer once. Sometimes she doodles on scrap paper, like she used to do when she came over for dinner, remember? She'd leave scribbled trails behind, hieroglyphs and computer formulas and words, here and there. Sometimes I'd try to decipher what she'd been writing before you dumped it all, along with the scraps. You weren't big on recycling.

We're watching Mrs Hardy digging in her garden. The stupid woman is digging up tulip bulbs and chucking them away, probably thinking they're onions. It's making Aunt Fleur laugh, which is a good thing. I suddenly remembered that time when I was about ten and I'd been playing outside making mud pies. Mum couldn't stand the mess and would forbid me to play in the garden unless I was garbed up like an industrial scientist monitoring Chernobyl. You didn't seem to mind so much. I even remember you getting down on your knees with me once and making your own mud pie. And you wiped your forehead and smeared it with dirt just like Aunt Fleur, but intentionally, to make me laugh.

The Thing That No One Is Telling Me is a constant presence. I've been asking Aunt Fleur questions about you and Mum and Gran and

Grandpa and it's not as though she refuses to answer, but it's obvious that the answers she gives are stand-ins for other, truer answers.

I'm a lawyer in training. I need to be able to get information out of people. The fact that I can't coax my own relative to tell me the truth isn't very promising. Why did I even go to law school? Maybe if I'd majored in English I'd be able to conjure up some beautiful words for the funeral tomorrow and everyone would be so enthralled they wouldn't notice the true sentiment behind them.

Oh my God. It's tomorrow.

The week before you died Professor Lexington gave a lecture about torts and car accidents. I'm sure you wouldn't be interested, but basically, torts are what happens when someone hurts someone else, either intentionally or through negligence. If the injured party can prove that the person believed to have caused the injury acted negligently – that is, without taking reasonable care to avoid injuring others – then they are entitled to compensation.

Still with me?

Anyway, Sexy Lexie (we have to pass the time somehow) explained that if there's an accident and one driver injures another because he or she wasn't paying attention, that would be a tort. The person who caused the accident would be called the tortfeasor, and the person who got hurt would be the victim.

Then I thought about the day before you died. When I came down to breakfast you were sitting eating your toast and reading the paper. You didn't say good morning. Neither did I.

And then I thought: Intentional harm and negligence are just as bad as each other.

I'm trying to remember some of the things we used to do together when I was small. I remember you taking me to school in the mornings. You never knew what to put in my lunchbox, so for years you always gave me the same thing – a sandwich, a packet of chips or some crackers, a banana, and a biscuit. Usually a gingernut. God, I got so sick of it.

When I was old enough to earn pocket money I used to throw my lunch out and order a pie and a doughnut as many days as I could. I can't even smell a banana now without feeling sick.

You want to know something? When you guys were getting divorced I used to sneak chocolate and biscuits from the pantry and hide them in my wardrobe. And when you and Mum fought and fought and fought and it made my head hurt I would go into my room and stuff my hidden treasures into my mouth as if their main ingredient wasn't sugar but safety. And then I'd throw it all up again. It helped, for a little while. Until the next argument.

Do they eat in Heaven, or wherever you are?

I have one clear memory. We were walking to school. I was about nine. We were nearly at the school gates when three of the big boys from Mr Aitken's class started shouting things like "Hey, fatso!", "What's up, Blubber Butt?", and "Andy Pandy, fat and randy". They always did this, and I was used to it. But obviously you weren't. I can't remember the details, but I think you told me to "Wait there" and strode towards the bullies. They kept on laughing until you reached them, round the corner of the main building. I didn't see what you did or hear what you said, but the boys ran off, and I remember you looking all dishevelled and disturbed. Those were the days when you had hair, and it was all over the place.

I'd like to say those boys never teased me again. They did, but not as much, and not as viciously, and any time you were with me they were nowhere to be seen.

I remember thinking you were my hero.

Andy

30

My usual tactic when any kind of unpleasant confrontation occurred was to pretend it hadn't happened. The argument with Kit had left me feeling distinctly uncomfortable, infused as it was with an earlier, more horrible earthly argument, but I tried to shake off the feelings at lunch by eating ten burnt gluten-free fish fingers in quick succession, washed down by three beers in the Boogie Bar. It had opened early to prepare for an afternoon karaoke competition. Adam was serving in Jezebel's absence and was making overly bright attempts to engage the only other two citizens at the bar in conversation. They weren't buying it: they hugged their drinks and fiddled silently with their bar mats. They looked frightened. Heaven had that effect on people. Peter's note was burning a hole in my pocket. Feeling slightly tipsy, I decided to chance it and go back to my cabin.

As I walked, trying to look inconspicuous, I wondered if Kit realised that he had inadvertently told me how he had died. I couldn't quite get my head around it. Someone had stabbed him to death and stolen his wallet. Who would do that to a boy?

I tried, without much success, not to think about the other things he had said. I was unwilling to believe that Andy had written all that about me. Kit had probably made it up in his fit of adolescent anger. Hardly any of it was true, anyway. OK, I hmm'd and haa'd about things sometimes, and I preferred to let others make decisions and take the lead on things more often than not. But I did stand up for things I felt strongly about. The day before I died I went to the supermarket and they had run out of lemon honey, and did I just let that one slide? No,

I made a fuss and insisted on speaking to the manager. I even yelled a bit. Turns out I had been looking in the wrong place (well, no one had told *me* that the lemon honey was now next to the honey instead of the jam). But still. No fence sitting on that one.

I sat down on the bed, reached for the Gideon Bible, and turned to Mark 1:17.

> Then Jesus said to them, "Follow me, and I will make you become fishers of men."

This was the moment when Jesus called the first of his disciples to leave their daily lives and spend the next three years watching him heal lepers and turn water into wine (as Robyn used to say on Friday evenings after getting home from the book shop and discovering the fridge was unapologetically free of alcohol, "Where the hell is Jesus when you need him?") and be crucified. How frustrating it must have been to have given up your livelihood and left the comforts of home for someone you thought was the saviour of the world, only to watch him dying like any other man.

Jesus had always seemed a little stern to me, akin to a grumpy schoolteacher who would whack you across the hand with a leather belt as quickly as heal you from a weeping skin affliction. But, hell, I would have left my job at the library to follow him. Which isn't saying much: I would have left the library for pretty much anyone.

I stared at Peter's note, half expecting the writing to dissolve and a more comprehensible message to appear in magical ink like on the Marauder's Map in *Harry Potter and the Prisoner of Azkaban*. When, astoundingly enough, it didn't, I closed the Bible, slipped it back into the drawer along with the note, and stared at the woman with bananas on her head. Then I reached under the mattress and took out my book.

I was a little afraid to see what else Andy would have to say about me, but I felt an unfamiliar and not unwelcome desire to be close to her. Why had I not felt that when I was alive? Had I let myself feel it? Ironic that I was making up for lost time now, when I was as far away from her as one could possibly be, with no way of ever contacting her again.

I thought of Kit, murdered. Kit, walking to feel better. Walking while planning. Moving; thinking; making progress. *Good luck with that*, I thought. *While you're figuring out where God has gone and how we're going to save our sorry asses, I'm going to sit on mine and think about what a crap parent I was.* It was hard to tell who was going to have more fun.

After a good half hour of absentmindedly scratching letters off God's "Welcome to Paradise" sign above the bed, I finally opened my book and read three new letters that had appeared since I had last looked.

Robyn's suspected new boyfriend didn't bother me as much as Andy's interpretation of the photo taken at her tenth birthday. I remembered it with surprising clarity: the cloying waft of Robyn's perfume as she marched past me towards Andy, birthday cake held aloft; the look on Andy's face as she prepared to blow, determined to get every single one on the first pop; the post-cake shouts and squeals of too many little girls on a sugar high. Andy thought I was bored, but I wasn't. I'm not sure exactly why, but at the precise moment she blew out the candles and someone snapped that photo (Fleur, perhaps), I was trying to bite back a sudden urge to cry. Maybe it was Robyn's perfume. Or maybe I was just a bit sad that my little girl had passed the single digits. Anyway, I was staring down the barrel of adolescence; anyone would have teared up.

I remembered when Robyn, gasping in snatchy, dramatic drags, had told me how she had discovered Andy throwing up in the toilet. It was not long after the divorce. Robyn had by then started her transformation into a new-age hippy, abandoning her accounting career ("It carries too many bad memories, Maurice. I'm sure you know what I mean.") and transferring her numeracy skills and anal retentiveness to the precise arrangement of furniture and incense sticks in her house. ("It's Feng *shway*, Maurice. Say it right or don't say it at all.") She had wound her kaftan around her henna-swirled hands and challenged me with liquid eyes. In what way would I let her down this time?

"Don't all teenage girls do that?" I had asked, with the determined ignorance of a father refusing to see his daughter in pain. Robyn looked at me as if I had just drawn a samurai sword and lopped off both her arms at the elbow.

"I'm getting the most expensive psychiatrist in town, and you're going to pay for it," she hissed. And I did. I didn't eat properly for a month. I had to walk to and from work every day because I couldn't afford petrol. And all so Robyn could feel better about herself. I wanted to help Andy but I didn't know how. I longed for the shrink to fix her, and when he didn't, I felt like even more of a failure.

In the third letter, written just an hour previously (it hurt my head to think about it), she described the time some bullies had called her names just as we were arriving at school. I remembered that day, but my memory was different to Andy's. These bullies were big boys, flabby and white and muscle-less; the kind who wash infrequently and torture incessantly. I had said goodbye to Andy at the gate. I never walked her to her classroom; she insisted on going alone, or maybe I insisted that she didn't need me. The bullies started when I was almost out of sight, and I sensed it wasn't a one-off. Their insults, not subtle but flawlessly cutting, were those of practised tormentors. With each assail Andy recoiled, clutching her bag to her chest. Her red hair was a veil over her face as she kept changing direction, trying to find an innocuous path to her classroom and safety. I remember looking at her back, no longer a child's but not yet an adult's, and something inside me lurched. I started to move.

"Wait there," a voice barked. There was a rush of wind as a man marched smartly past me and towards the bullies. I had seen him before; he was a parent of one of the special-needs children. He was five foot five at a stretch and thin as a whippet, but as he strode forward he was radiating something; something that made the bullies recoil as if an invisible force field was pushing them backwards.

I didn't hear what the man said to the bullies. I don't think Andy heard either; she was nearly to her building by then and still had her head down. The man repeatedly prodded the biggest boy in the chest as he spoke, punctuating his lecture. The bullies hung their heads lower and lower until they turned and skulked off towards the gymnasium.

The man turned and made his way back to the gate. As he passed me, he muttered with the complicity of two strong men colluding, "Creeps. That poor girl."

Then he took the hand of the little stunted boy who had been waiting obediently at the gate for him, and they walked towards the Special Needs Unit. The boy gazed up at his father with an expression akin to worship.

I looked up, and Andy was looking at me with almost the same expression. She thought it was I who had chased away her tormentors. She was regarding me the way a princess might regard her knight in shining armour. In that moment, just that one fraudulent moment, I felt strong and tall and fatherly.

She hadn't written the bloody eulogy yet. She needed to get a move on. She was right; we didn't know each other very well. But whose fault was that? Was she going to blame me for everything? Surely it had been up to both of us to make an effort; it wasn't like I was completely responsible. She could have spoken up. Told me how she was feeling. I wasn't the only one who wasn't communicative.

And anyway, I made a fuss about the lemon honey, didn't I?

I blinked hard as I closed my book, hid it under the mattress, and marched my mind back to the matter of Heaven and its absent God.

There was no way I wanted to get caught up in the questionable intrigue of finding the Almighty and leading him back, like an errant child, to wrestle his minions under control. Or finding Penelope's husband or the name of her grandchild or any of the other missing citizens. Nope. The safe position, my default position, was to let someone else sort it out. Heaven had me under no obligation. It deserved nothing from me. I was starting to feel very strongly that the only sensible thing to do was to remove myself from the situation entirely.

I must have fallen asleep. When I woke up around 8.30 pm, sweaty and disorientated, I had dribbled in soggy rivulets on my yellow pillow. It deserved it. My book was lying on the floor, open at the page of my face staring dumbly up at me. *Welcome to Heaven, buddy.* I looked up at the scratchily defaced sign. It now read:

L OME TO   ARA ISE! HAVE   ICE   AY! - GO

Here were my options: I could stay in Heaven and ignore the exhortation to "Have a nice day" every day for the rest of eternity. Or I could wash my hands of Kit and Adam and Eve and Moses and Penelope and the whole loony lot of them.

- GO

If God could do it, so could I. I was out of here.

Part Two
The Beginning and The End

31

Friday, 5 am

Dear Dad,

It's today. I hardly slept last night. I must have snatched brief segments because ragged dreams were just hazing out of my reach as I woke: you, running in a foggy mist but not getting anywhere; God with a giant whistle round his neck, refereeing a game of football between me and Aunt Fleur and Mum and Gwyneth (and, strangely, Barry Gibb); something involving a key and a tunnel and a ladder and Aunt Fleur climbing down it and saying you can't come down here, Andy, it's secret.

You can't discover the secret.

I haven't written the eulogy. Not one word. Everyone thinks I have. Aunt Fleur thinks I've read it to Mum and Mum thinks I've run it past Aunt Fleur. Gwyneth dropped a copy of the Order of Service round last night and it's there in bold black font:

Eulogy: Andrea Toogood.

Here are six things I know now that I didn't know five days ago:

1. *When your father dies life becomes surreal to the point that you are able to write him letters and post them via the mailbox down the road without it seeming strange.*
2. *Not having a father anymore feels like shit, even though having a father sometimes felt like shit.*

3. *You can lose two kilos in four days thanks to No. 2. (Grief has its silver lining.)*

4. *It is possible – only just – to survive on three hours' sleep a night.*

5. *The person who wrote "How to Write a Eulogy" on WikiHow is a smug prick who has obviously never had to write a eulogy for a family member.*

6. *Today I will get up in front of a group of people to give a eulogy for my dead father and when I open my mouth precisely nothing will come out.*

Maybe I should just avoid the funeral altogether. I could cry off sick. Then someone else – probably Aunt Fleur – will have to step in and do the eulogy for me. Which wouldn't be a bad thing. She'd probably do a much better job than me. And she knew you better, having grown up with you and everything.

I wonder what you were like as a boy. I wonder if you were like me. In one way, at least, you were: you liked to write. It's obvious how much you loved it. But what about in other ways? Were you shy? Were you overweight? Did you suck your thumb until you were thirteen? Did you like being by yourself a lot? I guess you had Aunt Fleur to keep you company. I didn't mind being an only child, but it would have been better to at least have had parents who loved each other. When you guys used to fight a lot I never had anyone to talk to and that was kind of hard. Really hard.

Maybe I should just make a run for it. Take off. Pack a bag and catch a bus. Who would care? OK, Aunt Fleur would worry, but I could call her and let her know I was OK. I'm sure Mum wouldn't give a shit. She probably wouldn't even notice, preoccupied as she is with her NEW BOYFRIEND and trying to decide whether vol-au-vents or sausage rolls would be more suitable for the "post-match function" (that's what she's calling the afternoon tea after the funeral).

She came round with Gwyneth last night to confirm last-minute details for the service. She started hyperventilating when she found out Aunt Fleur had forgotten to order the flowers. Gwyneth's fingernail tapping got more and more frenzied until Aunt Fleur screamed, "Oh for God's sake would you stop doing that with your fucking fingernails before I rip them off!" It was the only time I've seen Aunt Fleur losing it and Mum lost for words. There was quite a long silence with no fingernail tapping.

"I'm sorry. I shouldn't have said that," said Aunt Fleur after a stretch. "It's just…"

"No need to apologise, no need at all, not at all," twittered Gwyneth in a voice as bright and brittle as her nails. "It's a stressful time, a very stressful time. Agapanthuses are out of season, anyway."

I nearly fell off my seat when Mum spoke. "Actually, it's quite all right, Fleur. It'll be fine. Perfectly fine! I've got plenty of flowers in my prayer room at home. Lilies, hairyfruit musella…"

Aunt Fleur blinked.

"False, but no one will notice!" Mum shrilled. "I'll gather them up." She smiled at me, her mouth and eyes stretched wide. I looked away.

If you'd been there, we would have had a good laugh afterwards about Gwyneth. You would have imitated her spidery walk and her fingernail tapping and her raspy voice. We did used to have some laughs sometimes, except they were mostly at the expense of other people. But you were funny, I'll give you that. And it's something that we shared.

I miss you. I miss the longing for you: the longing for you to notice me more, to talk to me for longer, to ask me one more question. There's nothing to long for anymore, but the sense of longing has elongated, like a shadow desperately reaching for the one who cast it. Does that make sense?

Dad, wherever you are, I'm sure you think I don't miss you at all. But I do.

Andy

32

On the day of my funeral the White Guys came for Noah. It was just after breakfast and Noah was about to deliver a talk called "Facing the Flood: Basic Boat Building and You". I think Adam had decided to humour him with the fifteen-minute speaking slot in the hope that it would shut him up for good. Earnest and fidgety, Noah had just begun ("Can I start by asking how many of you get seasick? A show of hands, please?") when the doors slammed open and Michael and the others marched in. Noah didn't protest at all; he just quietly put down his tools and his *Animals of the World Almanac* and surrendered. The hall was pregnant with unspoken protestations. No one wanted to stand up and confront the White Guys this time in case they became the next citizen to disappear.

I had stayed awake most of the night figuring out my escape plan. When I say "figuring out", I mean wandering aimlessly from bathroom to bed, humming tuneless ditties and wondering if anyone would notice if I just ran as hard as I could in the direction of … nowhere. I scanned a sea of silent citizens. I couldn't see Kit anywhere, or Penelope. Perhaps they had gone to the library without me. I didn't care. I wouldn't be here for much longer.

Just as people were finishing eating, one of the Heavenly Hosts got up to make an announcement. Her face was a study in how to pretend to be enthusiastic when you are, in fact, scared witless. She tapped the microphone tentatively. Joseph had disappeared the day before and no one had used it since. It looked lonely, but relieved.

"Good morning everyone! Are we all feeling Hippy Happy today?"

She didn't pause for our reply; perhaps she realised how ridiculous the question sounded. "Our wonderful leaders, Michael and his team, would like to announce that there will be a compulsory gathering right here in the Hallelujah Hall at ten o'clock this morning. Michael has asked me to inform you that the purpose of the gathering is to share newly introduced rules and regulations, and to outline some changes in the way Heaven will be run from now on. He is sure you will find these changes … acceptable." The girl looked like she was about to cry. She blinked and gripped the microphone stand.

The announcement was met with silence. There was no muted muttering, no signs of unrest, no whispered questions. Everyone sat staring straight ahead, scared to move or cough or give any signal that might attract attention. The five White Guys who remained after their colleagues had exited with Noah were standing at the front of the hall this time. There was no longer any need for subtlety or pretence. Everyone was being watched.

The Heavenly Host continued. "Michael has also asked me to let you know that during the gathering there will be a cabin inspection. This is to ensure that all cabins meet recently introduced Heavenly health and safety standards. Thank you and have a nice day!"

That did it. No matter I didn't know where the fuck I was going. I was going, and I was going now. After we were dismissed, I forced myself to walk slowly out of the hall. All around me defeated shoulders drooped. Heaven was losing.

I accelerated to a gentle trot until I reached my cabin. I stuffed my book down the back of my trousers again, said goodbye to the banana lady, and left without looking back. The only plan I had, and it was a tenuous one, was to try to get out the way I had come in, and hope that whatever was beyond Heaven's gates was less ghastly than the dystopia I was leaving behind. A long shot, but it was all I had. I started to walk as quickly as I could without looking like a man on an escape mission.

And then I remembered Kit.

I have to tell you, I came perilously close to pushing him out of mind and carrying on. But then I remembered his face when he'd told me about his parents, and the way he'd helped me when I first arrived, and how he'd trembled as he revealed he'd been murdered. I was nearly at the reception building, and I glimpsed through two perfect trees the fire escape that he and I had climbed two nights previously. Ahead of me I could see the bend in the driveway around which a freshly dead me had stumbled four days earlier, speechlessly trying to keep up with a Heavenly Host. Just beyond were the gates.

I remembered Kit's mother, packing away sympathy cards, her grief illuminated by a cruel and glorious sunset.

Suddenly I found myself turning around and retracing my steps until I reached the path that led to Kit's cabin. Fucking hell. I couldn't even get an escape bid right.

Cabins 200 – 250, announced a sign perched on a stake in a terracotta pot. I picked up the pace. Something in my gut was squirming.

The front door of Kit's cabin, which was identical to mine, was wide open, and even before I entered I could see the overturned chair and the paper scattered like giants' confetti. The duvet and sheets, tangled and bunched, had been yanked down to the bottom of the bed. The duvet was ripped in several places: feathery evidence that Kit hadn't gone quietly. I felt ill, and guilty. I should have gone to him the night before and asked him to help with formulating an escape plan, and we should have put it into action that very minute. I sat down heavily on the naked bed.

I picked up the piece of paper closest to me, on Kit's pillow. It was a photo of Kit on his arrival in Heaven. He looked frightened out of his mind. I picked up other pages, edges jagged and wisped. The story of his life and death, reports on his funeral and his family. The sneaky bugger had taken his book from the library too, but someone – Kit himself perhaps, in a fit of teenage angst – had ripped out all the pages. A bold headline caught my eye, and I fished up a page that had partially slipped under the bed.

Kit Irwin – Eulogy

His father had delivered it. Brave guy. I skimmed through the first paragraphs about Kit's childhood and adolescence. It wasn't until near the end that I slowed down and read it carefully, word for excruciating word.

> I never thought I would have to say goodbye to my son. I always thought he would farewell me, carry me in a coffin (poor bastard, he probably would have dropped me), talk about me and what a wonderful father I was.
>
> But thanks to just one bad decision, one wrong turn, it is me standing here today. He was just going to post a letter; a love letter to a girl. Stupid bastard picked 10 pm to do it, and to walk through that park. I'm not angry at the lowlife who did it. Not today, anyway. Maybe I will be tomorrow. Today I am just here to say how wonderful my son was, how proud I was of him, and how gutted I am to have to say goodbye to him forever.
>
> Kit, mate, wherever you are, rest in peace.

The bedside clock ticked the seconds away. I sat back and thought about how I would have felt if I had had to stand up and speak at Andy's funeral. If Andy had been murdered.

I got up, shuffled the pages back together, and laid them on the pillow. Then I went into the bathroom for a pee. I was just shaking off, thinking about Kit (that sounded wrong. You know what I mean), when I heard voices. I hurriedly zipped myself up and peeked around the toilet door. Michael and Gabriel were coming up the steps. Luckily they were looking at each other and not inside or they would have seen me before I wrenched my head back and silently panicked. There was no way out. They were on the threshold. Inside. Close enough that I could smell Michael's cologne.

"Behold the mess," Michael said. "A spitfire, this one. Do not go gentle into that good night, and all that."

"What? Do not go what?"

"Never mind," sighed Michael. "Let's clean this up and get out of here. Everything in the bags, please. It has to look as if Mr Irwin has Gone On."

For a few moments there was the shuffling of papers, the whisper of clothing lifted and roughly folded, the clatter of stripped coat hangers.

A drawer was opened. "What's the story with all these pens? Who needs all these?" The click-clack of cheap plastic punctuated Gabriel's question.

"Dump them and check the bathroom," directed Michael. My bowels constricted. I looked around in frantic fast motion, almost dislocating my neck. Then I took refuge in the only place available. I leapt into the shower stall and silently pulled the door closed. Ridiculously visible, I held my breath and waited to be caught.

Gabriel pushed opened the door and walked straight to the basin without looking in my direction. He crouched down and opened the cabinet underneath, gathering a toothbrush, toothpaste, and a can of deodorant (unused, no doubt) into a bag. Then he straightened up and leaned towards the mirror, pulling his lips back and turning his head from side to side as he examined his perfect teeth. I half-expected him to kiss his reflection. He swished a hand though his hair, and as he did I glimpsed the welt on his inner wrist. His, like Peter's and mine, had healed, but not faded. He winked at himself before pirouetting out the door. I released my breath.

"Not much in there. Did you want this stuff?" There was a soft clunking as he opened the bag to show its contents to Michael.

"No. He wouldn't take those if he was Going On. Just his clothes and books there. Leave the Gibran one, it's complete bollocks. And for God's sake, fix his own book. Looks like the others were a little too enthusiastic when they came for him. Drama queens." I heard the shuffling of paper. "Fix it, then take it back to the library. Ask Peter to let you in. On second thought – give it to me. No one can know it hasn't been completed."

"Completed?" asked Gabriel, a papery swish indicating he had done as he was told.

"Don't you ever listen? We covered this in our staff seminar a month ago."

There was a long moment of silence, then an exasperated sigh. Michael spoke again, slowly, as if to a child.

"God used to give everyone their book to complete when they got here, whatever that means. He never told me." There was a sniff of indignation. "When it was done they were allowed to Go On, and they disappeared. But that's no use to us, is it? People with a giddy sense of closure, leaving in droves? How can we build our new kingdom without unhappy citizens to populate it?"

"Why don't we just get rid of all the books, then?" asked Gabriel.

"That, my dear uneducated friend, is the first sensible thing you've said all day. Make that ever." There was a small sound, a tiny click that sounded familiar but not immediately identifiable, and then a gasp from Gabriel.

"But that's…"

"It was his, but now it's mine, understand?" said Michael coolly. "Don't know why he gave it to the old lunatic; he'd destroy the whole of Heaven given a chance. I, on the other hand, will be a lot more targeted in my destruction." He chuckled. "Let's go. We've got another to collect today."

"Who's that?" asked Gabriel. I knew what was coming.

"Maurice Toogood. This one's sidekick. Frankly, I don't think he's much of a threat – librarian, mildly ineffectual – but better to be safe than sorry." There was another impatient exhalation. "For fuck's sake put that down and let's go."

I wasn't sure what "that" was, but it was duly put down and then they were gone. For a moment I was unable to do anything but stare wildly in front of me, blood thumping in my ears. When I was sure they weren't coming back, I opened the stall door and walked unsteadily back into the bedroom. All the papers were gone, and the clothes. Pens lay scattered like chubby Pick Up Sticks.

One piece of paper had been left on the bedside cabinet. Still trembling, I picked it up. It was the page with the photo of Kit, newly murdered and scared as hell. They'd missed it – or perhaps Michael had considered it unimportant, and it was this that he had crudely dismissed. And then three rather significant thoughts that had been hiding at the back of my mind as I cowered in the shower stall felt safe enough to present themselves.

First, I reached under the mattress and pushed my hand around, searching. After a moment I had it. Predictably – or perhaps it only appeared so because it was precisely what I would have done – Kit had hidden the misappropriated library key under his mattress.

Second, I walked back into the bathroom and stood in front of the shower stall. Something wasn't quite right. My subconscious had registered the fact when I was hiding but had been too terrified to let my conscious self know. Until now. There were three words written on the stall door:

next to God

I thought about the sign on my own shower stall, and I realised that Kit had been busy scratching as well. He had scratched off all the other letters of:

Remember: Cleanliness is next to Godliness!

until he was left with only this economical phrase – which, I mused, was a handy response to a number of life's pressing questions, such as: Where the Hell is Jesus, anyway? Where would the Devil least want to be seated at a dinner party? Where would one be safest during Armageddon?

Third, I remembered Peter's note. *Read the signs.* An icy resonance of possibility nudged me.

I was reluctant to admit it to myself, but I was terrified. Once again I considered washing my hands of the whole sorry business and simply bolting. But then I thought about Michael and his perfect smile and smug cruelty, and all those uncompleted books and their owners living in ignorance, and I thought of Kit's father reading the eulogy at his own son's funeral. I thought of my daughter. And I realised that along with feeling frightened I was also extremely fucked off – so fucked off, in fact, that I was, unbelievably, going to try to do something about it.

I looked at the three words on the shower stall door one more time. And then, armed only with a key and a flimsy negligée of an idea, I set off.

33

Friday, 8 am

Dear Dad,

Oh God, it's hopeless. I'm hopeless. I'm just going to have to tell Mum I haven't done it and watch her crow and fuss and triumph that she knew I couldn't do it, and how dare Aunt Fleur even ask me to do it in the first place, and who needs a eulogy anyway? It's not as if there's much to say about him. He never amounted to much. We'll all just sing a hymn and eat a savoury and go home.

No. Something has to be said. You have to be there. You may have been absent from my life for years, and from Mum's, and perhaps even from your own, but you can't be absent from your own funeral. I've got to get up and say something, *however flimsy.*

I've got seven hours.

Perhaps I could structure it like a book. I could separate it into chapters: Chapter One, you were born; Chapter Two, your childhood (I'd have to make most of this one up, but who would notice? Aren't all childhoods the same? The endless stretch of summer, the dripping cones from the corner dairy, the school assemblies, the longing for your parents to be happy); Chapter Three, the teenage years (again, made up, but I could write for hours about adolescent angst); Chapter Four, meeting Mum (subtitle: My Marriage and Other Regrets). My birth would be Chapter Six. Chapter Seven, My Unbearable Career as a Librarian. And then the final chapter of all.

Did you notice that Chapter Five is missing? What happened, Dad? What are Mum and Aunt Fleur not telling me? I have a feeling, somewhere deep inside of me, that if I only knew that I might be able to finally write this thing. I have a feeling that everything would change.

You can't come down here, Andy. It's secret. You can't discover the secret.

That's it. As soon as Aunt Fleur wakes up I'm going to insist that she tells me everything, every last hidden detail, and I'll threaten to run away and not go to the funeral if she doesn't.

Andy

34

I didn't have long. The meeting in the Hallelujah Hall was about to start, so I was counting on the fact that Michael would be busy for at least an hour before I was missed. Unless he had already been to my cabin and found me MIA, in which case I was a fugitive already. The endless intrigue, I mused as I left Kit's cabin and started to run, was exhausting.

I passed my own cabin and kept running (well, jogging and fast-ish walking) until I reached the signpost to God's Glory Glade. I turned down the pebbled path, panting my way through the corridor of giant topiary. As I passed the bush that Moses had burned, a flash of white winked. I skidded to a halt. Sticking out of the charred skeleton, propped up by a latticework of burnt twigs, was a white card with writing on it. I stood still for a few moments, afraid to move. Then I plucked the card from the bush. It read, in scribbled ballpoint:

Revelation 20:11. And I saw a great white throne, and Him that sat on it.

My heart gave a giddy thump. I squinted at the message. Was it Kit's writing? It was either confirmation that I was on the right track, or a random Bible verse stuck in a bush. I preferred not to dwell on the third option, which was that I was walking into a trap.

I put the card in my pocket and carried on into the Glory Glade. Ducking under the ropes, breathing hard, my knees aching, I made my way towards the throne. I looked around to see if anyone was spying on me, then, for the second time, walked up the three stairs and sat down. Nothing happened. I felt suddenly and acutely stupid. I had rushed here on a whim, prompted by a randomly scratched sign in Kit's bathroom. Had I really expected him to miraculously jump out from behind a flowery trellis, shouting "Surprise!"? Once again I shifted around in an effort to get comfortable, absently at first and then with increasing curiosity. Something was pressing, subtly but insistently, into my buttock. I stood up and looked closely at the cushion. I was expecting to see a pebble or perhaps a loose stud, but there was nothing obvious. I looked closer. There appeared to be some sort of raised bump under the cushion. I lifted it up. Lolly wrappers and a crumpled tissue were hiding in the crumby corners.

The bump I had felt was a raised wooden knob, bang in the middle of the seat. I ran my hands around the seat's edge. Three hinges at the back. It was built to be lifted, but no matter how hard I tried it wouldn't budge.

I needed something to jimmy it open. I looked at the umbrella stand again. Could I break off one of the hooks? I ran my hands over the stand's smooth surface. And then, under one of the hooks, my fingers found something. A switch. An old-fashioned one, like the plastic light switches I would flick up and down when I was a boy, bored, to annoy my father. "Want me to come over there and break your fingers?" he would say in a low growl, hidden behind his newspaper. I stood back for a moment, my heart hammering. I pushed my hair left, then right. Then I flicked the switch and the knob in the middle of the throne's base started to turn. After a few seconds it gave one final click and the seat popped open. There was another scribbled white card taped to the underside.

Mark 1:17. Then Jesus said to them, "Follow me…"

I peered downwards. There was a ladder. And I knew without a shadow of a doubt that it was my destiny to climb down it.

35

Friday, 10 am

Dear Dad,

I got sick of waiting for Aunt Fleur to wake up, so I went and knocked on her door. There was no reply, which was unusual. She always answers when I knock. I knocked again and then tried the door, which opened to an empty room. Perhaps she had gone for a walk, or to buy milk. Her bedsheets were tangled, her pillow a scrunched lump, pummelled into sleepless submission. I had a sudden urge to wrap myself in the cocoon of her duvet and hide there until the day was over. I crossed the room, kicked off my slippers, and pulled back the duvet. There was an A4 pad and pen under it, hidden perhaps by design but more likely by accident. I could see Aunt Fleur's handwriting, and my name. Dear Andy. I knew I shouldn't look at it, but today is the day I fail to deliver the eulogy for my dead father, and there are no rules on a day like this.

I grabbed the pad, climbed into bed, pulled the sheets tight around me, and started to read.

Dear Andy,

Today will be one of the hardest days of my life. I am so very proud of you for agreeing to deliver the eulogy. I could never do it. But you have always been strong, and so very brave.

My darling girl, there is so much I need to say to you. I

want to wrap you in my arms and never let you go, and never let you be hurt by the things that have been hidden from you.

When we were young, your father and I would sit at the top of the stairs at night and listen to our parents – your grandparents – fighting, and we would hold on to each other to make the world seem a fraction more stable. Your father would grasp my hand until it hurt, and I would think how lucky we were to have each other, at least.

I never had children – never met the right person, you see, and then all of a sudden it was too late, and I was sweating my way through hot flashes and perimenopausal jogging. So you have always been like a daughter to me. A precious daughter who deserves to know the truth. Your mother has never given you that gift – not because she's a bad person, but because she's scared – and maybe I'm a fool for thinking I can somehow compensate for her very human failures. Maybe I'll never show you this letter. But I need to write it all down, right now, because my heart is so heavy and so sore that I'm afraid I won't wake up tomorrow if I don't relieve it of some of its burden.

Where do I start? The beginning, or the end?

As I told you on Tuesday night, your dad wanted desperately to be a writer. I think I got up to the bit about him going to university.

What I didn't tell you was that your grandpa was outraged at the thought of his only son studying a "useless" subject like English. By then, of course, he and your gran were separated and living in entirely different universes, Gran with her books and he with his anger. He had been let down by an artistic, impractical wife, and now by a son who insisted on existing in a mother-made literary cocoon (as he saw it) of vagueness and indecision. The day Maurice started university was the day Dad stopped speaking to him.

I was a step up, but a minor one. At least I had chosen graphic design, and Dad didn't have to make an excuse for me every time someone mentioned my name. But he knew I had stayed in contact with Maurice, and he resented it, I think. We spoke, but rarely, and never about things that really mattered. Have you ever wondered why "family" events never involved your grandparents? Or why, when Gran died, your father and Grandpa sat with you between them? And why, when you used to visit Grandpa at the home, he got that look on his face when you mentioned your father?

Maurice met your mother at university, and they fell in love. Oh, she was beautiful then, Andy. Beautiful and fierce and generous to a fault. They were like chalk and cheese: he the absent-minded dreamer, she the practical, outspoken action woman, but something about it just worked. I remember asking her once, in a tipsy moment of womanly chit-chat not long after they had met, why she had fallen for him, and she said: "I don't know how it happened. All I know is it felt like the first chapter of the best love story ever written, and I was determined to be the lead character." Then she laughed that enormous laugh of hers and hugged me.

She really did love him, Andy, and she was marvellous company back then. She just had to win at everything. I accepted her for what she was, and I saw how Maurice adored her, and I was happy for them.

They both graduated with good marks, and your mother got a job in a reputable accounting firm. Your father toyed with the idea of doing a PhD, but his first love was fiction writing. All he wanted to do was write, but Robyn insisted she didn't want to be the only breadwinner. So he bought a book shop. Dad left us both a sizable amount of money –

years of hard work had yielded a healthy income and he was a scrupulous saver – although he would have turned in his grave if he knew Maurice had bought a book shop with his share. It was a beautiful shop, close enough to the centre of town to entice customers but far enough away that it had the air of an undiscovered treasure. It had comfy couches and little nooks and crannies and a tiny courtyard with a fishpond and a trickling water fountain. It specialised in "lost" books – books people couldn't find elsewhere. Maurice would go to the ends of the earth to track them down. He loved everything about it. He loved the smell of books and the swish of pages and the thrill of mystery and discovery. It was his pride and joy.

It also helped to finance his writing. By now he was writing his first novel. It was something he had always dreamt of doing, and the modest but steady income from the shop was making it possible.

At first, your mother was a faithful ally in the business. She coached and lectured, filed and advised. Maurice relaxed into the pillowy comfort of her capability. He had always been hopeless with money and figures. Ledgers and bank accounts and financial updates didn't interest him, so he put zero effort into understanding them. He spent his spare time with his imagination, brooding over the pages of his unfinished manuscript that covered the floor of his pokey office at the back of the shop like clothes shrugged off in haste.

The shop did well for a while, but Robyn became increasingly unhappy. As Maurice slipped away more and more to his writing haven, Robyn was finding it harder and harder to let him go. She would make snipped comments to me and others about all the work that needed doing on the shop floor, or a new order coming that morning, or the fact that she couldn't possibly keep up with the cataloguing. She started to complain about how often Maurice left her alone in the evenings. She didn't like him writing all the time; it made her anxious. When he wrote she felt abandoned. As she saw it, I think, all his creative energy, his passion, was directed at something other than her. She was desperate to be close to him but scared to make herself vulnerable enough just to tell him that, plain and simple. But the more she clung and pulled and cajoled, the more she pushed your father away, and he basically set up home in his office, writing. But the bookshop wasn't going to run itself and he knew it. He needed more staff.

Janine came on the scene. She was young and pretty and very, very bright. She was enthralled by Maurice's writing talent. And so began his badly written contribution to one of the oldest, sorriest entries in the Encyclopaedia of Human Fuck-Ups. She and your dad had a short affair. Don't hate him for that – he was just a foolish man who made a mistake in a moment of weakness. Then, of course, your mother found out and threatened to leave. Your father begged and pleaded with her not to. Janine was fired, and he promised never to contact her again. There were nights and nights of tears and shouting and exhaustion. They went on an expensive cruise to try to sort things out, but it didn't work. Then your mother made a bargain. She would forgive him, take him back, and try to forget about the affair – if he sold the shop. She said she couldn't live with him, knowing that he and Janine had been "carrying on" there. So Maurice sold. It broke his heart, but that wasn't the worst of it.

The worst of it is hard to write, even now.

That was it. The page was blank from there. My heart throbbed in my ears and I realised I was gripping the sheets so hard my knuckles hurt. And then there was movement in the hall and Aunt Fleur was in the doorway.

Andy

36

The climb down seemed interminable, guided only by the shot of light falling through the open throne. My breath came in shallow bursts, the sound magnified in the narrow enclosure. After endless rungs a dim wash of light appeared beneath me, insubstantial but welcome. It came closer, flickering, growing stronger, until finally my foot found solid earth, and I let go of the ladder. I had gripped on so tightly that my knuckles hurt and my fingers were cramped and red.

I was standing in a dirt tunnel, lined on both sides with dozens of yellow candles, the chattering flames of those disturbed by my movements casting ghoulish shadows on the walls. The candles all looked brand new and previously unused. There was not a wax rivulet in sight.

Tiny fires giggled and fidgeted, pointing up to a sign on the wall in front of me. The sign said:

←← **Reception and Exit**
Toilets (7 am – 7 pm) →→

I pondered for a nanosecond then set off to my left, hitching my stride to a trot. Flames stuttered and danced as I passed. The tunnel was relatively straight with just a few gentle curves and rises, but I couldn't see very far ahead of me because the further I went from the ladder the further apart the candles were spaced. It was all very *Harry Potter and the Deathly Hallows.*

After about ten minutes, my steps becoming more tentative as the light grew dimmer and dimmer, my shadow elongating and warping like a Halloween caricature, I sensed the air changing. I could still smell dirt, but now there was the smell and taste of air conditioning and papery administration. I wondered what my library colleagues would think if they knew I was about to break into a heavenly stronghold and possibly fight a legion of evil angels in a brave attempt to rescue a fellow dead person I barely knew. They'd probably just wonder if it was fiction or non-fiction and then go back to their shelf stacking. Or they would ask one another, without much interest, "Maurice who?"

The tunnel curved to the right, and I stood in front of a plain wooden door lit from overhead by an electric sconce in the shape of a leafy crucifix. I reached out and grasped the door handle, not really believing (or hoping) it would move. To my surprise, it turned. I wondered for one pee-inducing moment if I was walking into an ambush. And then, as if someone on the other side had been waiting for me, the door was pulled open and a face appeared.

"They're already looking for you. We don't have much time. Follow me."

It was Peter.

He grabbed my arm and pulled me through the doorway, shutting the door behind us. Without saying another word he turned and set off. I followed him through a musty labyrinth of corridors. Our feet thumped damply on cheap linoleum. Cobwebs swooped in lazy skeins above us. Intermittent light bulbs blinked on and off, a morse code gone haywire. We walked swiftly, silently, until curiosity got the better of me.

"Was it you?" I asked. "Who left the cards?"

"Yes. I hoped you would figure it out. I wondered if you had seen me go down the throne that day you were hiding in the Glory Glade. If you had, I knew the messages might make sense."

"You saw me?" I puffed.

"Cherubs were bobbing, Maurice. You were pretty hard to miss.

And besides, I was right behind you most of the way. I hid behind the harp during your conversation with Moses on the Topiary Trail. I thought you'd heard me cough, actually."

My mind started to rewind in an effort to put puzzle pieces together. "Why did you slip that note in my pocket? That day after breakfast?"

"To warn you. You and Kit were getting careless. They noticed the two of you huddling and talking. And they suspected someone had broken into the library, via God's office. Someone who knows his apostrophes."

"What is this tunnel?" I panted, tiring.

"God's passage. Runs between reception and the Glory Glade. Adds to the sense of majesty if he just … pops up, apparently."

We turned a corner and started up a set of stairs. My breath was loud as I struggled to keep up with Peter, who was taking two and three steps at a time.

"I also scratched the letters off the sign in Kit's bathroom," he said. "I finished just before you arrived."

"So…" I hesitated, as much from breathlessness as uncertainty. "You *are* a good guy?"

We had reached the top of the stairs. A sign on the wall in front of us presented its limited menu:

Library, Reception, Exit →→
←← Conference Room

Peter turned and looked at me, not unkindly. "There are many who would dispute that." We turned left and followed another beige corridor to a dead end. In front of us stood a yellow door secured by a sturdy padlock. Peter reached into his pocket and drew out an enormous keyring, keys of all sizes and colours bulging around it. "Matthew chapter sixteen, verse nineteen," he sighed as he flicked to the correct key, fitted it into the padlock, and pushed open the door.

37

Friday, 10.30 am

Dear Dad,

Aunt Fleur stood in the doorway holding two hessian bags filled with flowers from the Friday farmers' market on Keep Street. For a moment she just stared at the pad in my hand and at my shattered face. Then she put the bags down and slowly walked over to sit on the side of the bed.

"I'm sorry," I whispered. "I didn't mean to…"

"It's OK. I understand." She reached for me, but I held myself rigid. I could feel myself trembling, and I gripped the sheets even tighter. There was a strange whistling in my ears. Bookshop. Janine. Affair. Novel. Affair. Writer. Janine. Dad, a writer. Dad, an adulterer. Dad. The words and letters jostled in my mind, muddled and hazy, like an insane game of mental scrabble.

"What came next?"

Aunt Fleur swallowed and reached for my hand again. "Sweetheart, I…"

"What. Came. Next?" I pulled away, ripped back the duvet cover and stumbled to standing, the pad still in my hand. There was silence for a long minute as Aunt Fleur looked up at me, her glasses reflecting me back to myself, my head in a crooked angel's halo from the overhead light.

"The truth." I held out the pad to Aunt Fleur and dropped it in her lap. It slid to the floor in a dull rustle. "Finish the letter. Right now."

Aunt Fleur crinkled her forehead. "Now? You want me to write the rest now?"

I almost screamed then. "It's a metaphor, for fuck's sake! Tell me what happened or I swear I'll … I'll …" And then Aunt Fleur stood and pulled me close, and I felt something in me let go, and all the grief and the hate and the love and the hope and the anger just sighed up and out and away like air from a week-old deflating balloon, and all that was left was sadness.

"Please just tell me," I whispered into Aunt Fleur's jumper that smelt of cinnamon and freesias. And then Aunt Fleur started talking, and after that everything happened very, very fast.

Andy

* * *

He takes out a match and holds it like a pen. He strikes it against the matchbox, but it doesn't fire. He tries again. Again, it fails. Something else I am useless at, he thinks.

The third match hisses to life, the flame immediately searing against his palm. Clumsily, he throws it. Greedily, the fire starts feeding.

He imagines his characters scrambling to escape the flames, screaming to the edges of the pages, leaping off into the unknown. A World Trade Tower of pages, collapsing in on itself now, the edges curling up as if to hug themselves goodbye. He thinks of his parents, his mother, his childhood. He thinks of his wife.

He watches as the flames leap higher, licking and slurping. Fahrenheit 451, Ray Bradbury, Fahrenheit 451, Ray Bradbury. He repeats it in his head, over and over like an incantation as the smoke blurs the outline of the fence in front of him and his wife behind him, running. He is hot, so hot, but he doesn't move further away from the flames.

Maurice, watch out! Oh my God, Maurice no no no no!

He hears Robyn's voice, but it is like an intermittent radio frequency that he is choosing not to tune into. After the fire has died and the smoke-ravaged earth has been left lifeless, he will choose never to tune into it again.

* * *

38

Loud fluorescent lighting made me squint after the relative gloom of the corridor. For a moment all I could see was glare and movement and lots of grey and white. Then my eyes adjusted. It was the kind of nondescript conference room used for team-building courses held at two-star motels, but on a grand scale. Smaller tables had been set end to end to form two giant tables, chairs on both sides regularly punctuating their length. The end wall was one huge whiteboard, the high-tech kind you write on then press a button and it magically prints. On my left, halfway down the room, was a small kitchenette area, delineated by yellow and white lino. A sign read **Leave this kitchen as you would wish to find it.** Another sign said **Toilets**, with an old-fashioned hand encircled by a frilly cuff pointing to small corridor beside the wall-mounted microwave. A door to my right stood ajar, and I glimpsed a smaller room, its walls lined with rows of camp beds, blankets strewn untidily across them.

One table in the main room heaved under piles of books just like the ones in the library, and thick, coverless piles of pages. The other held stacks and stacks of scrap paper covered in close handwriting. It was a sea of paper and words, waves of movement passing books and pens and paper from hand to hand. People rose and fell, ducked and reached, calling and chatting and walking purposefully back and forth.

There was Noah, passing a wad of paper to a woman on his right. It was Penelope, and next to her was her husband John. There was Jezebel halfway down a table, stacking books and flirting openly with a young man I didn't recognise. She looked sober, at least. I spotted

Eve, still naked, and my heart gave a jolt as I watched her enact every librarian's worst nightmare. Muscles worked in her arms and chest as she tore the cover off a book, eying Jezebel as she ripped. Jacob limped from his seat to feed a wad of papers into a shredder, one of several standing against a wall. A group of young men, ten of them, worked together, looking scared but determined. They seemed to be taking turns carrying piles of coverless books to the corridor leading to the toilets (surely no one needed to take *that* much reading material), casting furtive glances towards the front of the room as they went. I followed their gaze and saw Judas standing on his own, partially obscured by a Health and Safety noticeboard.

Peter clapped his hands once and all movement stopped. And I realised then that staring at me, without a trace of surprise, was every single person who had disappeared from Heaven, taken prisoner by the White Guys. And sitting at the end of the table on the left, partially obscured by an enormous bald man with muscles the size of Christmas hams, was Kit. "Took you long enough," he called.

Peter was immediately all business. "Kit, fill him in. The rest of you, keep shredding. But slowly."

Everyone turned back to their work. Kit gestured me towards him as Peter left, clipping the door neatly behind him. I heard the padlock click shut.

I walked the length of the table to the back of the room, grabbed a spare chair from a stack in the corner and sat down next to Kit. When had he last slept? He smelt electric and sweaty. His eyes were bloodshot and his fingers were covered in plasters.

"Paper cuts," he explained. "We've all got them."

"What the hell's going on?" I asked. I pushed a small bowl of individually wrapped mints out of the way. "I thought something awful had happened to you." The next words came out rather gruffly. "I came to rescue you."

Kit blinked, then smiled. "Wow. That's… Thanks, Maurice. Really.

But right now we're all a bit busy to be rescued."

I looked at him blankly for a moment, feeling deflated. *If you're going to go out of your way to rescue someone,* I thought, *then the least they could do is need rescuing.* Then I remembered Michael and his stupid companion talking in Kit's cabin. I gave Kit a Reader's Digest version of what I had heard. He nodded rapidly as I talked.

"The White Guys, they're archangels," he said. "They're trying to overthrow God." He threw a glance around the room. "Getting the trouble-makers – that's everyone down here, apparently – out of the way was the first step." He snatched up a book, looked at the front, then scribbled a name in Vivid marker on a large scroll of butcher's paper that ran down the middle of the table. The scroll was covered in names; a heavenly roll call. He passed the book to the extremely large man sitting next to him, who ripped the cover off, back and front, and threw the discarded cover under the table.

"Maurice, meet Samson. Samson, Maurice." Samson nodded as he effortlessly peeled the cover off another book. These didn't just *look* like the books from the library, I realised. They *were* the books from the library.

"So they picked us off one by one," continued Kit. "Most of us were taken from our cabins during the night and brought here. Peter said it was going to be you next."

"I know," I said. "I heard Michael say it." I jumped as an old man with a long and matted beard dropped a paperweight in the shape of a sceptre. "But what are you all doing here? Why aren't you chained up, or in prison or something? And what the…" I gestured at the table. "What are you doing to the books?"

I reached round to check on my own book, still snugly tucked down my trousers, its cover now slippery from sweat. There was no way I was ready to see it destroyed.

"They need us to do their dirty work for them." Kit looked up, as if the answer might be inscribed on the ceiling. "We're under the reception building. Three or four floors down. Apparently God used to use this room for staff meetings and such until someone suggested it was a bit inappropriate to hold 'Reach for the Stars' motivational workshops underground." He grabbed another book, noted down its name, and handed it to Samson. "We're being held here until we've shredded all the books in the library. The archangels want to destroy them, to make sure none of us can Go On." He paused, then asked eagerly, "Do you know what that means? To Go On?"

I cast back to what I had heard as I cowered in Kit's shower stall. "I … I think Michael said something about people completing their books then disappearing? But I don't know where to, or…"

Kit lifted books and sorted piles with renewed vigour. "It means, Maurice, that there *is* something more than this." He gestured widely with one enormous hand. "I told you. I *knew* it. We're all going to get out of here! But apparently the only way it's going to happen is if we save the books – all of them, if we can. You need to do something with your book before you can Go On; I don't know what, exactly, but Peter said he'll explain more when it's time."

He pointed at the piles of scribbled-on paper on the other table, and at the shredders steadily devouring every page. "So we're shredding all that scrap paper instead. Then we rip the covers off the real books and hide their pages behind panels in the men's bog." I watched as one of the ten young men picked up another pile of naked books and headed to the toilets. After a few minutes he emerged empty-handed.

Kit unwrapped a mint and slammed it into his mouth. "Apparently we're all tagged for Going Down."

I didn't think I wanted to hear the answer, but I asked anyway. "What is … Down?"

"I don't know, but it sounds bad. They can't kill us, obviously. That job's already been done for them. It must be worse than that. Peter's doing what he can but we're running out of options."

"So Peter's definitely not one of them?" I asked, as Joseph, still sporting his brightly striped jacket, stopped by Kit's chair to collect a pile of coverless books. He headed towards the toilets, humming a cruise ship tune as he went.

"Peter's on our side. Has been since this all started. The archangels think he's with them but they're wrong. Says he owes God, or something." Kit leaned in. "Tell you someone else who's on our side." He nodded towards Judas. "Keeps to himself," he said in a low voice, even though we were far enough away that Judas was unlikely to hear. "Doesn't seem popular. I think the other disciples – " he nodded at the group of ten young men " – wonder why he's even here."

I watched as Noah fed pages two by two into a shedder. "Where did you get all the scrap paper?"

"Judas found it in the archive room by God's office. Screeds of it. Early drafts of the Bible."

I spotted Moses near the front of the room. The old man was working away, shredding pile after pile of white paper, but tears were running down his long face in a steady stream and into his beard. "What's up with him?" I asked.

"Apparently in draft number eight he actually made it to the Promised Land," Kit said, frowning. He gestured for me to follow him to the kitchenette, where he dumped a tea bag into a yellow mug and poured in hot water from a zip. "Basically, this is a Heavenly holding pen." He spooned sugar into the mug and stirred, sloshing hot liquid onto the floor. "I reckon as soon as the archangels think we've shredded all the books, we'll be … disposed of." He attempted a quick laugh, but it stuck in his throat. He looked down and stirred more slowly.

I swallowed. "How much more scrap paper is there?"

Kit sipped and gestured at the piles on the table. "This is the last of it. We're trying to take as long as possible, but best-case scenario? I reckon one more day, two at the most. Peter says there are still hundreds of books left in the library. He lets the other White Guys in, and they bring us a new batch every few hours. But we're running out of room to hide them." He barked out a tired laugh. "You think when you die all your troubles are behind you, right? Rest in Peace? What bullshit."

The door opened. Peter was back. He closed the door precisely then clapped twice. Everyone stopped what they were doing and turned towards him.

"Listen up, everyone." He glanced around the room, eyes resting on me before moving on. "The archangels know Maurice is missing. They think he's tried to escape." There was a collective intake of breath. "They're searching every cabin. We've got time, but not a lot."

Peter cleared his throat. "The archangels are determined and dangerous, but they are not infallible. They are unsettled. They – with the exception of their leader – are scared." A buzz of excitement reverberated around the room. Judas, who had moved to stand next to Peter, raised his hands and gestured for quiet. Peter nodded at him then continued.

"Michael knows he needs to strike now or it'll be too late. He's ordered all the Heavenly Hosts to gather the citizens of Heaven on the cocktail lawn, and at midday he's planning to declare himself God. Anyone who stands against him will immediately be Sent Down."

There was silence as everyone took this in.

"I've managed to plant a few whisperers amongst the citizens. Most have lost hope and will accept Michael as their leader without challenge. Some, however, are curious, and are starting to wonder. To question. The tide may be turning. We have to act now."

Peter found my eyes. "But first, we have to save as many books as we can. Maurice, do you have my library key?" I stood, nodding dumbly. How did he know? "Good. I had to borrow Judas's after I lost mine." He glanced at Kit then looked back at me. "It's time to use it. Go up and grab as many books as you can and bring them down here. Hopefully the archangels won't notice they're gone. We'll hide as many as we can today and tonight. We'll sleep in shifts. Take Kit, and…" he quickly scanned the crowd of faces. "Eve, Joseph, Moses, Noah, Judas, go with him. The rest of you, slow right down on the shredding. Let's hope they won't notice the discrepancy between the number of covers and the amount of shredded paper."

Eve stood immediately, her face grim and determined. Kit put down his mug and walked with her to the front of the room, and Judas moved to stand beside them. I stayed put in the kitchenette, my feet apparently glued to the floor. The other three whom Peter had nominated remained seated, their faces a study in avoidance.

Eve's eyes flashed. "Well come on, you nincompoops! Do you think I'm happy about going up there? Do you think I want to get caught and Sent Down? But I'm doing it. And I'll tell you why – there is no way those fuckers are getting away with this, and no way we're Going Down without a fight. Trust me, you do *not* want the archangels to win this war. Under their rule Heaven would be Hell."

"It's not exactly all beer and skittles right now," I thought, unfortunately out loud. "Unless you like yellow, and egg and spoon races."

Eve regarded me, one severely arched eyebrow disappearing under her fringe. A fresh bloom of red was spreading across her throat. "You choose, then, Maurice. Go on." Her voice was loud and precise, every word stapled into the silence. "You're so clever and witty, how about you make a joke while you're at it? You're just like my fucking husband, useless when it really counts and no doubt a wiener the size of a toothpick." Jezebel snickered. Eve swung to face her. "That's right, you lard-arsed hussy, go ahead and laugh. Go on!" Her eyes blazed around the room. "Anyone else think this is amusing? Anyone else want to share a cosy snigger over the state of my marriage?" Everyone looked anywhere but at Eve. Some were staring with distaste at Jezebel, who had bent her head in a pantomime of contrition. From where I was standing I could see one of her hands slink to the knee of the young man next to her.

Peter moved to put his hand on Eve's shoulder. She grasped it and hung on. The red was receding, whispering back to its placated corner. When she spoke again all the punch had gone.

"Listen. Just listen, you fools. Very soon the archangels are going to be down here, and they're coming for us. We act now, we might just save our sorry arses. We do nothing, Heaven loses. God's out of the picture permanently."

For a moment all was silent.

"Shall we take a vote?" I said, finally. "All those in favour of doing nothing *and* saving our arses?"

Eve looked at me, incredulous. Samson cracked his knuckles. I looked at Peter and read disappointment. The rest of the room seemed to sigh, once and heavily, and I surprised myself by wishing I was brave enough to apologise.

In the end, it was Kit who was brave.

"Yes, but where the hell *is* God?" he cried, his huge hands stiff at the end of outstretched arms. That question was for Eve. The ones that followed were for every human in the room, and perhaps beyond. "How do we know he's even coming back? How do we know he actually exists? Where is he? What the hell are we all doing here? *What the fuck is going on?*"

39

Dear Maurice,

I am struggling to hold a steady image of you in my mind. Is it happening already? They say that when a loved one dies, after a while you forget what their face looks like. Then their voice. You can't hear it anymore. And then there's nothing but what you imagine. You rewrite and rewrite the memories until you're left with nothing but a grubby palimpsest; a patchwork fiction of a person you once knew.

I can't picture you as you were when you died: middle-aged, sad, angry. All I can remember – maybe all I want to remember – is you at five, then at eight, then at fifteen. Then twenty. You, before you completely lost your sense of wonder.

There are two incidents that stick in my mind.

One, when we went to the beach on my tenth birthday. Do you remember? It was about a year before Mum and Dad separated, although they were already far apart. You were seven and Dad was starting to wonder what he had done wrong to have bred a son like you: a son who didn't want to play ball, who had little interest in "manly" adventures, who cried when sent to school camp because he missed his mum. A sissy who preferred books to toy guns and dirt and rough and tumble.

We were walking back to the car, skin sticky and prickled with heat and sand and salt, all of us mildly irritated and sad after a long day in the sun with people and screaming and the infinite, crowded sea. Mum carried her books as she hid under a giant hat, wrapped like a mummy in her kaftan. She was terrified of the sun, which she said made her ill and weak, but had agreed to come because it was my birthday. She had read all day under the green and white umbrella that Dad was juggling along with deckchairs and a picnic basket, lighter now but cumbersome all the same.

As we approached the car, Dad fumbled for his keys, trapped in his trouser pocket. (Do you remember how he never wore shorts, even when it was sweltering?) The umbrella tipped on an awkward angle, a deck chair clattered to the asphalt, and as the picnic basket tipped to eject two rejected ham sandwiches his ankle twisted and he crashed to the ground.

We stood, the three of us, watching as Dad tried to disentangle himself from beach equipment and embarrassment. We knew not to try to help him. Other beachgoers stared.

Then you stepped forward. I heard your small, nervous voice as you picked up fallen sandwiches and tried to right a crooked deck chair. "It's OK, Dad." You reached out your hand.

Mum spoke then. "Maurice. Don't, love." She was clutching her books like they were a lifeline.

Dad stopped struggling with the umbrella, pushed everything aside with an almighty heave, and limped his way to standing. Blood from a nasty graze on his right elbow stained his white shirt. He brushed at himself with two urgent slaps, then thwacked your hand away.

"Yes, well at least I know how to get up again," he said. "You? Don't even bother. Weak little boys grow into weak men." He pointed at Mum. "And it's your fault. You deal with it."

He limped to the car as the sun, having seen enough, dipped behind the red and white changing sheds. On the way home you held Mum's hand that she reached through to the back seat without Dad seeing.

The other incident I remember was the night before you started university. We visited Mum in the rest home and she struggled to remember our names. You held her hand as I arranged wildflowers from my garden in a vase and placed it on the grubby windowsill. The room smelt of cabbage and disinfectant and bodies that were washed, but only just.

Before we left you leaned over to kiss her. Silver hair spread over her pillow, every trace of auburn now extinguished, the tired strands greasy and stiff. As your face got close to hers she grasped it, her eyes growing wide. Then she whispered, and I had to bend in from my neutral position by the ensuite door to hear it.

"My books. My books."

You pulled away slightly, nose wrinkling. Mum's breath was sour.

"It's OK, Mum. I'll look after them. They're safe with me," you said.

You had to prise her fingers from around your hand before you stood up.

As we walked down the corridor to the reception area, I asked you where her books were.

"In my apartment."

"Do you want me to help you get rid of them?" I asked.

You stopped and stared. A young man pushing a wheelchair, which cradled a tiny woman in a dressing gown holding a teddy bear, weaved around us.

"You heard what I said. I'm looking after them. At least there's one thing I can do." You started walking again, with more purpose. "Now I just need someone to look after me, and I'll be fine." You ran your hand through your thinning hair and coughed out a laugh as you opened the door to the car park.

I tried, Maurice. I really tried, but God, you made it so hard sometimes. And now I'm trying to look after Andy. I'll do better this time. I promise.

Fleur x

40

Kit's last line strangled its way out as his face turned an interesting shade of pink and huge tears threatened at his eye brims. All the teenage invincibility had drained from his face, his shoulders, his enormous fledgling hands and feet. He was a boy; a murdered boy suspended indefinitely in the cruel joke that was Heaven. He could have been Andy. And something in me quietly went *ping*.

I didn't yell. I didn't try to make a run for it, or collapse in a corner and weep. I walked to the front of the room and put my arms around Kit (a little awkwardly; my head came up to his shoulder), and for a soggy minute he cried in my arms like a baby. Everyone looked carefully the other way or busied themselves with paper – except for Moses, who pushed himself up determinedly with this staff and came forward, holding out a handkerchief. I saw Penelope smile. This time it was Kit's turn to accept one. He parped and wiped and looked at the ground.

"I'd rather you didn't give it back," said Moses, his attempt at humour a small but generous gift. A few of us smiled, and the room felt kinder, and I felt ready.

I turned around, smoothed my hair to the right, and spoke.

"I don't know about God," I began. "Never knew what to believe when I was alive. Turns out my daughter was right. Never had the strength to get off the fence, really. If he does exist, then he's got a lot to bloody answer for, if he comes back. And I don't really know what this place is." I gestured above me, trying to indicate all that was beyond the white, fly-specked ceiling and fluorescent strip lighting. "It's not what

I imagined Heaven to be. And right now – " I could hardly believe the next words that came out of my mouth " – I'm pretty frightened." I looked at Kit, and he gave me a watery, grateful smile. I was surprised to see more than a few heads nodding in recognition. I took a breath and carried on. This would probably be the first and last time I would ever have a literally captive audience.

"I guess what I want to say is, we have nothing to lose. We're already dead. How much worse could it get? And we can't let them destroy everyone's stories, can we? It's not … it's not right."

I felt like I was having an out-of-body experience, incredulously watching an unfamiliar me put his stake in the ground. What on earth was I saying? Who did I think I was? A middle-aged, slightly chubby librarian with a broken marriage and a daughter who despised me, thinking I could play a part in a Heavenly war? I wasn't the leader of a revolution. As Robyn and Andy would say, I wasn't really anything at all.

I glanced at Eve. She nodded once, smiling grimly. Tears fought with my eyelids. What was happening to me? Surfing the wave of incredulity, I addressed the six people whom Peter had shoulder tapped.

"So, what I'm saying is, let's go. Fuck it. Let's go and save those books. Are you with me?"

After such a stirring speech I expected the room to erupt into action, everyone standing as one and rushing to follow me as I triumphantly led them forward, a leader valiantly leading his troops into battle. It didn't happen. After I finished talking there was a smattering of applause, led by Kit, Moses, and Eve. I noticed Noah picking his teeth. Judas, looking vaguely impatient, moved towards the door and held it open as Moses promptly tripped over a pile of books and cursed loudly as a trickle of blood ran down his knee.

Finally, after a few messy minutes of sponging and plasters, we were ready to file out into the corridor. As Peter closed and locked the door we stood in an uncertain half-circle, like awkward office workers around a water cooler.

"Good luck," said Peter, turning to go.

"What are you going to do?" I asked, wondering why he wasn't coming with us.

"Distract the archangels. I'll do my best, but it may be too late. Just do what you can. Do it for Him."

The rest of us looked at each other for a few uncertain seconds. Then we set off to save the unfinished stories.

<h1 style="text-align:center">41</h1>

Dear Maurice,

When you and I were young, I would creep into your room at night and sit by your bed while Mum and Dad argued downstairs. Do you remember? You wouldn't say a word. You would just sit upright in the half-dark and I would sit next to you.

"What are they arguing about?" you used to ask in a tiny voice. "Is it us?"

"No," I would say. "Try not to think about it. It's best not to know."

Should I have told Andy what happened? I remember her face that morning, the day of your funeral, as she sat and trembled on my bed. Her bruised and beautiful face with its halo of glorious hair, sadness and anger and disbelief passing over it like clouds in a greying sky, swirling and twisting, unpredictable shapes at once forming and disintegrating. Would she have been better off not knowing?

We can only speculate. In that moment, I could do nothing else.

"After your father sold the shop he changed completely," I began, after she had clung to me and whispered into my jumper. "All the fire went out of him. He stopped writing. He packed away all his drafts and scribbles and manuscripts and notebooks into boxes and hid them away in the garage.

"Not long afterwards he started working at the library. Your mother knew someone who knew the boss there. Dreadful woman, but at least she took him on. I watched him wither, Andy – wither, and at the same time bloom with bitterness." I winced. "Oh God, what an awful metaphor."

She sniffed. "It wasn't great."

I smiled and kissed the top of her fiery head. "He and your mother tried to fix things, they really did," I continued, as I led her back to the bed and sat her down. "I think initially your mother regretted her harshness, and in her own way tried to make it up to him by buying him books and pens and expensive notebooks. Perhaps she realised that his affair had been his mistake, but also hers." I handed some tissues to Andy, who clutched them, dry-eyed.

"But he didn't seem interested. He would come home from work and just sit on the couch and stare at the TV. He didn't read anymore. He and Robyn would make perfunctory conversation, and they went and did married couple stuff now and then, and perhaps they made love now and then to try to not feel so lonely."

"Marriage sucks," deadpanned Andy.

"Why do you think I never did it?" I smiled gently.

"Don't blame you. I'm never getting married. Ever."

I squeezed her hand. She nodded for me to continue.

"This went on for a while. Months. They were both so bloody miserable, Andy. And then one day your Mum rang me, sobbing and almost incoherent, and said that she needed me to come over right away. She opened the door and her right hand was bandaged from wrist to elbow. She told me that two days previously she had written Maurice a letter saying she had lost all respect for him and could never forgive him; that the marriage was over, she wanted a divorce. She hadn't given it to him, though."

"Why not?" asked Andy, crumpling and squeezing the tissues.

"She said she'd discovered something that had changed her mind; something that made her decide to try one more time to fix things, that she was planning on ripping up the letter, never letting him see it. Only, she didn't do it right away. You can guess the next bit. Your dad came home from work with a bad back – apparently that awful boss of his at the library had cleaned the shelving ladders a bit too zealously – looked *in Robyn's bedside drawer for painkillers…"*

"Oh God," muttered Andy. "How could she have been so stupid?"

"Your mum told me they had a massive fight; a ghastly, violent argument, and that at one point Maurice accused her of destroying his dream of being a writer, and Robyn yelled that he had nothing important to say anyway and would never have made it, and that he had failed at marriage and a career and he might as well stop trying to be good at anything…"

Andy stared at me, her eyes wide.

"I'm so sorry, sweetheart," I said. "But if you're going to hear it, then you need to hear it all. So you understand."

"I hate her," said Andy, so quietly I could hardly catch it.

"You think you do, love, but deep down you long for her. Just like your dad did. He couldn't bear the thought of losing her."

"But why? She said such ghastly things to him. Why did he even want to be with her anymore?"

"We all fling words in anger when we're hurt, Andy. We can be cruel, but it doesn't mean we're bad through and through. Nobody is. Despite everything, if she had left, I think it would have broken him. Our father leaving our mother started the process. Robyn's leaving would have finished it."

I continued with the story. It had to be told. It was too late to rewrite it.

"As your Mum was talking, I could smell something burning. I thought she'd had a kitchen misadventure – she couldn't cook to save herself – until she took me out to the back garden.

"There was an old tin crate by the back fence that Robyn had tried to grow herbs in. Never worked, so it stood, barren and weedy, awaiting her next attempt. Today it was smouldering and black, puffs of ash and smoke still drifting from it." I paused. Took a breath.

"Robyn told me she'd gone to bed after the fight, drained and sick. She'd woken up to the smell of smoke and the sound of crashing and ripping."

Andy went rigid. "Dad. What did he do?"

"He … he was burning all of his writing. Everything. The almost-finished manuscript of his first novel, early drafts, journals packed full of notes and scribbles, discs, USB sticks, all his half-finished stories and story plans … every single piece of evidence that he had ever tried to be a writer. I learned later that he'd gone into his computer, too, and wiped everything from its memory. He even burned all his writing books from his childhood. The one you have is the only one Robyn managed to save. She grabbed it from the flames before it was completely destroyed. It was too late for everything else. She gave it to me, eventually. Maurice didn't want it and I don't think she could bear to keep it.

"A few days later I asked him why he'd done it. He shut me down immediately. 'Dad was right, and Robyn was right,' he said. 'I'll never amount to much. Mediocre Maurice, a small-time librarian. Let's leave it at that.' He never wrote again. Not one word."

Andy and I sat in silence as the clock ticked over to 9 am. She was as white as a sheet.

"He burned it all? He destroyed all his writing?"

"Yes, love," I whispered, desperately biting back tears.

Minutes passed. I could almost hear her mind working, frantic and bruised and desperate.

"Why didn't Mum give him the letter? What stopped her?"

I paused. "You did. She'd found out that morning that she was pregnant."

Andy blinked. "When did she tell Dad?"

"After the fire. A few days later."

"Did…" She swallowed, and to my surprise I saw tears gathering in her eyes. Andy never cried. Her next words were very small. "Did they … was she … did they want me?"

I took her hand. "Oh, my darling. My dear, sweet Andy." And suddenly she was crying, really crying after years of not, and she was in my arms, and I was stroking her head and whispering that in all the awfulness and anger and sadness of that day and all the days before and after it, she was the only thing, the only one, the only happiness.

And that you and Robyn wanted her more than anything else in the world.

I wanted to stop there. I wasn't sure I could go on. But Andy wanted to know what had happened after she was born. As the tears slowed down she pulled away, wiped her face, hitched in a shaky breath, and demanded I tell her. You know her. Stubborn beyond measure. Like a dog with a bone.

I went to the window and looked out at the day of your funeral.

"Your father made his choice: to stay," I said. "Both of them did. Then you were born, and for a time he was a new man. He would hold you in his arms for hours in those early days, exhausted and lost and bowled over with a love I don't think he even knew he could feel. He would stroke your hair – you had so much of it, right from the start – and call you his little Fire Princess, over and over. But after a few months the hurt and the anger and the bitterness took hold of him again. Of both of them. It never extinguished his love for you, but it made it almost impossible to recognise. Your parents struggled on together for years, mostly for your sake. But I don't think they ever forgave each other."

I walked over to the bed and sat down again next to Andy. She wouldn't look at me. Her face was blotched and pale. "Your mother gave up accountancy, went all New Age, or Buddhist, I don't really know which. Maybe it made her feel less guilty. Maybe she was frightened by her own power to destroy and needed something more powerful than herself to believe in. Eventually they separated, then divorced. You know all about that. He swore he would never tell you what had happened, and he made me swear the same. Maybe he was ashamed that he had lost everything and failed at everything. How can you admit that to your only daughter? But above all, I think he wanted to protect you from the whole sorry mess. And when you're hiding your pain from someone you love you end up hiding the other parts of yourself as well, because it's all an inseparable whole. And then you become unknowable. Unreachable."

Andy balled her fists. "I hated him. I hate him."

"You didn't hate him, Andy. You longed for him. And he longed for you too, but I don't believe he could let himself know it. All he knew to do was to shut down, and I stood back and let it happen."

I started to cry, then. I apologised to her, over and over. I said I was sorry for keeping the wrong secrets. For not stepping in earlier and telling the truth. For not trying to fix something between the two of you. I should have taken each of you by the hand and led you back to each other, and now it's too late.

I'm sorry, Maurice. I'm so sorry. I thought she finally had a right to know, and, besides, she wouldn't accept no for an answer. But if I had known what was going to happen that day, the day of your funeral, I never would have told her, and I'm not sure I can ever forgive myself.

Fleur x

42

We had only been in the library for a few minutes, the seven of us greedily scooping books into our arms, when there was a knock on the door. Looking back, none of us seemed surprised. We all thought it was Peter.

"I'll let him in," said Noah, who was closest to the door. He walked over and, as if suddenly remembering what one does in such a situation, whispered intently at the door. "Who is it?"

There was no answer. I caught a renegade whiff of aftershave. In the same second that I yelled "Don't open it!", Noah opened the door.

Michael appeared first, his beautiful face aflame with fury and triumph, and he flung Noah to the floor with one effortless arm-sweep. As his fellow archangels followed him in and lined up in front of the entrance, each one more radiant than the next, I felt a strange paroxysm of relief. The thing I had dreaded the most was finally happening. It was almost easier to face it than it had been to fear the possibility of it.

"Put the books down," said Michael, his voice poisoned silk. "It's all over."

I slowly placed my jumbled pile on the ground and put out my hand to steady Kit, who was next to me. "It's OK," I murmured. "Just imagine them without their clothes on."

There was a muffled, slightly crazed guffaw from Moses, who was standing on the other side of me. It cut off abruptly at a razor glance from Michael.

Out of the corner of my eye I saw Eve inching towards a bookshelf, the first one on the left as you entered the library. Her face and upper body were blooming as hotly scarlet as boiled blood. She didn't look frightened; she looked furious. She caught my eye, and a current of understanding ran between us, a flash of complicity so sharp, so exquisitely primitive, that the hairs rose on the back of my neck. *Why did I never make it with a woman like that,* I thought for a crazy second as I moved in the opposite direction, trying to draw angelic eyes away from her. And even though I didn't have the first idea what to say, I coughed a little past the lump in my throat and started talking. Without realising it I had raised my hands in an attitude of surrender.

"Right, people, let's all just calm down for a moment." The archangels, suspicious, feral, looked at me. "Can we just talk about this? How about we take the discussion outside, perhaps. We are in a library, after all. Please keep noise to a minimum, haha. I know this, you see. I was a librarian." I flung this last sentence into the air between me and the archangels. It hung there like a cheap epitaph. I had a weird urge to laugh. Kit let out a tiny groan. I wasn't sure whether it was from fear or exasperation. Michael stepped forward, his smile a gash of pearls.

"I know exactly who you are, Maurice. Oh yes, I know. I know everything. How you tried and failed to be a writer, then a husband, then a father. How you spent your days cowering between stacks, stamping and filing and shelving books that you hadn't written, wallowing in paper and ink but hating it because you were too useless, too lazy to add your own story. Right, Maurice?" He was coming closer. I could hardly breathe. "How you think that in this moment you're going to somehow salvage a part of you that's worth something and fashion yourself into a … hero. How awfully redemptive." He was at my shoulder now, the beauty and terribleness of him making me feel faint.

"So here you are again, Maurice," he hissed on the last syllable. It was all very *Silence of the Lambs*. "Here you are again in a library, only this time you do have your own story – through no virtue or talent of your own, mind you. A pathetic, limp little tale." He tossed out a sharp laugh, which was echoed by the other archangels. Then he lent into me and whispered tenderly in my ear like a lover. "And today, my friend, your story ends."

Suddenly my arms were behind me and halfway up my back and I was bent double, the pain brittle and breathtaking. I heard Kit cry out in protest, and there was a rush of shellsuits and courage as Moses and the others started towards me.

"Stop! Let him go!" The voice was sharp as a gunshot. I craned my neck up as far as it would go and saw Peter standing in the doorway, a carbon copy of the other archangels in all but intent.

"It isn't going to work, Michael. You can't win. Let him go, and let's talk."

A high, nasally voice whined from the line of angels. "See? I *told* you not to trust him. Bloody traitor."

"Ah, but there are all kinds of traitors, are there not, Gabriel?" said Michael smoothly, his eyes daggering towards Peter. He let me go suddenly and shoved me away. I stumbled and straightened up with a small moan, rubbing my wrists.

Michael whispered at Peter, moving slowly towards him. "There are spies everywhere, watching. Listening. Waiting." Without taking his eyes off his opponent, he said softly, "Judas? What news?"

Judas stepped forward, away from us and towards the archangels. His face was impassive.

"They've been shredding scrap paper for days now instead of books. God's draft copies of the Bible. They're hiding the real books behind the walls in the men's toilet. Peter and his helpers are trying to incite the citizens towards revolution. They think they can overthrow you." He paused, then played his trump card. "They're frightened."

There was a ghastly silence as Moses, Noah, and Joseph wilted, slack-jawed and betrayed. Peter stood in the doorway, bewildered and uncertain. Looking back, that was the most frightening moment. Our leader, the strong and steady symbol of our fledgling revolution, was losing his grip, and, obedient followers that we were, we started to follow suit. Michael sensed it, and his eyes widened in triumph. He reached into his pocket and pulled out a small golden square. Kit, snaring a small reserve of defiance, muttered an incoherent word that sounded like "No" and stumbled towards Judas, his fist curled.

And then the library started to collapse.

Eve's scream, bestial and deafening, broke every librarian's cardinal rule as she torpedoed her body into the first bookcase and it toppled backwards onto the one behind, and then that one smashed onto the one behind it, the shelves recruited as giant dominoes. On and on it went, a deafening procession. Books started to topple crazily, slapping and diving and thudding, some across the room, some into archangels and humans. The procession picked up speed, down to the window at the far end, across the back wall, back up towards us, quicker and quicker as it approached its end, a tidal wave of stories.

Judas started towards Eve, all pretence banished, his eyes feral, his mouth twisted in a vengeful leer. I heard a shout of desperate protest before registering it had come out of my own mouth, and suddenly I was leaping over piles of books towards the traitor. With strength I didn't know I possessed I grabbed him by his dreadlocks, and with an inelegant grunt and pirouetting hop, flung him as far as I could across the room. Taken by surprise, Judas's arms cartwheeled as he tried to regain his balance and alter his trajectory. A toppling shelf jarred out of line and tumbled on an angle, striking him. He fell soundlessly, his body trapped from the waist down. He didn't scream.

A few of the archangels rushed to his side as Michael and Peter started circling each other. "Run, you fools!" Peter hissed at me, and in that giddy and awful moment he managed to throw me his bunch of keys, and I raised my hand and clumsily caught them. Then I was stumbling out of the library, Eve and the others behind me, through the tiny vestibule and down the stairs, down and down and along the corridor until I reached the locked conference room. And then the door was open and after a brief, desperate explanation the captives were finally free, and all of us were swarming upwards towards the strange sun then dashing out onto the cocktail lawn, until we all stopped and wheezed a bit and realised that none of us had the foggiest idea what we were supposed to do next.

All the citizens of Heaven had been herded into a messy circle, the Heavenly Hosts surrounding them like yellow shepherds. No one was trying to run away. It was nearly noon.

And as if one entity, every single person turned at the same moment and looked at me. The expectation was palpable. Even Eve, who had so openly doubted me in the conference room, was staring at me with something akin to hope, her naked bosom heaving.

Moses stepped forward, next to me, and raised his stick. "Let my people go!" he cried, his voice wavery but resolute. Nothing happened. A Heavenly Host sniggered. Moses cleared his throat and nudged me. "What now?" he whispered.

I blinked in the fire of the strange midday sun and felt the first fragile buds of bravery starting to shrivel. The fresh, vaguely antiseptic air, the vast expanse of emerald AstroTurf, the open faces, the impossible sky stretching as far, perhaps, as another, better Heaven; the *nakedness* of it all started to drain me of my underground bravado. How could one be brave up here, laid bare in the light?

I used to have ambition, I thought. *I was a passionate man, once. I remember the excitement of beginning to read a new book, my delight tempered only by wistfulness that I would never again experience the joy of discovering that particular story for the first time. I remember the thrill of mastery that was the writing process – the fist pump after snaring the perfect word as it whispered past; losing myself in the zone and resurfacing hours later, dazed and full of wonder; finishing a paragraph and knowing it was special. I can recall those first surreal minutes after Andy's birth; the magical, giddy terror of holding her in my arms. I was passionate once. Robyn and I made breathtaking love. Once upon a time.*

I looked around in the suspense of silence at these people who were counting on me to go all Che Guevara, and all I felt was tired. I wanted to go and lie down on my bed and listen to Gospel FM and get up and wear yellow in the morning and eat gluten-free pancakes in the Hallelujah Hall and play checkers with naked people and have my eternity dictated by angel despots. I didn't care. It didn't matter.

Most people just live their lives, I thought, *and then, vaguely content but not quite, they die and that is that. And they are remembered for a month, a year, possibly a little more, and then the memory of them is fondly and only a little wistfully packed away. What happens after that means nothing. Because what are you if no one remembers you after you die?*

I was opening my mouth to let everybody down when Eve screamed again, and our collective gaze followed her voice towards the reception building door.

Michael and the other archangels were advancing slowly down the steps. Peter wasn't with them, but Kit was. Gabriel, trumpet slung over his shoulder in its elaborate halter, had one arm tightly around him and was holding a dagger to his neck. Kit's head was tipped slightly towards the sky, his pupils ping-ponging in the whites of his eyes. Slowly Gabriel led him down the last few steps, pushing him slightly with each descent so that the tip of the dagger pressed upwards into Kit's flesh, threatening to break the skin.

"Maurice. We need to do something. Now." Eve was right behind me, her breath hot on my neck.

"Then *you* do something, for fuck's sake," I hissed over my shoulder, feeling as desperate and helpless as Kit. "Why does everyone expect *me* to come up with some brilliant plan? What the fuck would I know?" I pinned on my incompetence like a badge of honour.

Eve pushed me aside with a grunt of impatience and strode towards the archangels. She drew herself up, filling the space, owning her position. "Let him go! I am Eve, first woman created, Mother of Humankind, and I am ordering you to let him go!"

Gabriel started laughing, and one by one the other archangels joined in, a braying angelic chorus.

Eve stopped at the bottom step. "What are you going to do, asshole? Kill him?" And her laughter joined her opponents', shrill and defiant.

Michael raised one hand and his troops gradually quietened down, some wiping their eyes with merriment. Kit was breathing hard, his skin pale. Tiny pricks of blood now laced his neck, punctuation marks to Gabriel's jerky laughter.

There was silence, and Michael addressed Eve as a patient teacher might address his most trying student.

"Well, well, well, first woman created, Mother of … whatever." He tipped his head to one side, thoughtful. "Perhaps we should add lover of snakes or eater of apples to those impressive titles?"

"Don't you dare talk to my wife like that!" Adam pushed forward out of the crowd, shaking his finger hard at the archangel. "It was one time! And it was my fault too!" The archangels whooped and cheered. Adam wilted a little and moved back towards the other citizens, but not before he and Eve exchanged a glance that said more than might be said in a fifty-minute couple's therapy session. *Thank you. Forgive me. I was a fool. Me too.*

Michael, smiling benevolently, threw his arms out wide as if to embrace the two of them. "My, how terribly touching. The weakest man in all creation stands up for his ball-breaking wife. I think I might just shed a tear. Or not." He sniffed once, then turned to Eve. "But back to your question, my dear. Yes, we're going to kill him."

Kit's eyes opened wide, and he stared straight at me. I stared back. There was a giddy *woosh* in my ears.

Eve faltered for a second, her frown forming tiny hills between her eyebrows. Then she rallied, shook her hair back, and looked directly into Michael's eyes, something I had not seen anyone do, human or angel, since I had arrived in Heaven. And for the second time in that insane day, I fell ever so slightly in love with her.

"Ha!" she barked, hands on hips. "Good luck with that. In case you'd forgotten, that particular train has already left the station."

Michael held her gaze as he smiled, as gently as a mother to her baby. My bowels turned to liquid and I thought, *Oh God. Oh God, she's wrong.*

"Oh no, no, no, my beautiful girl. No, that train is most definitely still waiting to depart." Michael walked down the steps to meet Eve. She held her ground. He leaned in close to her, but his voice carried. "Can't you hear the whistle? All abooaaard…"

The archangels started to laugh again, gently, madly. Gabriel gripped Kit tighter, and another red bead appeared at the tip of the dagger. Kit cried out quietly, like a newborn kitten mewling for its mother.

Michael straightened up and spoke to the crowd. The mad fire in his eyes was prancing and panting, eager to be let off its leash.

"Come now, citizens of Heaven. Time to surrender. Haven't we all had enough of this childish display?" He shook his head, an indulgent father regarding his disobedient children. "You're never going to win. Never. And why even try? We are not the enemy." He held out his hands, palms up. *See? Nothing bad in here.*

"Citizens, we are your friends. We want to *help* you. We want to make the afterlife *better* for you." Michael gestured to himself and to his fellow archangels above him on the steps, like a conductor introducing his orchestra. "We are here, and God is not. What does that tell you?"

"That God had the right idea, that's what," offered an intense, throttled voice. It was Kit's. "If I were him, I'd want to get as far away from you as possible."

Gabriel grunted and shifted the dagger until it lay horizontally along Kit's throat. A few citizens cried out. I felt my mouth shaping itself into a silent O. Michael poured up the steps – that is the only word that comes remotely close to describing how quickly, how fluently he moved – to stand beside Gabriel. He stayed the hand with the dagger and turned back to the crowd, and this time there was no attempt to win them over. The leash was off. He yelled into the terrified silence.

"Let me tell, you, citizens of Heaven, what happens when someone dies in Heaven. Let me tell you before demonstrating on our young *friend* here." He spat the word out as if it were rotten, eyeing me as he said it.

"You die here in Heaven, you don't Go On. There's no salvation. No God. No Happily Ever After. You die here and you are reborn on earth, to live your whole life again. The whole sorry affair, from messy birth to messier death. With no chance to change things – *and knowing that the whole time.*"

Whether it was true or not, we believed him immediately, all of us. The most dreadful things are the easiest to believe. The citizens, the archangels, Heaven itself seemed to fade into sepia as memories took their place: my mother and father fighting endlessly, fear and anxiety making me wet the bed; the way Robyn and I played out the almost identical scenes years later despite my desperate, impotent struggle to be nothing like my father; the day Andy was born and I rushed back to the library an hour later, too scared to hold her in case my heart might break with love and longing and too bitter to explain that to Robyn; the divorce; Andy's lost childhood; the days and days of stamping and filing and stacking in my cemetery of books. And the fire.

I thought of living all this again and being powerless to change any of it; greeting each new day and month and year and milestone not with ignorance or foolish hope, but with horrified recognition.

Faster and faster the memories filed past, an old-fashioned movie reel clacking furiously through scene after scene until the reel ended and snapped out, slapping uselessly against metal again and again and again. And then the movie was over and here I was, a useless little man standing on a lawn in Heaven, powerless to be anything but a failure. I looked around at my new friends. Noah was pacing slowly back and forth, clutching his back. Jacob was leaning heavily on a Heavenly Host, his face slack and exhausted. Samson's hugeness seemed incongruous and redundant, his posture tiny. Jezebel stood alone, arms crossed to hug herself, tears streaking her dusty, slutty face. I caught Kit's eye. His fists were relaxed now, and his gaze was steady and compliant. It was over.

I thought again of the fire, the flames leaping and consuming, burning and destroying and defeating. I looked at Moses anxiously picking his teeth, his staff lying on the ground before him where he had laid it down in surrender. I thought of his desperate efforts to part the lake and to burn down the topiary. I thought of Michael in Heaven's library, his eyes burning as he reached into his pocket to take out something golden and shiny. I thought of him knocking on the library door.

Let me in. Let me come in.

The big moments, the most vital realisations, the most exquisite turning points: these are always the quietest. The noise and the fanfare and the orchestral climaxes are reserved for moments that need noise and fuss to make them matter. And so it was, that standing in the midday sun that Friday in Heaven, on the verge of surrendering to murderous archangels, another something in me quietly went *ping*.

And in the next second – fellow writers, please forgive the cliché – all Hell finally and gloriously broke loose in my heart.

"YEEEAAAARRRRRRRWWP!" My Whitman-esque cry rang in my ears as I started running towards the archangels. Gabriel and Kit were on the second to bottom step. I was nearly level with them and Michael was grinning, Heaven's Joker, as his cohorts moved in to grab me, but nothing was going to stop me now. I ducked and barged my way through them, glimpsing the flash of bewilderment and then the slam of realisation on Michael's face as he guessed where I was going. "Stop him!" he screamed, which distracted Gabriel just long enough for Eve to leap to Kit's rescue, wrenching him out of the angelic grip and flinging him to safety. And then I was at the top of the stairs and running through the reception building door, and I heard Eve's second battle cry, wild as a banshee's, and the tentative response from the awakening citizens of Heaven, and I kept running.

I ran for my life.

<h1 style="text-align: center;">43</h1>

Dear Dad,

I feel like I did the day you died. Was it just five days ago? I feel as though my heart is in a hundred pieces, a puzzle that no one knows how to fit back together. I don't know whether to be mad at you, or to feel sorry for you. To hate you or love you. To long for you with every tiny broken puzzle piece, or to be glad that you're gone.

I hate Mum. I hate her. I hate her. I hate her. I hate Aunt Fleur. I hate you, too.

When Aunt Fleur told me everything, I cried. Hear that, Dad? I cried, for the first time in years. I never let myself cry in front of anyone. Not even when you left my sixteenth birthday party early. Not even when you forgot the name of my best friend. Not even when Andrew Greer used to poke my stomach and screech with laughter when it wobbled. Not even when you kissed Mum on the cheek at my seventeenth.

Not even when you died.

Is that why you never liked to talk about books? Do you remember the times I tried to reach out to you when I was younger, coming to you with a book I was reading, longing to share with you my love of words and stories, only to be shut down with a glance, or a cutting comment, or a turning away? I didn't know it was the books you despised. I thought it was me.

Perhaps that's why I never told you I wanted to write. I was scared of your scorn. But perhaps you were scared too: scared to see anything but failure in me, in case seeing success was too painful. Scared to see the real me in case it reflected back to you everything that you had lost.

Anyway, what's the point of going all psychiatrist. You're gone and you're never coming back. And today I'm expected to stand up and "commemorate your passing", like you're a train whooshing through a station and I'm a struggling artist on the platform, desperately trying to sketch at least an outline; a sense of your form and your features as you wallop past, blurry and unreachable, hurtling towards a distant station.

I hate you and I love you. Hate you, love you. Hate, love. Love.

The last thing Aunt Fleur said to me this morning before leaving to get ready for the funeral, was this: "Please don't be angry at him, Andy. He loved you. And so do I, and your mother. And I'm so sorry. So sorry. Please forgive me. And them."

Why the fuck have I been writing these letters to you and posting them? You're gone, dead. Forever. You won't ever read them.

I know what I have to do now. Goodbye, Dad.

Andy

44

As I entered the library I saw Peter lying, crumpled and twitching, by one of the fallen shelves. He opened his eyes for a moment and saw me, then closed them again. Judas hadn't moved, abandoned to his fate by the White Guys.

The library looked like a battleground with its enormous toppled soldiers spilling out their lifeblood. The lives of all of us. I started to step and skid over them to get to Peter when I heard the archangel coming.

I turned back towards the open door, breathing hard, and waited.

When Michael appeared, his breath even, the silk curtain of his hair impeccably draped, he stood just inside the doorway and again took the small golden square out of his pocket.

"You know how this works, Maurice. I know you do." He held it out to me like a gift. "I want you to burn them. All of them."

I moved slowly towards Michael and took God's lighter from his outstretched hand. The lighter he had stolen from Moses's bedside, and boasted about to Gabriel in Kit's cabin.

"Thou shalt not steal," I said.

Michael smiled his killer smile. "Thou shalt not commit adultery," he countered.

We considered each other, the evil archangel and the plump, panting human.

"I'll do you a deal," I said. Michael's eyes widened. I teetered, took a breath, and leapt.

"Let me burn my own book. Right now, right here." I patted my buttocks, hinting at my book's hiding place. "I'll burn it so I can never

Go On. I'll stay here forever and work in the library, under your rule. I'll let citizens in to read their books, but I'll make sure that no one ever gets to complete their story. I'll make sure that no one ever Goes On, ever again, so that your kingdom grows and grows and grows."

Michael tilted his head slightly, stroking a lock of his hair. "Why on earth would I need you, Maurice? I have plenty of followers already. I can just assign *them* to library duty. Well, the ones I don't like, anyway."

I silently flung a desperate prayer into the beyond. "Because you can't." Michael stopped stroking. "I think I've figured it out. I think only a citizen can get into the library. Only the people whose stories are inside it can open the door. And only if he or she is given a key by the keyholder. That's why Kit and I could break in that night. Kit had Peter's key."

Michael's mouth twitched, and his eyes flicked to the door, once.

"You ordered Peter to get the books out of the library, to destroy them, because you couldn't get in there yourself," I continued. "He's a citizen, just like us, even after you recruited him. And more than that: he's got the keys to the Kingdom of Heaven. It's in Matthew somewhere."

Peter moaned. He hoisted himself up on his hands and knees and then slowly onto his feet. I could see a hateful gash above his left ear, oozing blood. He faced Michael, his gaze steady. "Matthew chapter sixteen, verse nineteen," he said quietly.

"That's it," I said, snapping my fingers and pointing at Peter. "I read it the other night." Peter nodded at me, a small but enormous confirmation. I felt my heart thud once, a thud that reached my knees, and I turned back to Michael.

"Before, when we were getting the books, you could have just stormed in and taken us all by surprise. But you knocked. You knocked because you couldn't get in by yourself. Someone has to unlock the door for you. Not even Judas could, because he'd given his key to Peter, that day in the Glory Glade." I huffed out a tiny laugh. "You know, it's funny. I think you've been trying to figure out how to get into your library for years, while for years I've been trying to figure out how to escape mine."

The fire in Michael's eyes was starting to dance. "You don't know what you're talking about," he hissed, but he shifted on his feet and his nostrils flared. "And even if you were right, I have Judas … and Peter." His insane eyes burned as he flicked them towards the man who had betrayed him. "The traitor will die, of course – but not before he gives the key back to Judas … who can then open the library for me any time I wish. Why do you think I recruited the fool?"

I pointed to Judas's body, broken and trapped. "He's dead, Michael. Gone to repeat his earthly life, according to you. Maybe this time around he'll steer away from kissing men in moonlit gardens."

Michael strode over to Judas and kneeled by him, touching his wrist. When he stood once more, his beautiful face was paler than snow.

I was delirious with fear but determined Michael wouldn't know it. Time to put on my mask. *I'm too stupid to be scared.*

I slapped my trembling hands together, clutching them tightly to steady the shaking, God's lighter trapped between them. "You need me, Michael. You know it, and I know it. I'll burn my book and stay here for eternity. But in exchange, you have to agree to let all the *current* citizens complete their stories and Go On. All of them. You can have all the arrivals from now on."

I held my breath as Michael's came in tightly knotted ejections. "How can I trust you?" he asked, his voice a razor. "How can I be sure you will not betray me to the new citizens?"

I needed no mask now. The next words I spoke were the truest words I had ever spoken.

"Do you really think I would be capable of doing that, Michael? Of leading a rebellion all by myself? Of having the courage to betray you?" I loosened my hands, dropping them to my sides. The trembling had stopped. My limbs felt limp and loose. "I'm not brave at all. I'm just not cut out for it. As my daughter and my ex-wife and probably everyone who has ever known me would say: I'm nobody." And then I played my trump card; the card that all my life I had believed to be a hateful liability; the card that would now quite possibly save my soul. "I'm just Maurice Toogood, a small-time librarian."

Michael stood still and considered. He didn't take his eyes off me. Then he strode forward, pulled me into a violent embrace, and put his hand down the back of my trousers.

"Why, Michael, this is all so sudden," I said, my adeptness at inappropriate humour surreally intact. He pulled out my book and pressed it roughly into my chest.

"Well, well, my librarian friend," he said. "I'll accept your proposal. How heroic. How wonderful. How stupid."

I clutched my book. My story; my life. Andy's letters. My last chance. Finally, in Heaven, this was how it might end. I felt detached and at peace and all liquid: my body was giving up its lines and bones and brittleness. *How beautiful,* I thought, my mind outside itself, observing. *This is how it should feel.*

I flicked open the lighter's cap, catching movement out of the corner of my eye as Peter winced and started forward. I glanced at him and shook my head with as minute a movement I could manage. *Don't move. I think I know what I'm doing. I hope.* Peter stopped, nodding imperceptibly.

I heard rushing footsteps and suddenly Kit was in the doorway. Pearls of blood dotted his neck but the fire was back in his eyes. He paused for a moment as he took in the scene, then with a shout of shock rushed towards me. Michael was quicker. He grabbed him and yet again Kit was captured in the arms of the angel. *There's a song in that,* I thought, gripping the lighter.

I hesitated. I closed my eyes and prayed quickly to an absent God that this was going to work.

"Do it, Maurice," said Michael, his eyes wide, on fire. "Do it now or the boy dies. Again."

"No! Don't do it! Maurice! No!" Kit sobbed, thrashing against Michael's chest.

Did I pause, just for a moment? Did I wonder, just for a second, if Kit's life was a small sacrifice to make for saving my own? Here is what I remember: as my trembling thumb flicked the tiny flame into life, I looked at the young man who felt just a little like my own son, and I was ready.

"It's OK, Kit. You were murdered once. Can't let it happen twice." And I touched the lighter to one corner of my book.

We watched as fire started to lick and pull at the pages, Michael glowing with triumph, Kit with dribbly tears turning his ruby neck to pink, me with a dumb fascination. Peter moved closer to me, wincing. I slipped God's lighter into my pocket. I thought of Robyn and of that day years ago on the back lawn of our house; the day my faith in the world and my love for my wife and my writing ambitions had perished. And then I thought of the birth of my daughter, and the letters she had written me, and I closed my eyes and started reciting The Lord's Prayer in my head:

> *… and forgive us our trespasses,*
> *As we forgive them that trespass against us.*
> *And lead us not into temptation,*
> *But deliver us from evil.*
> *For thine is the kingdom,*
> *The power, and the glory,*
> *For ever and ever.*
> *Amen.*

The flames were threatening to leave me only one small corner in which to crowd my fingers. I looked for a bare space of floor. I was desperate not to drop my book on any of the others for fear I would set the whole library alight, possibly condemning all our stories to eternal cliffhanging.

"It is a pleasure to burn," whispered Michael, the fire matching the crazy dance in his eyes. "Such a pleasure, Maurice." Then, dragging Kit with him, he covered the space between us in three strides and knocked my life out of my hands. Flames sparked and jumped and hissed. Hungry for fresh flesh, they leapt immediately to the nearest scattered pile and started feeding.

Kit screamed in horror, struggling to escape from Michael's grip. The archangel reached up with the arm not holding him captive and softly stroked my head from front to back, his face inches from mine.

"Trust you? I don't think so, Maurice. Do you think I'm stupid? And now, let us watch every book burn and my kingdom begin. Let us watch."

Michael, Peter, Kit, and I stared at the spreading flames. I held my breath. Slowly, as if transfixed, Michael let Kit slip from his embrace. I heard a rush at the door and Moses, Eve, and Noah stood breathless and horrified in the doorway. I held out my hands as if to ward them off.

"Wait," I whispered. "Wait."

Michael ignored us all. As Kit, Peter, and I moved back towards the door the archangel closed his eyes in rapture and spread his arms wide, inviting the books to turn down their charred corners in adoration.

I stumbled across toppled books to Moses. "I used God's lighter." My words were desperate, urgent. "Please tell me I'm right about this. Please." Moses looked at me, then at the books, then back at me. Then he gasped, his eyes wide and fixed. He started to whisper, and we all leaned in to hear.

"… and behold, the bush burned with fire, and the bush was not consumed…"

Moses slowly raised his hand and pointed. We all turned to look. The fire had passed over the books on the ground and three bookshelves already, but where there should have lain piles of ash and charred remains, there lay books. Intact books.

I searched for my own book, my heart racing, daring to hope. It, too, was still in one piece.

The fire was moving in a very definite direction – starting on the right of the room, at the last bookshelf to fall, and moving back the way the tumble had happened, like a game of giant dominoes in reverse. The flames were not randomly jumping and leaping and tumbling. I focused on the highest, most fierce flame, and realised that the books within it were not being blackened and burnt. They were being enveloped, and licked, and engulfed, but not consumed. Not destroyed. What's more, the fire wasn't damaging the wooden bookshelves. It was passing over them and around them.

"… and behold, the bush burned with fire, and the bush was not consumed…"

Moses said it louder this time. His cheeks were turning pink. I grabbed his trembling forearm. "You're sure? You're absolutely sure?"

"What? Sure of what?" Kit hissed. "What do you mean?"

I saw a flicker of realisation cross Peter's face, and then Eve's, and they both gasped. And then Moses was striding towards the archangel, who stood like Jesus above Rio, his eyes still closed.

"Wake up! Wake up and witness the power of your absent God!" Moses cried, shaking his staff inches from Michael's face. The shower of spittle alone would have alerted Michael to the fact that all was not going as planned. He opened his eyes and for a moment seemed nonplussed by Moses's presence, then his arm shot out and grabbed the old man by the throat. Moses shouted, choking, through the stranglehold.

"They're not burning! Not burning! Look around you! The fire cannot consume them! *And behold, the bush burned with fire, and the bush was not consumed!*"

Michael ripped his eyes from Moses. He let go of his throat and the old man fell, spluttering and coughing, to the ground. Kit rushed to him but Moses pushed him aside and immediately stood again, tall and fierce, tears streaming down his vindicated face.

The fire was at the top of the horseshoe now, straight in front of us. LMN. IJK. Irwin. Iscariot. It twirled and leapt but stayed contained and controlled. It knew what it was doing.

For the first time I looked directly, with no fear, at Michael's face. The phrase "incandescent with rage" had been written for it. He was trembling, his mad eyes burning, his skin white-hot, his terrible beauty breathtaking. He started to tremble. And then he tipped back his head and let out a deafening, demonic scream that walloped the breath out of me, the bitter taste of bile filling my throat. He turned to face us, four helpless humans against one archangel. *This time,* I thought. *Surely this time there won't be any escape.*

Eve stepped out from behind me, clutching her own undamaged book that she had retrieved from one of the shelves. Smith, Eve.

"It's over, Michael. You've failed. The books won't burn." She held her book above her head and shook it in triumph. "*We* won't burn, and we won't bow down to you, ever. We will bow only to God, even if he has left us."

Michael's face was illuminated like a million terrible stars. He looked round at the people who had trapped him. Then he looked directly at me and said, "You will pay for this. If not you, then her. She is coming." Then he streaked past us all and out the door.

"After him!" I yelled, scrambling in his wake.

Peter put out an arm. "Let him go, Maurice. There's no way he can win now. Leave him to his fate."

"Who did he mean? She is coming. Who is *she*?"

Peter frowned. "I've no idea. I haven't been in the gatehouse today."

Kit came to stand in front of me, his face alive, his neck still streaked with blood. "How did you know? How did you know they wouldn't burn?"

"I didn't," I said. "I took a punt. Remember when Moses told me about the fire of God? How it didn't consume the burning bush?" Kit nodded. "And remember he also told me that God's lighter had gone missing?" He nodded again.

"I guessed Michael had stolen it and was going to try to burn down the library. Bloody Alexandria all over again."

Kit frowned. "What?"

"Never mind. I was pretty confident that Moses was right – that the fire of God can burn things without destroying them – but I wasn't certain. So I decided if he just burned mine, and it was destroyed after all, then at least everyone else would still have a chance."

"But you'd have been stuck here. Forever."

I shrugged. "Can't be that bad, can it? Anything's better than the Bressington Heights Community Library. Believe me, if you'd worked there, you'd understand."

Kit held out his hand to shake mine. Then he muttered, "Oh, for God's sake," and hugged me instead. "Thank you," he said, pushing back to look me straight in the eyes.

I blinked several times. "You're welcome," I said, carefully clearing my throat.

We turned then and watched as the fire reached the last bookshelf, the one that Eve had tipped over not half an hour earlier. As the last pile of books surrendered to it and then emerged miraculously intact, the flames trembled and warped like the edge of a forcefield. Slowly, gracefully, they began to shrink, not so much going out as allowing the room and the books and the presence of us to come and take their place. There was a soft swoosh of sweet-smelling air, which felt for a moment as if it had leapt into me and through me, and I gasped dizzily for breath. And then the flames were gone.

Our small band stood close together, knowing we had just witnessed something holy and absurd. Moses was wiping away his last exultant tears as Noah patted him gently on the back. Eve was staring where Judas had fallen. The traitor's body was no longer there.

45

On our way up to join the others, Kit explained what had happened after I made my break for the library. After rescuing Kit from Gabriel's grasp, Eve had attacked the archangels with such speed and fury that they were caught off guard. Kit immediately rushed back to help, stamping on Gabriel's foot, pulling his hair, and then punching him so hard in the mouth and nose that the angel dropped the knife and fell backwards to the ground, bleating about broken teeth and trumpet damage and ripped hair extensions. A few other citizens whose bravery and belief were still intact surged forward to join them, flinging punches and kicks. The Heavenly Hosts, with a sensible instinct for self-preservation, promptly changed sides and joined the citizens in overpowering the archangels.

"It didn't take long," sniffed Kit. "Cowardly bastards, as it turns out."

A few minutes later we emerged (again) into the light. This time it was the archangels who had been corralled into a circle. Triumphant and panting, many dishevelled and some bleeding, the citizens and Heavenly Hosts cheered as we made our way down the steps. I felt like Harry Potter after defeating Voldemort.

The archangels were grubby, diminished, and silent. Gabriel was holding a handkerchief to his nose and daggering Kit with his gaze. Michael was nowhere to be seen.

Once again pairs of expectant eyes swivelled towards me. But this time, I was brave enough to speak. With some help from Moses, who retrieved a whiteboard from inside the reception building's front office and proceeded to sketch detailed diagrams of shrubs and flames and trajectories, I explained what had happened. Kit stepped in and told them how I had burned my own book as a sacrifice. Eve then embellished a little, insisting that it was she who had chased Michael out of the library. I nodded solemnly as she spoke. She had earned the lie.

After further cheers and a great deal of back slapping and calls of "Well done" and "Congratulations", Peter stepped forward and raised his hands, palms facing the crowd. Heaven fell silent.

"Citizens of Heaven. Listen carefully."

One of the archangels hissed.

"About three months ago, God disappeared." There were gasps of shock from the citizens and Heavenly Hosts. "All of us who lived long ago – those of us who feature in God's book – can vouch for this. We were here. But the rest of you arrived after that day. None of you have had the chance to see the Almighty."

A ripple of unrest passed over the crowd. Peter raised his voice and continued.

"When God left, Michael and his fellow archangels made a plan to overthrow him and establish their own kingdom, here. Their strategy was to recruit all of you and every new arrival as their servants, and to rule the heavenly realms. Their plan has failed."

Another cheer went up but ended abruptly as Peter signalled for quiet.

"This place … this place we call Heaven … it does not have to be your final destination. If you choose, this can simply be another … doorway. There is more."

Incredulous chatter erupted. Kit nudged me and grinned. Again, Peter raised his hand for silence.

"You've heard about the fight in the library. About the books. Each of you has one, with your name on it. That book holds all the unfinished business of your life. All the things not said, the wounds unhealed, the decisions left unmade, the knowledge incomplete."

I looked out over the crowd and spotted John and a wide-eyed Penelope, clutching her handbag in one hand and the little knitted rabbit that had fallen out of it in the other.

"You will now have the opportunity to find your book, and to read and complete it: to put things right once and for all. And then you will be able to Go On."

It was clear that most of the citizens had had no idea that the library even existed. There were murmurs of anger and then incredulity and then excitement and many, many questions. Most of them Peter could answer; some he could not. He did not know where God was, nor did he know what happened once one Went On. He did not know if there were other places like our Heaven, and if so, why we were all chosen for this one.

"How exactly do we 'put things right'?" asked a young man with a severe haircut. I recognised him as one of the ten disciples who had been working together in the underground conference room. "We can't exactly change anything we did when we were alive, can we? I have to say, Peter, I'm a little sceptical."

Peter looked thoughtful for a second. "All I know, Thomas, is what I observed many times, before God went away. He would invite citizens into the library, one by one. When they had been there a while – a few hours, a day – one chap was in there for almost a week, on and off – they came out changed. They looked … complete. And very soon after – usually within a day – they disappeared. And their book was no longer on the shelf."

Gabriel stood up. "But God's dot here adymore, is he? So who's goid to help theb fiddish their stories dow?" He laughed once, loudly, then winced.

Samson, who was taking his guard duties very seriously, placed an enormous hand on Gabriel's shoulder and forced him to the ground again.

The citizens waited for an answer.

"The right person will appear when it is time," said Peter. Then he looked at me and smiled.

"What about God? Is he coming back?" asked John, clutching his wife's hand.

"Yes, but no one knows the day or the hour," said Peter.

"You'd think he would have come back to help us, instead of riding in like The Big Hero when it's all over," muttered another citizen.

"What do we do with the prisoners?" grunted Samson.

An old man I hadn't noticed before stepped forward. He looked pale and exhausted and his hands were covered in paper cuts. "I say we show them mercy. Everyone deserves a second chance, don't they?"

Eve leaned in close. Apple-scented shampoo and feminine sweat mingled, making me slightly giddy. "Abraham, the old fool," she whispered, not unkindly. "Always standing up for people, even when they don't deserve it."

Peter thought for a moment, then spoke again. "We give them a choice." Everyone stared. Someone booed. Peter continued. "They can choose to stay here, forever relinquish their attempt to rule, and live peacefully alongside us – " there was great grumbling and much head shaking amongst the citizens " – or they can follow their leader."

At that, a profound silence fell.

"But where did he go?" asked Joseph. His colourful jacket was unbuttoned and ripped down one sleeve. "Michael, I mean. He ran out of the building and towards the gates so fast we just saw a blur. Did he escape?"

Peter addressed the crowd.

"I obtained this information from Michael when he trusted me. He was given this information by God himself. Outside the entrance gates – in the area we call The Gateway – there are three paths. One of them, you have all taken to come here. It is, with few exceptions, a one-way street." He paused, perhaps so each of us could take a moment to remember our arrival in Heaven.

"The path on the right leads On. No one knows where, but each of us will walk it one day, God willing. The path on the left leads …

Down. This, I suspect, is the one Michael has chosen. What he will find at the end of it will be determined by the choices he has made here. That is all I know."

Gabriel took the handkerchief away from the marred perfection of his face just long enough to whine another question. "Will he be deh boss, dowd der?"

Peter looked at him with contempt. "Possibly. No one can know for sure. Nor can we know the kind of dominion over which he would rule." Then he addressed all the archangels. "So now you have to choose. Living here as equals with all of us … or taking your chances with Michael. What will it be?"

The archangels stared at the ground, or nervously at one another. No one seemed willing to be the first to make a decision.

Peter spoke again. "If you don't make a choice then we will make it for you. You will all stay here and live with us in peace and do your share of duties. Even archangels have to clean toilets." I could have sworn he threw me a small wink.

That broke the stalemate. One of the archangels stood, shaking out his hair and smoothing his trousers. "Well, I'm not staying here. I will follow Michael. He never made us do toilets." One by one the others stood and declared that they, too, would follow their leader.

Peter turned to us. "Kit, go back to the library reception area and get the Departures file, please. Maurice, Eve, Moses, Noah, and Adam, come with me." He turned to the crowd and raised his voice. "Heavenly Hosts, split into two teams. Team One, see what you can do to fix up the library. Team Two, proceed to the underground conference room." He threw his keys to the young woman who had welcomed me into Heaven. "There is a large hole in the wall in the men's toilet. Retrieve the books you find in there and start matching them to their covers on the tables. Bookbinding skills may come in handy. They all have to go back to the library."

The clearly confused Heavenly Hosts quickly organised themselves and trotted off, ponytails and skipping ropes swinging. Peter turned back to the citizens left on the lawn.

"Citizens, go to your cabins. Throw out everything yellow." A huge cheer went up. "Then let us meet in the Hallelujah Hall at three o'clock to discuss the future of Heaven."

The crowd started to move off. Our small group – I felt like one of the Magnificent Seven or Ocean's Eleven or similar – walked towards the archangels as Kit emerged from the reception building with two files under his arm. He handed one of them to Peter, who directed us to surround the archangels and walk them towards the front gates. Not that they needed such supervision. It was obvious they couldn't wait to get out of Heaven and be with their leader again, and they trotted along obediently.

When we reached the gatehouse I had passed on my first day, Peter stopped, took out another keyring, unlocked the door, and went inside. A few minutes later we watched as the giant yellow gates groaned open.

We walked, counterintuitively, out of Heaven. We rounded a bend and came to a three-way junction, just as Peter had described. The path ahead was straight, but a few metres in it was obscured by a dense, lazily swirling mist. The two paths on either side curved away to the left and right respectively.

A silence fell over the group as Peter flipped to a fresh page in the Departures file. Borrowing one of Kit's pens, he carefully inscribed the names of the seven archangels:

Michael (departure presumed)
Gabriel
Raphael
Uriel
Simiel
Oriphiel
Raguel

Then he passed the file back to Kit and turned to the archangels.

"We wish you no evil," he said. "Go in peace."

They didn't look so keen to leave now. They looked terrified, their bravado and beauty having faded in the strange silence of The Gateway.

"I've heard it's a really exclusive club down there," said Eve. "Only for beautiful people. They hold contests, you know, to judge who's the most stunning. Winner gets his own salon."

That did it. The archangels hurried down the left-hand path and disappeared around a corner. A whining, "Ouch! Who pulled my hair? Watch the extensions, you idiot!" drifted back to us, and then there was silence once more.

Smiling, I turned to Kit. I was keen to share the satisfaction of victory with him. I felt brave and heroic. These were unfamiliar, unsettling emotions, and I wanted, for the first time ever perhaps, to process them with someone I cared about.

His white face stared back at me. The Imminent Arrivals file was hanging open in his hands.

"I just wanted to see if God would come back, now that Michael's gone," he whispered. I grabbed the file from him and looked at the only name written at the top of the first page.

Andrea Toogood.

She cannot feel her limbs. She can hear nothing but her own endless longing, her life force calling to itself, a wild cry of desire. She does not know if her eyes are open or closed, if her body is broken or whole, if she is alone or borne by legions of angels. All she knows is this moment, this heat, this tumbling, this intoxicating comfort. The whorls and lattices of her fingerprints have become her own personal stars, a heavenly panorama inscribing itself on the backdrop of forever. She breathes in the universe. She is not afraid. She is travelling.

46

Andy is dead. My daughter is dead. Blood thumped in my ears. The file fainted from my hands to the ground. There was movement around me, I think, and urgent whispering, and then Peter was grabbing me and steering me back into Heaven.

He marched me towards the gatehouse. My legs pistoned up and down, feeling weirdly disconnected from my body. The building was larger than it appeared from the outside. I registered a row of small computer screens, a large desk, and a few plastic chairs. Peter pushed me down into one of them. Kit was there, and Eve, and Moses. Snatches of urgent conversation scurried in and out of my hearing. "How long have we got?" and "What happened?" and "Can he do it?" and "They're still fighting!" and "It's beating! It's still beating!" and "Torch! Someone get a torch!"

"Maurice. Maurice? Look at me. Look at me right now." Peter was crouching on his haunches in front of me, gripping my shoulders until they hurt.

I focused my eyes on him and said once more, out loud this time: "My daughter is dead."

Peter gently but firmly pulled me up and over to the row of screens. There were a dozen of them, embedded in the wall. They were each the size of an average paperback. Only one of them was turned on.

"No she's not. Look, Maurice. Look at this."

As I watched, a lazy blip moved across the screen from left to right. Then another. Then another.

Underneath the blip scrolled a line of text, which read:

Toogood, A. ETA: 20 minutes. Status: Wanderer.

I blinked, comprehending nothing.

Peter pointed at the blip. "That's her heartbeat, Maurice. Andy's heartbeat. She's still alive."

There was a strange ringing in my ears. I turned to look at Peter, finding it hard to form words. "But she's coming. The file says she's coming. In that case she must be ..."

Peter tapped on the scroll of text. "See this? We see a few of these. From time to time. They're the ones hanging in the balance; the ones with a question mark over their heads. Sometimes – just sometimes – we can send them back."

I glanced at Kit over Peter's shoulder. He looked as stunned as me. "So that's what I was fixing? *This* is the programme I was working on?"

Peter nodded at him. "The whole system breaks down sometimes. If there are too many. So I did need your expertise. But ... it wasn't just that. I suspected you might be able to ... help." He and Kit stared at each other, understanding passing between them.

I wiped a hand over my face. "Hanging in the balance? What the hell does that mean? What happened to her?"

"It means she is going to die," said Peter.

I whimpered.

"I don't know how or why yet; we don't find that out until they arrive. She'll be here in about ... fifteen minutes now. But that may not be the end of it."

"What do you mean, not the end of it?" asked Kit.

Eve stepped forward. "You know those stories of near-death experiences? I died then came back to life? My heart stopped for ten minutes on the operating table? I went to Heaven but my dead aunty sent me back?"

Kit and I nodded.

"They're all true."

Adam interjected. "Just like those people who get abducted by aliens. That's true too."

"Oh for God's sake, you blathering idiot," said Eve. "Just because it's in *Readers' Digest* doesn't mean it's gospel."

Peter cut a flat hand through the air in front of them, closing down the argument. He turned back to me.

"She's a Wanderer, Maurice. Which means there's a chance she can be sent back to life. This may just be a short stopover before she heads back home. But that is largely up to you."

I looked at the screen again. The blip was taking longer and longer to cross the screen. "Just tell me how to save my daughter," I said, the words cotton wool in my mouth.

"You have to go and wait for her," said Peter. "When she appears, you have to tell her that it's not her time and she must go back."

I was puzzled. That didn't sound too hard. Andy would do what I told her to do, especially once I told her what Heaven was like.

Peter gestured for me to follow him outside. We stood by a falsely perfect tree as the strange sun started to track away to the far side of Heaven, where God should have been.

"There's a catch, Maurice."

I grunted. "Of course there is. There's always a catch."

Peter smiled faintly. "You can't tell her about this place. You can't say anything about what your afterlife is like."

I puffed out a desperate sigh, then looked back at the gatehouse and saw the faces of my new friends staring out at me. I looked up at the sky. The marvellous, ghastly, heavenly, yellow-tainted sky. I looked at the gates of Heaven standing open, preparing to embrace and enclose my daughter.

"What do I say to her," I said, dropping the statement at Peter's feet with no expectation of an answer. "She's never listened to me, ever. What if she doesn't listen to me this time?"

"Tell her the truth, Maurice. That's all you have to do."

I thought about this for a moment; what it would feel like to tell Andy the truth.

"Will I be able to come back here? After I've sent her home?"

"Yes," said Peter. "You will find your way."

The gatehouse door opened, and Kit, Moses, and Eve came out to stand beside me.

"Take this," said Kit, handing me his torch. He took a pen from the few still perched in his shellsuit jacket pocket and scribbled on a small slip of paper, then held it out to me.

"Oh God," I said. "Not another bloody cryptic message."

Kit laughed, and it sounded a little like a sob. "Could you give this to her? If you get a chance? Please … don't ask what it is. Just … if you get a chance."

I nodded and put the piece of paper in my pocket. I wasn't curious about the note, nor about why Kit was asking me to give it to Andy. I wasn't afraid, either. I was … ready. That is the only way I can describe it now, looking back. I was ready.

I turned once more to Peter. "How will I find her?"

From the gatehouse came Adam's over-excited announcement: "Five minutes! Incoming in *five minutes and counting!*"

Eve rolled her eyes. Peter nodded towards the gates. "Go to The Gateway and take the path straight ahead. Walk into the mist, then stop. She'll come to you."

I took a couple of steps with legs that felt like silly putty. Then I stopped and turned back to Peter. I had tears in my eyes again. I was turning into an emotional wreck.

"I don't know if I can do this," I said.

"Yes, you can. As soon as you arrived in Heaven, I saw it in you."

"Saw what?"

Peter smiled. "Potential."

And so it was, that after saving Heaven from evil archangels, I walked out of its gates to save my daughter from dying.

47

As soon as I turned the first corner and entered the mist I realised why I needed Kit's torch. A dark chill clutched at me, hurting my chest when I breathed. I could see nothing. I pressed the torch's switch. It took a couple of slaps for it to reluctantly flicker on. I willed its batteries to live long enough, then held it out in front of me in a trembling hand. Lazy tendrils of fog whispered through the thin beam of light, disappearing again into blackness.

"You're a brave man, Maurice. I underestimated you."

I whipped round, turning in messy circles, holding the torch out like a talisman to ward off danger.

"What a brave man, to sacrifice his own life twice in one day. Except this time, there really is no hope of a happy ending." There was a chuckle, and a caress of cologne whispered past my nostrils.

Michael was here with me, in the mist. I circled and breathed and circled again. Where was he? Should I call out for Peter and the others?

"Where are you?" I cried, although it came out more like an awkward stammer, sounding strangely powerless in the damp air. I waved my torch and turned this way and that, blind and stupid. "What do you want?"

Michael's voice was closer this time.

"Listen to me, Maurice. You're making a fool of yourself, my friend. A fool." A pause, and then, "Did he tell you that you can send her back again? Peter, I mean. Is that what he told you?"

I nodded to the darkness.

Michael tsk-tsked. "Really. That naughty Peter. And did he tell you that you can re-enter Heaven after the fact, and all will be well? That you won't be stuck here, in The Gateway?"

Again, I nodded.

Suddenly Michael was standing in front of me, his beautiful, savage face illuminated by my torch, making him look like a demon, or a god, or both. He appraised me with false pity.

"Poor Maurice. Off he trots to be the hero all over again, thinking he'll earn his reward at the end of it. Only … there is no reward. Just more sacrifice."

"I … I don't understand." I shifted the torch to my other hand. It was heavy.

"He didn't tell you everything, Maurice. He's a very … naughty … boy. He should be crucified … maybe even upside-down." Michael smiled and his focus wandered a bit, as if to savour the vision more fully.

"What do you mean, he didn't tell me everything? What more was there to tell?" I sounded frightened.

Michael leaned in very, very close. "Oh, Maurice, only *the* most important thing about this wonderful rescue mission upon which you've embarked. The thing you really *should* have been told, my dear librarian friend."

Then he raised his hand and touched my cheek, tender as a lover. "If you manage to send your daughter back – and believe me, there's no guarantee of that – you will indeed be able to re-enter Heaven. But, as our mutual friend Peter would say, there's a catch." He paused, ball suspended, racket high. Then he smashed the ace.

"In order to send back a Wanderer, a citizen must waive his right to Go On. Permanently."

I stared at him. "That's not true," I whispered. "I don't believe you." A thumping pain was taking up fierce residence behind my eyes.

I believed him. I believed him because this had all seemed too good to be true. Overthrowing the archangels, finding out about Andy's imminent arrival just in time, the chance to save her with impunity. I believed him because this was right; this was just. I didn't deserve to get off scot-free. There was always going to be a punishment for the father I had been.

I believed him because I was the kind of man who always believed bad news before good.

Michael smiled again in the way one does when one knows, absolutely, that he has just ruined everything for another. "Yes you do," he said. Then he stepped back and appraised me as if sizing me up for a new suit. "You don't have to do this, you know. When you see her, you can choose to welcome her instead. A loving father welcoming his beloved daughter home at last. Almost makes you cry, to picture it."

My hair ruffled for a moment. My shellsuit trouser leg brushed my shin. The mist started to swirl, delicately picking up speed like a lazy dancer, until it was pushing towards me, through me, around me. I thought of a trip Robyn and I had taken to England before we were miserable, and how we had loved taking the London Underground, standing waiting in the tunnels with the world pressing down above us, waiting for the first breaths of wind to wash over our expectant faces. I recalled perfectly the particular promise of that wind, pushed forward by an approaching train, bringing with it its curious sweet stench of fuel and under-earth and electrical currents; the wind that whispered, "It's coming." The wind that would bear us on.

"I have a proposition for you, Maurice," said Michael. He came and stood by me, facing into the mist-wind, as if we were travelling companions standing side by side.

"You have three choices. One, you can try to send your daughter back, and in so doing condemn yourself to staying in Hippy Happy Heaven for the rest of eternity. Feel free. I'm not stopping you. Two, you can walk back into Heaven with your daughter. OK, she'll be dead, and no one likes to precipitate their child's death, but at least you'll be together. You'll be able to build many happy memories, I'm sure."

I grasped the torch so tightly the sharp metal grooves around the hilt cut into my fingers, breaking the skin. Michael continued to gaze straight ahead, the wind blowing his hair back until he looked like a vicious shampoo commercial.

"Three. You and your daughter can come with me."

I quickly turned inwards towards him, stumbling in the swirl of the mist and wind. I was convinced I hadn't heard right.

"What?"

Michael now turned towards me until our faces were almost touching. We could have been an ABBA music video.

"Here's another thing Peter didn't tell you, because he doesn't know. God himself told me this, long ago. Down isn't what you think. It's the real one."

I paused, not comprehending. "The real … what?"

"The real Heaven. You think that crap – " he gestured back the way I had come " – is the real deal? Are you kidding me? It's a holding pen for people who aren't quite good enough; who don't quite make the grade. People like you, Maurice. A man who failed at everything and didn't have the balls to try to put it right. Who destroyed his own ambition because he was too scared to fight for it. Who stopped believing in himself because it was the easy way out: easier then fighting back, getting his hands dirty, standing up for something. He's got high standards, this God Almighty of ours. Very high. You think he'd let just anyone near his real throne? His real seat of Majesty?"

Michael swept hair out of his face as the mist swirled, picking up pace with every second.

"I've figured something out about you, Maurice. You're bright. You're a lying bastard, but you're bright. And what a hero. God would love to meet you. Wouldn't you love to meet God, Maurice? That's where he is, you know. Down." He fluttered his long fingers. "Adam and the rest of them are buzzing round like busy honeybees, trying to figure out where he's gone … and all the time *he's been right there under their noses.*"

The wind was now so strong we both had to dig our feet into the ground to prevent being blown over. The torch sputtered.

"Come and meet him, Maurice. Come and join us in the real Heaven." He tipped his head coyly and winked. "You know you want to."

Disorientated and confused, I shook my head and turned back the way I thought I had come. A gust of wind pushed me over, and I was on my knees, crying out as my hands struck sharp earth. The torch skittled out of my bloody fingers and away, throwing weakening shards of confettied light. I heard myself scream, thin and insubstantial.

"Peter! Kit! Help me!"

Michael picked up the torch and kneeled down beside me, shining the weak light into my face. "No one's coming to save you, Maurice. They can't hear you. And even if they could, would they actually risk it? What good have your friends ever done you? Peter's a deceiver; Adam's a loser; Eve's one of these mouthy, unshaven feminist types who'll break your balls without a second thought; Moses ... well ... he's a loyal supporter of the Almighty, I'll give him that, but he's unbearable. No wonder nobody listened to him in the wilderness." The archangel put his hand solicitously on my shoulder. "And Kit. Well now ... Kit's just a boy, Maurice. He's not your friend; not really. Why would a teenager want to be friends with a fat, good-for-nothing, fifty-something librarian? He befriended you only so he could stay close to Andy."

The wind raged. Tears ran down my face, and I swiped at them with scraped and punctured palms. "Wha ... what?"

"He loved her, Maurice. Well, he *thinks* he loved her, in that sweet, stupid, deluded way adolescents think. He wanted to tell her; for weeks and months he wanted to tell her, but he didn't have the courage. Sounds like someone we both know, doesn't it, my friend?" Michael squeezed my shoulder until it hurt. I cried out and tried to pull away, but he gripped on like a determined dog.

"You want to know how he died, Maurice?"

I screamed again as his perfect fingernails started to bite through my shellsuit jacket into my skin. "He was murdered! In a park! In Australia! He was murdered!"

"Yes, he was," said Michael, matter-of-factly. "But here's the thing, my friend. He wasn't in that park by coincidence. And here's where it gets real pretty, Maurice; where the whole big, beautiful puzzle starts to fit together." He pressed his lips to my ear, momentarily strangling the wind, and whispered with ghastly clarity. "He was on the way to post a letter to Andy, to tell her he loved her." He sat back on his haunches, beaming. His teeth were a beacon in the roaring darkness. "Isn't that adorable? The thing is, he never got to send it. So sad. Sad for Andy, too. She missed out on her first and only love affair, albeit long-distance. Ain't life a bitch when you're young? And then you die."

Michael stood, leaning again into the wind. "So you see, Maurice, he doesn't really care about you. You were just a conduit to Andy. That's why he took you to the library. I saw you both go, you know. I let it happen. I was curious to see what you were capable of. Not much, as it turns out." He huffed a little pant of laughter. "Kit thought your book might tell him how Andy was doing; how she was holding up. If she still thought of him. If she was missing him more than she was missing you. And let's face it, Maurice. *She probably was.*"

I stayed crouched on the ground. My stomach turned and I leaned forward and vomited, a single violent hurl. I didn't look up at Michael until he put his hand down and tipped my chin up. Blinded by the torch light, I could only make out his shape, and in the swirl and the tears and the confusion I saw two giant shadows slowly unfurling behind his head.

"Come with me, Maurice." Michael's voice rose to compete with the wind. "Put your hand in mine and let us greet your daughter together. Then let me take you and Andy to the real Heaven. God's just dying to see you."

I wiped my hands over my grubby face again, blood mingling with tears and dirt. Michael reached out one elegant hand and waited, his face so desperately beautiful, so devastatingly glorious, I almost did as he asked. But then the torch sputtered and its ray arced and distorted in the screaming mist and its beam lit up the archangel's hair so that for a moment it was a flaming halo, and suddenly it was my daughter's face before me, her voice calling to me, her empyrean hair blazing, her hand reaching. Reaching for me.

Everything Michael had said seemed to fall into its proper place. I pushed myself up, refusing his help, and stood before him. Then, embracing the wild push and clamour of the wind, it was my turn to lean in close; so close I could see every perfect pore.

"I'm not fat," I panted. "I'm just short for my weight. And I'll tell you something else I'm not. I'm not afraid of you." Michael's smile grew a little crooked. "You can't harm me, or you would have done it long before this. I think you've been bound by God not to harm any citizen, or something like that. That's what I think. You can brand a wrist or a forehead or two, but that's about it. You're an impotent angel. You're all bound up in knots and feathers and hair spray." The angelic face was turning red, and the flames in his eyes were starting to dance.

I breathed though my nostrils, deeply, gathering momentum. My voice grew stronger. "I'll tell you something else. I don't care how useless my friends are. I've never needed friends much anyway. I don't even really care about Kit deceiving me, if what you say is true. I've trained myself not to care about things for most of my goddamn life. Seems I'm doing well, with one rather major exception."

Michael raised one fabulous eyebrow. "Don't tell me. Your illustrious career as a librarian?"

"*My daughter*, you fucking glorified *freak*!" I yelled, and the exuberance, the blessed *luxury* of this realisation, as well as my sudden ability to embrace it, sent a dizzy, wild thrill tearing through me.

I was the one on fire now. The light, the heat, the craziness of it, pumped though me. I punctuated my next words by poking Michael repeatedly in his granite chest. With each poke he retreated a step.

"Good try, Michael. Good. Fucking. Try. Yes, I'm a good-for-nothing, failed-at-everything, adulterous, chicken-shit, pathetic, can't-write-to-save-myself, small-time librarian who gave up on himself and destroyed any chance he had at happiness. But you know what else I am? *I'm a father.* And I am going to save my daughter, whatever it takes. And if that means missing out on some new and improved version of the afterlife, I don't care. Get it? I. Don't. Care. My life was crap. Why shouldn't my death be as well? Why should I have expected nirvana? Why should any of us? Do we deserve it? If we're honest, don't we all deserve *that*?" I poked a resolute finger in the direction of the path back to Hippy Happy Heaven.

The feathery shadows behind Michael's head had almost fully unfurled to reveal wings as glorious and horrifying as his inferno eyes. The wind screamed. I had never felt more alive. I was incandescent with rage and elation, and nothing, not even a demented archangel, was going to stop me.

"But I'll tell you something for free, freak. My daughter doesn't deserve it. And I don't believe for one minute that you know where God is, or where the real Heaven is, if there even is one. I think you're just trying to pay me back for what I did to you in the library. You're going Down, Mr, and you want to take me Down with you. Well, fuck that. I'm going to save Andy, right here, right now, and send her back to the rest of her life. And then I'm going to walk back through those gates into my own personal nightmare. And you can Go Down and find whatever it is you're going to find there. Maybe God. Maybe the Devil. I don't care. But you're not taking me or my daughter with you. Not now, not ever. Because if I have to look at your face or smell your goddamn aftershave one more time, *I'm going to go batshit crazy!*"

The archangel rose into the mist and spread wide his monstrous wings. Terrified, exultant, I stared into his face, a face now drunk with fury and ugly as sin. The flames in his eyes seemed to spread until he was engulfed in their insane, blazing embrace. The wind was a hurricane, forcing me to my knees again, walloping the breath out of me, the howling demonic and unbearable. The last thing I saw was Kit's torch as it fell to the ground and smashed into pieces. I covered my ears and screamed – for Andy, for my life, my death, for the universe. Time was gone and all was darkness and noise and more than that, horrendously *more*, and this was it, this was death at last, the real death, and I was nothing in the face of it, and suddenly I understood that nothing mattered, nothing was, nothing would be, nothing could be. And then an impossible screech of the most transcendent, most ineffable madness pulsed exquisitely through the hurricane and through my body, and I heard, or maybe felt, my own shriek rise to meet it, and I knew this was the end. And then, as suddenly as the flick of a switch, it stopped. There was silence. Michael was gone.

I was alone.

I scrabbled towards the torch, feeling my way, my hands dancing wildly over the ground.

And then I heard, or perhaps felt, a voice.

Daddy

Andy. I started whimpering, then calling out wildly, screaming her name, groaning and sobbing. I could see nothing, feel nothing. I stood up, stretched out my arms, and stumbled, running and tripping, forwards and back. I couldn't find her.

And then, in the grief and the panic and the terror, I registered another voice that wasn't Andy's. (*It's bloody Central Station in here*, I thought for an unhinged second.) This voice was still and bright and clear, like the kiss of a coin into a freshwater well.

"Pocket."

I froze. My sob rose at the end, a soggy question. Then I thrust my hand in my trouser pocket. I felt the note that Kit had given me and the white card that Peter had stuck in the topiary bush. Nothing else. I thrust my hand deeper, panicking, snapping seams.

"Other pocket." This time there was a tinge of exasperation.

I reached into the other pocket, and felt the small, sturdy shape of a lighter.

Daddy, where am I?
Is this Heaven?
Are you close?

Daddy

She is standing on solid ground now, but she doesn't know how she got here. She looks behind her and sees darkness.

Ahead, a light. It is becoming brighter, coming closer.

Her body is light, seamless, strong. The light is nearer now. It is brighter than the stars, than the sun, than a thousand suns. Yet her eyes drink it in, letting it fill every part of her with white brightness and quench every thirst she ever had. It is cool and gentle and more powerful than a thousand gods, and it is beautifully breaking her heart.

She hears a voice now, calling her name.

I'm coming, Andy. Hold on, sweetheart. I'm coming for you.

She wonders without hope or fear if it is God or the Devil. She does not care. She is content to bathe in the light and be still.

The voice calls again.

Andy.

And she realises that it is her father's voice. He is holding a light and the light is upon her, it has become her, it has created her. And then her father steps from the light and stands before her, and she is home.

Daddy, she says, and her voice is just as it was on earth, but more. Am I dead? Is this Heaven?

Her father's face is illuminated and beautiful and not at all what she expected. It is as if the light has entered into him too, making him the father he always was in her dreams.

She asks again: Is this Heaven, Daddy?

Her father speaks, and his voice is everything she ever wanted but never knew it.

Sweetheart. You have to go back. It isn't your time yet. You must go back.

She realises she cannot grasp a single memory of her life on earth. It is like a distant frequency caught intermittently on an ancient radio. Her mother, her aunt, her friends, her life; all of it is fading. She does not want to go back. She wonders briefly, abstractly, who will find the unfinished stories beneath her bed. So many unfinished stories.

She looks into her father's face, and, for the first time, or maybe for the millionth time, she knows how much he loves her. She feels his imperfect, desperate love, and now, here, in this place, it is enough.

I read your stories, Daddy.

And I read your letters, he says.

She does not wonder how. She knows.

I'm sorry I said those things, she offers.

No, you were right. You were right about everything.

They stand very close, without movement, without breath. Light rejoices within and between them, blurring their edges, holding them safe.

You were writing a book, she says after a pause that lasts for a second, or an eternity. Before the fire destroyed it.

Yes.

What was the book about, Daddy?

About us. About me, and you. I didn't know it then, but I know it now. It was about a little boy who fights with angels, and then finds his true love.

And she realises she has already read the very early first draft of this book, and she understands why it sang its way into her heart and made a home there.

I'm sorry, she says. It was all my fault.

No, her father says. No, sweetheart. It was all mine.

A current, or a breath, or an eternity passes between them, through them, reaching out to the other, reaching into the other with all the words unspoken, the stories untold, the hurts unforgiven, the hearts unknown.

You must go back, he says again.

I don't want to go, Daddy. I want to be with you.

You will be, one day. But right now, you need to live. Don't be afraid. Live.

Will you be here waiting for me, Daddy? When I come back?

Her father looks away for a moment, off to the right. He is searching for something, something he desperately desires. He relinquishes it, then looks back into his daughter's face. He is at peace.

I'll be right here. I promise.

He pauses, desperately not wanting her to go. Then he slips something into her hand. She fingers it without curiosity, as if it were an extension of herself. He puts his arms around her and pulls her to his heart.

The mist starts to slowly swirl once more, heralding a moving on. A returning. He senses there will soon be an ending, and so he says what he has always meant to say, what he has longed to say, but never knew how.

I love you, Andy. I know I was hopeless at saying it when I was alive, but I'm saying it now. I love you. I always have and I always will. Never forget it.

She lets the words sink into her, enfold her, become her. The mist whispers and starts to dance with the stars, twisting and pulsing and shocking around her and through her, drawing her away.

Back to herself.

48

I let go of my daughter as she drew away from me. I caught a glimpse of her face, her hair, her eyes as they searched for me. I felt myself fading. I sensed her becoming more solid, returning to the living, leaving me. She raised her hand, perhaps to wave, or perhaps because she had something more to say.

Then she was gone.

49

Two and a half weeks after the accident

Dear Dad,

I did at least make it to the funeral home. The service had been set to start at 3 pm, with refreshments afterwards, but in a fit of Domestic Goddess insanity Mum had decided to serve afternoon tea beforehand. ("Nothing worse than a stale sausage roll, now, is there?")

Rewind to the morning, though. After Aunt Fleur had told me everything, I got up, walked to my room, shut the door very quietly, and locked it. She tried knocking several times but I refused to open the door or even answer her. Finally, at 12 pm, after I heard her crying through the door as she pleaded with me one more time to come out, I said, "I'll see you there."

"What about the eulogy?" she asked.

"I'll think of something," I answered. Which was a lie. The only thing I could think about was how she and both my parents had lied to me, about everything, for so many years. Everything I thought I knew about you had been blown out of the water. You were a passionate man, once upon a time. And my mother, the one I despised but also pitied for having married someone like you, had suddenly taken on a new layer of cruelty; an unrecognisable mantle of awfulness. It was like watching an old familiar movie only to find that it had been dubbed in a foreign language. Everything had shifted.

As soon as I heard the front door click at 12.30 pm, I opened my door and headed for your alcohol cabinet – the cardboard box next to your bed, hidden by Gran's ancient and faded tea towel with An Irish Blessing printed on it. (*And until we meet again, may God hold you in the palm of his hand. Yeah, right.*) You thought you had cleverly camouflaged the box as a bedside table. I wasn't stupid. Sometimes at night I would hear you in your room, the dull clunk of bottles pushed together, the gurgle of liquid into a glass. You kept your beers in the fridge but apparently the Southern Comfort needed to be hidden from me. Perhaps you feared having a daughter who was a lawyer and a spirits drinker. Or perhaps you were just selfish and didn't want to share it.

By the time I was ready to catch a bus to the funeral home, I was swaying a little, and rather warm. I passed Mrs Hardy's house just as she emerged, wrapped in a yellow polyester dress – the kind I would wear to a bad taste fancy dress party – and a redundant green raincoat.

"You off to the funeral then, dear?" she said as she stepped around the garden gnome on her porch. Pants around its ankles, it was bent over as if preparing for a rectal exam. A clay bird perched merrily in its crack.

I stopped and swayed. "No, I'm off to blow up the Town Hall with the explosives currently strapped to my body under this unusually padded funeral attire."

She stared for a moment at my Bee Gees T-shirt, denim jacket, and jeans. "That's nice, dear. Where's Mrs Toogood?" For a moment I thought she meant Mum, then I realised she was talking about Aunt Fleur.

"Gone on," I said.

"Gone on? Well, I never. Would you like a lift?"

For a moment I thought I had misheard. "I beg your pardon?"

"Would you like a lift?" She jabbed her keys towards her carport. "I'm going to the funeral, dear. Your father and I weren't close, especially after the paperweight incident – " she sniffed " – but you have to pay your respects, don't you?"

I felt something in me soften. Maybe it was the Southern Comfort.

"Besides," continued Mrs Hardy, "There's usually a nice afternoon *tea, and I haven't been grocery shopping for a few days."*

I considered stabbing my spike-studded skull ring into her eye. I looked at my watch and then, with a kind of surreal calm, observed the 249 to Cliff Hills rumbling past the front gate, accelerating like an old man clearing his throat as it headed down the slope leading to the intersection where you died.

"Yes, please," I said to my surprise and the even greater surprise of my neighbour. "A ride would be superb."

We drove in silence as far as the first intersection. Mrs Hardy smelt of cheap perfume and tinned salmon. This, along with the alimentary antics of the alcohol, made me take rapid and deep breaths in an effort to stave off the churning nausea. I closed my eyes and the world spun.

Mrs Hardy's hatchback hopped and limped through the intersection. Gear changes were clearly not her forte. "You know, dear, if it hadn't been for all that rubbish, your father might still be with us."

My eyes snapped open. "What do you mean, rubbish?"

Mrs Hardy sniffed, as if the memory were olfactory. "The morning he died, dear," she said, with not a trace of sensitivity. "He left thirty minutes later than usual. He normally leaves – oops, left – at eight o'clock every morning, but on Monday he left at eight-thirty. I remember, see." She took both hands off the steering wheel and tapped both sides of her head. "I remember because at eight o'clock every morning I'm usually on the toilet, which is right by the driveway, but on Monday I was busy in the living room, rigging the bingo cards. Constipation, see."

A horn blared and Mrs Hardy, unperturbed, veered back into our lane. I swallowed a gob of saliva. My heart was trying to race but nausea was making it sluggish. "What do you mean, rubbish?" I heard myself ask again.

Mrs Hardy braked suddenly as a bus pulled out in front of us. I jerked forward and snapped back. "Goddamn buses. Selfish bastards. All foreigners, no doubt. Eggshells and gravy dinners and cans and fizzy drink bottles and sweet wrappers. Took him a long time to clean it all up.

By the time he'd finished he was running late. Bastard! Selfish bastard!"
She shook her fist at a cyclist who had emerged out of a side road and
swayed into our lane momentarily. "Not your father, dear. Although,
having said that, he did hose eggshells onto the boundary. I watched him
do it."

She continued shouting at drivers and the occasional hapless
pedestrian, but I didn't hear another word. I was breathing hard,
desperately trying not to puke, trapped back in the previous Sunday, the
night before you died, the night we had an argument after dinner and I
stormed out to the university library, the night I arrived home and saw
the full rubbish bin on the kerb and knocked it over to piss you off or
make you notice me or just because it was there, I don't know; the night
I set in motion the events that would lead inexorably to my own father's
death.

It was all my fault.

We arrived at the funeral home, Mrs Hardy jolting into a mobility
carpark. As we walked towards the front door, where an awkward, self-
consciously earnest Gwyneth was welcoming guests, the smell of sausage
rolls and coffee mingled with the scent of air freshener and a third, more
sinister scent.

A brief nicety and we were inside. A large yellow banner hung over
the door on our right, leading into the chapel. It read:

RIP, Maurice. May you find books in Heaven.

Suddenly Felicity's eye was in front of me. "Andrea. We are *just* so, *so*
sorry. The *banner is* from *us. It was* the *least we* could *do.* There *was a*
special on at *It's a Sign."*

Your colleagues stood to the side, looking vaguely embarrassed. That
young guy with the weird name gave me a smile that said "Sorry. Nothing
to do with me." Briefly, horrifically, I was distracted by the realisation
that he was handsome. I hadn't noticed it before.

I weaved my way down the hall, the walls of which were lined with pastel paintings of landscapes and Helen Steiner Rice poems framed in raffia, and into the reception area. There were about fifty people spaced around the room, most of them close to the tables, trestled anchors in a sea of awkwardness. Ladies were twittering, their husbands looking at the carpet. Mrs Hardy had followed and was now helping herself to half a dozen savouries. Gwyneth appeared, click clack, click clack, all brittle nails and screechingly high black patent heels. In a morbid nod to funereal colour coordination, she was wearing glasses with black frames. Her fingers kept pressing them to her face, as if she was scared she would lose them. She went to stand by Mum, who took her hand and hung on. I couldn't see Aunt Fleur. She was probably in the chapel organising the flowers.

I was suddenly enveloped in a pillowy cloud of face powder and Karma Oil.

"Oh, my dear, I am so very, very sorry for your loss. Please, if there's anything I can do, let me know, won't you? I just … Oh my goodness, I feel so …" Barbara's voice tailed off. She let go and plugged a flowery hanky to her pink mouth, her eyes watery. As was often the case at funerals, friends had come to seek comfort from the family.

Mum appeared at my side, her wrap floating behind her like Galadriel's at Caras Galadhon. She reached for Barbara's hand. "You loved him, Barbara," she said with a dramatic sniff. "We all loved him." With her other hand she reached for an asparagus roll. "Could you just check on the portable Buddha? Last I heard, the delivery van was late. Foreign driver, no doubt. Typical." She plunged the roll into her mouth in one swift movement as she turned to me, then abruptly stopped chewing. "Andy, what on earth are you wearing?" she gobbed, the words squeezing out with some difficulty past plump asparagus. "A T-shirt? The Bee Gees?"

I swayed.

She narrowed her eyes, then leaned towards me and sniffed. "Have you been drinking? *For Buddha's sake, young lady, have you no respect?"*

The dam burst.

"Respect? Me show some respect? Oh my God, Mum, for Christ's sake would you just shut the fuck up! Listen to yourself! You didn't respect Dad at all, you didn't even love him. You hated him so much you made him want to burn all his books! All his writing, everything! You told him he was nothing! And now here you are trying to play the part of the grieving widow when all you want to do is get everyone out so you can go home and fuck your new boyfriend! And I'm worse than you because I killed him! I killed him!"

If there's one way to plunge a politely chatting funeral home crowd into silence, that's pretty much it. But it lasted only a second. I picked up a platter of pumpkin and feta tartlets and smashed it to the ground. The lamingtons went the same way, then the asparagus rolls.

I heard a rush from the kitchen as staff emerged to survey the scene. I continued to spit accusations into the incredulous quiet, hurling all my grief and guilt and anger at Mum, who stood with her mouth hanging open, shreds of half-chewed asparagus roll dropping to join their fallen colleagues. No one knew how to stop me. After a while the words no longer made much sense, mixing with sobs and tears until they were nothing but a mumbled, soggy paste spilling from my mouth.

Then I felt Aunt Fleur coming up behind me and laying her hand on my shoulder. Rigid with rage and grief, drunk and disorientated, I shoved it away and turned from my speechless and eviscerated mother. I pushed through Barbara and Felicity and the other funeral goers standing around her like extras who hadn't learnt their lines. I stumbled out of the reception room, past the reproachful paintings and poetry, and towards the front door. For an awkward moment I pushed instead of pulled, then I was out. By then the tears were coming in desperate, hiccupping jags and I all I wanted was to get away, as far as possible. I ran across the road, throwing a cursory glance to the right. But not to the left. And then … nothing.

And then you.

Andy

50

Three weeks after the accident

Dear Dad,

Your funeral was cancelled. The funeral home gave us your ashes so that we can hold a small family memorial when I'm well enough. I don't mind. I know you are not in that urn.

When the van hit me it threw me in the air and delivered me, broken and gasping, to the opposite pavement. I landed on grass and a pile of leaves, which was the first thing that probably helped save my life. Despite the relatively forgiving earth, however, I still broke my clavicle, my right leg, and my left arm (not my writing one). I cracked a number of ribs and sustained massive bruising everywhere, inside and out. I have fourteen stitches on the back of my head thanks to the van's wing mirror. They had to shave the back of my hair off. I look like a bogan now, with tufts of renegade-red hair at the back and long hair at the front.

The van had been carrying the portable Buddha Mum had planned to place on the altar, next to the cross. It was slowing down to turn into the funeral home car park. The fact that it was slowing down was the second thing that saved my life. The driver was taken to hospital as well, suffering from shock and minor scrapes. She was discharged the same day and sent the Buddha to my hospital room as a gift. It's as bruised as me but looks surprisingly serene sitting cross-legged in a corner, benevolently watching over the Get Well Soon bouquets. I think I'll keep it.

At one point, in the ambulance, just as we reached the hospital, they thought they had lost me. For a few seconds, or an eternity, I was technically dead, until a mad gaggle of paramedics and a defibrillator jolted me away from you and back to life. After the operating theatre I was unconscious for the first few hours, embraced by that strange ether-limbo of anaesthetic and barely tamed pain. When I surfaced, thrashing and nauseated, moaning that I wanted to go back, I didn't want to leave, No, Daddy please, I knew immediately that what had happened had not been a dream. I had seen you.

Aunt Fleur told me that Mum's behaviour in the hospital was a huge surprise. No dramatics, no hysterics. She was quiet and pale and didn't leave me, not even to smoke. Forced withdrawal from nicotine and a nearly dead daughter: normally they would have been enough for her to compose a melodrama of mythic proportions. Instead, she simply sat and breathed and held Aunt Fleur's hand.

"She's wandering," said Aunt Fleur at one point when the hospital room seemed to expand with a vast, starry distance. "Let her find her own way back."

Apparently Mum looked like she was about to faint – genuinely, this time. "What if she doesn't come back?" she whispered. Aunt Fleur said her voice was like that of a lost little child.

She took Mum's hand and the two women held on to each other. "Then she'll be with her father, Robyn."

I haven't told anyone about what happened. Not yet. They'll want to reduce it to a category, an "after-death experience". It was more than that. You were more than that.

I'm being discharged today. This morning they gave me back the clothes I was wearing on the day of your funeral. The T-shirt is ruined; they had to cut Barry right down the middle. The jeans are a write-off. But my jacket's surprisingly intact. Mum offered to get it drycleaned, so I cleared out the pockets. In one of them I found a note. I swear it wasn't there before the accident. It was scrunched and grubby and scribbled in weird handwriting, perhaps because you were in a hurry. It said:

Beautiful, talented Andrea, I love you. Keep writing.
– From the guy who believed in you

I love you too, Dad. And I will.

Andy

51

Four weeks after the accident

Dear Dad,

I'm still sore and moving slowly, and I haven't been back to class yet. In fact, I'm debating whether I'll ever go back. I don't think I'm cut out to be a lawyer. I'm even thinking of changing my major to English. There's a great post-grad course in creative writing.

I've been resting a lot on Mum's front porch. (I've been staying with her for a while. I can't say she's suddenly turned into Mother Teresa, but she's making an effort. She hasn't commented on one thing I've eaten.) Today the sun is making a brave attempt to shine through stubborn clouds. It's warm enough, though, and Mum has spread an old red and green tartan blanket over my knees so I can sit outside and write.

Guess what? I never did write your eulogy.

Yesterday we gathered in Mum's living room, just Mum and me and Aunt Fleur and Gwyneth. Turns out it was Gwyneth Mum was talking to that night when I walked in on her. They've grown very "close", as Aunt Fleur put it when I asked. Mum seems happy. I'm happy for her, I guess; nothing would surprise me anymore (although if Gwyneth doesn't cut her fingernails soon, I swear I'll lop them off with a hedge trimmer).

Everything that happened still sits between us, acknowledged but not discussed. Aunt Fleur told her at the hospital that I knew about the fire, and everything else. Apparently Mum lay her head next to mine and just whispered "I'm sorry" over and over. One day, when I'm ready, we'll talk. In the meantime, we're trying to be kind to each other. Some days it's easier than others.

We put some Bee Gees on the stereo and cried a bit and hugged. Gwyneth made a little speech about how the dead are always with us in spirit, and Mum made another one about how grateful she was that I was there in the flesh, not in spirit. It was quite nice, actually. There was a bit of hysterical crying near the end, but when Aunt Fleur said "Robyn" in a low, patient voice, Mum calmed down a bit. And then, I read the poem I wrote a few days after I came home from hospital.

Love Letters

When my world began, you were there.
When my world ended, you were there.
But in the in-between years,
In the living and the longing and the silence, you sent me
Poorly written love letters
Half-complete
Perhaps you were waiting for me
To finish them and send them back to you.
I never did.
So now, now that I know it is not too late,
I am writing my own love letter
To you.
It will never be finished; it is my life.
It is enveloped in flesh and failure
Stamped, and delivered most longingly
(standard mail; I know you will wait)
To you.
The stars stretch, the planets spin,
The moons circle and satellite, etching perfect arcs.
We blink, incredulous, at the same sun,
And love eclipses all distance.

After I had read it there was silence for a few seconds, until Mum said, with minimal dramatics, "That was beautiful." She paused. "You'll make a fine writer." And I reached for her hand and held it for a bit.

We're going to put a plaque up in Bressington cemetery with your name and dates and stuff. There's a special room where you can go and they're all there, lining the walls like books on a library shelf: silent testaments to lives lived well, or badly. We're going to put a quote on the plaque too. Mum said I could choose it, so I chose the one I found in a book of love poems I bought from that second-hand book shop on Marsh Street, about a month before you died. Don't laugh, OK? I don't know why, but I was thinking about that boy I fancied at school, and how I never told him how I felt. Kit. Maybe one of these days I'll try to track him down.

Anyway, the book is called 'How We Love Each Other'. On the front cover two hands reach out towards each other, encircled in a love heart. The book smells faintly of mints, or maybe lavender. The man in the shop said he thought it had come from a deceased estate. Oh, the irony.

Inside the front cover someone has written in slightly shaky blue biro:

To my Poppet, Penelope, on your 65th birthday. From your John.

And then John (I presume) has printed in large, bold letters (perhaps to give the quote more weight than his own, less eloquent dedication):

**Love pours life into death and death into life
without a drop being spilt
– Author Unknown**

Yes, yes, I can just hear you now: "If you're going to put a quote on my plaque, then people should at least know who bloody wrote it!" But I think you would have been pleased, all the same.

Rest in peace, Dad. I will see you again.

Andy x

Part Three
The Last Letter

52

After the revolution, and after I sent my daughter back to life, Hippy Happy Heaven became a vastly different place. For one thing, nobody wore yellow shellsuits anymore. There was a glorious ritualistic burning of them on the cocktail lawn, sparked this time with a normal lighter. Moses was on fire extinguisher duty. The next thing that happened was that in the space of just two days Heaven changed hue. Joseph put his colour scheming to good use, mixing various remnants of paint he kept in his cabin (you should see his walls) to create a striking blue-green, and we held a forty-eight-hour painting bee. Then he found some pearly white paint and we attacked the gates of Heaven. It was a vast improvement.

After that we started on the lawns and gardens. We couldn't do much about the grass and the existing trees, but Adam raided the pantry for all the apples he could find, and we planted the seeds in beds of loamy dirt dug and hauled from the underground tunnel by dozens of willing citizens. Someone found packets of sunflower and poppy seeds in God's office, and we planted them in as many places as we could. The chef, who withdrew his resignation after a great deal of persuasion (Peter) and apologies (Jezebel and Adam), planted a vegetable garden at the back of the kitchen. Heaven was coming alive again.

Jezebel and I decided that the Boogie Bar needed a complete makeover. We started by getting rid of the statues. (I didn't tell Jezebel, but I kept the cherub. It's in my bathroom.) Then we ripped down the fairy lights and painted the walls, and replaced some of the tables with couches, and sloshed beer on the carpet. The karaoke machine stayed, but I vetoed the song selection. *The Creation of Adam* stayed as well, but Eve insisted that Joseph, who had painted it, A. work her into the picture, and B. cover up Adam's nether regions. He did both, and at the same time put a pint of Guinness into God's hand. God looks pleased. The Boogie Bar is now a dark Irish pub with hidden nooks and crannies and questionable pub food. It reeks. Jezebel's still the quintessential flirty barmaid. (Would you want them any other way?) It's perfect.

The Heavenly Hosts are a lot less perky. They've lost the tacky costumes and badges and play a more low-key role in the day-to-day running of Heaven. I think most of them just feel grateful to have been offered a second chance. They've formed an acapella choir, and it's rather good. They performed the Hallelujah Chorus the other night after dinner. Someone found a backing track for it on a USB in God's office. The things the Almighty keeps in his drawers.

Moses doesn't try to part the waters in the lake anymore. He spends much of his time reading in the sun or reminiscing with Noah and Jacob and a few others about the old days. He loves to potter in the vegetable garden, but the chef has to ask him repeatedly not to carve the pumpkins into biblical emblems. Noah has been appointed chief of water activities, and most days you can find him down by the jetty, fixing this boat or that, watching with amusement as John the Baptist tries to dunk unsuspecting citizens under the water during Samson's aqua aerobics classes. There's always a faint air of melancholy about the old man. I asked him about that one day as we sat under the strange sky, watching a group of citizens canoeing up and down.

"I miss my animals," he said.

"Have there never been animals in Heaven?" I asked.

He shook his head. "Never seen a one. I always wanted to ask God about that. Maybe they get to go to a better place. Heaven knows they deserve it." He got up as the canoeists approached the shore, their workout complete. "Ever see a giraffe be intentionally cruel to anyone?" he asked.

Nonplussed, I shook my head.

"There you go. We could learn a lot from giraffes."

Adam's not in charge anymore. He stood down of his own volition, although he was issued an ultimatum by Eve, who told him if he didn't prioritise "working on their relationship" he could forget about even having one. He gave in, and things appear to be getting better. I haven't seen her cleavage flare red for some time, although I do spend a fair amount of time checking, just in case. Occasionally, for a few moments, she looks at me and I at her, and something passes between us, and I have a fleeting sense of what might have been. But as Peter says, the universe really is as it should be, and as I watch Adam and Eve walking towards the Glory Glade at twilight, fingers tentatively entwined, I feel only a little bit lonely.

You'll be wondering what happened to Kit. After I returned from The Gateway, I told him about Andy and how I had managed to slip his note into her hand. He hugged me then, and held on for a long time.

"I know you loved her," I said eventually.

Kit drew back in surprise.

"It's OK," I said. "I did too." I took a punt, guessing the content of the note. "And now we've both told her."

We didn't need to say anything more.

He spent a good few days after that with Peter in the gatehouse, helping refine and perfect the new programme for detecting and sending back Wanderers. At breakfast or lunch I often observed them, heads together, scribbling formulas, Kit's big hands gesticulating above his head as he pontificated on the finer points of computer programming.

He and I passed the evenings together, looking out over the lake from the clearing where we first spoke. Sometimes he would bring his book and read it, occasionally sharing memories of his parents, imagining what they would be doing if he were still alive. He told me the things he regretted, and the things he wished he had said. There were a few tears, and I was all right with that. I mean, I didn't take him in my arms and wail with him, but it felt almost natural to pat his back and tell him it was OK, and that I was sure his parents knew that he loved them.

Not long ago, Peter, Kit, and I were enjoying a quiet beer in the Boogie Bar after a busy afternoon removing all the false flowers from the Glory Glade (Hallelujah). A few citizens were fooling around on the karaoke machine. As "Living on a Prayer" came on for the third time we took our drinks and potato chip packets outside. Samson had shifted some of the trestle tables from the reception building and erected a sheet of corrugated plastic as a makeshift shelter, fashioning a crude but serviceable garden bar area.

We sipped and ate in silence; the intimate silence of friendship formed in adversity and promising much. The false grass stretched before us in waves, the false trees punctuating the crests and dips.

"Can we do anything about them?" I asked.

Kit took another salt and vinegar chip. "Nope, they're all stale. Must've been sitting out the back for months."

"I mean the trees."

"Oh," he said, reaching into the packet again. Stale, then, but not inedible.

"They didn't seem so fake when God was here," said Peter. He stared into the middle distance. "Nothing seemed quite so bad when God was here."

"Do you know why he left?" I asked.

Peter took a gulp, draining the last of his Guinness. Caramel foam sneaked up the side of his glass then down again.

"No," he said, placing the glass carefully on its beer mat. "I don't think anyone knows."

I finished my own glass and placed it next to Peter's. "What's he like?" I imagined Dumbledore, striding forward to save Harry from the Death Eaters, arms wide, face furious and powerful. I imagined long white robes and a beard to match. I imagined benevolence mixed with terrifying expectation. I imagined Santa Claus and the Godfather.

Peter looked at the ground. "I don't know that either. I never met him."

My jaw dropped, and Kit coughed as he choked on a chip. I banged between his shoulder blades. Before we could speak, Peter continued.

"Sometimes I would think I had caught a glimpse of him, from a distance. Sometimes, in the middle of the night, I would jolt awake, and I could swear someone was standing at the end of my bed or just vanishing out the door. Sometimes I thought I heard him laughing, just beyond the pétanque court, or by the lake, or behind the gatehouse. Or in my dreams. But I never actually met him."

"What about at Cocktails with God? Or in the Glory Glade?" Kit asked.

Peter crumpled up his chip packet and stuffed it inside his beer glass. "He was never there. He was away on business, or at a conference, or the Glory Glade was closed for renovations, or cocktails were cancelled due to lack of interest." He looked at us and his expression was as confused as ours. "I don't know if any of us saw him. Maybe we thought we did, or we thought everyone else did and we were the only unlucky sod who missed out."

Kit and I sat in incredulous silence.

"You know that bit in *Harry Potter and the Order of the Phoenix*, when Sirius dies?" Peter asked in a rather disconcerting non sequitur.

I nodded immediately. I was back on familiar ground. I could picture the exact location of the earmarked copy in the Bressington Heights Community Library.

"Luna Lovegood asks Harry if he can hear the dead, whispering, beyond the veil. You can't see them, but you can almost hear them, like a radio station just off its proper frequency, and you know they're there, just out of reach…" he drifted off for a moment. "God is like that, I think. There, but not there. Just beyond the veil." He wiped his hand across his eyes.

Kit coughed and excused himself to go to the toilet. Eventually I asked Peter if he would like another beer. He cleared his throat and said yes, and I returned with three more beers and three packets of chips, chicken flavour this time. "Jezebel swears these ones aren't stale. They've only just come in." I knew chicken was Peter's favourite.

He smiled gratefully. "I really wanted…" he began, after we had ripped open our chips and settled back in our chairs.

"Really wanted what?"

"I really wanted to talk to God and say … and say I'm sorry." He was gripping his glass so tightly his fingers were turning white.

I stopped crunching. "You? Sorry? After everything you did to save Heaven? What on earth do you have to be sorry for?"

Peter straightened a little in his seat. "Never mind. It doesn't matter. I shouldn't … I shouldn't have burdened you with that." He cleared his throat again and took a manly gulp. Kit returned with more chips.

"Heaven Help Us All" came on the karaoke machine, and I could hear the raspy, inebriated warbles of Moses and Noah. Kit started tapping one foot and humming under his breath.

Then I had a thought.

"As I see it," I said, "there were three things that were key to saving Heaven."

Peter looked at me sideways. "What three things?"

"Your three notes," I said. "The one in the burnt topiary bush, the one in the throne, and the one you slipped in my pocket. We wouldn't be here now without them."

Peter was still for a long moment, his face contorted, obviously struggling with strong emotion. Then he gave me a small, grateful smile. "Thank you," he said.

"Forgive yourself, Peter," I said. "We all have to. You too, Kit. For everything you're sorry for." Kit looked down at the table, but I saw a hint of a smile. "We'd go mad otherwise. And what use would that be?" I pointed at myself. "A mad librarian? God help us."

We laughed together and had a few too many more beers, and not much later we all ended up on the karaoke machine. Let's just say "Too Much Heaven" will never be the same again.

The next day, after breakfast, Kit came to the library to put his book back. He hugged me so fiercely I gasped, then loped out the door, his numerous pens bulging from his pockets. He wasn't at lunch. I miss him a great deal. I've stapled a photograph of him onto the banana lady's face.

Penelope and her husband John Went On just a few days ago. After things had settled down they came to me and asked if I could take them to the library. They were there for a good hour or two. When they left they were holding hands, and Penelope was clutching her little crocheted rabbit.

"What a beautiful name," I heard her say as they pushed the lift's UP button. Her husband's face had opened like a bud unfurling to greet the light. They weren't at breakfast the next morning.

And me? Well, I'm now Head Librarian (and not a wobbly chin or misplaced emphasis in sight). But here, it's a whole different story. People come to the library whenever they like. Some of them write their own pages, adding them to their books. Or they talk to me as Kit did, sharing their regrets, their loves, their most precious memories, their most heartbreaking losses. And then, one by one, I notice that they haven't been for a while. Or I miss them at dinner. Or they're not at the weekly Trivial Pursuit (the biblical version) night anymore. Their books have gone from the library shelf. And I am happy for them.

Heaven is emptying out. There have been no new arrivals since the revolution. I'm not sure what that means, other than the possibility that one day it will just be me and an empty library. Although, no one from the Bible has Gone On yet. I'm not sure why. Perhaps there is more for them to do. Perhaps they like it here. Perhaps they're waiting for God to come back to finish their books on their behalf. He is the one who wrote the original version, after all.

I sleep with my book under my pillow. From time to time I check for new letters, but there haven't been any from Andy for some time. I choose to see that as a good sign. She is alive, and at peace. I long to hear from her, but I'm delighted that I don't.

There were two letters from Fleur. I wanted to write back and say, it's OK. I forgive you. I love you.

Perhaps that means that my story, too, is complete.

53

Dear Andy,

Last night I had a dream. It may have been fuelled by a long evening session with a Southern Comfort bottle, a darts board, and a drunken gaggle of disciples wailing their way through the karaoke version of "Don't Stop Believing". Regardless, it felt very real.

I dreamed God came into my cabin and sat on my bed. I can't describe how he looked, because it was more a … sense of him. I wouldn't be able to remember one thing about his face or what he was wearing or whether he had a beard or was black or white or whatever. I *felt* him more than saw him, if that makes sense. His voice was the same one I had heard in the mist; the still, tiny-but-enormous voice that told me to look in my pocket. He smiled, and for once in my life I was speechless. It was like this guy just knew me through and through, and saw all the ghastly parts too, and liked me despite of them (or even because of them). Maybe even loved me.

"Maurice," he said. "You did good. You did real good."

I started to modestly demur that it was nothing and that others had played their part in saving Heaven and also that it was "really", not "real", and "well", not "good", when God interrupted. "No, Maurice, I'm talking about Andy. Because at the end of everything, there's only love left, right? Only love, and human hearts to feel it. That's it. And until you guys figure that out, things aren't going to change a great deal."

"Where did you go?" I asked.

God crossed his legs and wrapped his top knee with latticed fingers, leaning back slightly on the bed. "I just stepped aside for a while. You guys have to figure things out by yourselves, even up here. Sometimes everything gets out of kilter in the universe. Everyone forgets stuff, like how to love and make connections and so on and so forth, and all the planets go haywire, and I have to get out of here and leave you to it for a while. Went to Tijuana last time, had a blast, but that's a whole other story. Everyone thinks that when the proverbial hits the fan the Big Guy will step in and take over, sort everything out immediately. You know what? It's up to you."

"We have to fix everything? You mean, you don't help at all?"

"Ah." God gave a hint of a smile, then knitted his eyebrows. "It's a bit more complicated than that. It's like … now let me see … it's like, say, an echo. An echo always comes after your own voice, right? You must be the first to reach out, to call into the unknown. It's usually a bad yodel, to be fair, but that aside: you speak first, the echo always answers. It's a law of the universe. The echo will always come." He shifted and recrossed his legs. "But the first step is yours to take. Or in your case: the first word is yours to write."

I thought about this, and about Heaven, and about the rest of eternity.

"How do people … Go On?' I asked. "How do they complete their stories?"

"They rewrite them. Especially the endings. And then they send their stories back."

"Who to?"

God uncrossed his legs and leaned towards me, animated, gesturing.

"To the people they love the most. They don't literally send their stories back, of course. The simple act of retelling, rewriting their own histories, daring to forgive themselves, re-imagine themselves … it changes things. It makes something happen in the universe … opens endless possibilities. It's a gift." God grinned and sat back. "One of the best ideas I ever came up with, if I may say so myself. That, and free wine at communion. And it's 'To whom.'"

"Where are my parents?" I ventured. "And the rest of my dead relatives, and other people I knew? And all the famous people? Why are some people from the Bible here, but not others? And what about writers? Chaucer. Shakespeare. Kafka. Frame. Why are they not here?"

God looked mildly exasperated. "Whole families, together in a confined space? All the world's writers self-importantly scribing their impressions of the afterlife? Give me some credit." His expression softened, and his voice was then so kind and so wise it almost hurt.

"Heavens within Heavens, worlds within worlds, time inside out and upside down, love within love within love. There's a right place for everyone, Maurice. Sometimes that right place is just very unexpected." He raised both arms to gesture around him. "For you, it was here: a Heaven on the brink of revolution. It needed a hero, and you needed to be one. As for my biblical friends: only a smattering was needed. And just as you needed them, they were the ones who specifically needed … you. Case in point: Peter. I forgave him centuries ago. Three times, no less. But there's no telling some people. They won't believe it until they hear it from somebody else." He sniffed.

I blinked. Heaven needed me. I didn't know whether to feel important or inadequate. I hesitated, then risked my next question. "Why … I'm sorry, but why is this Heaven … so ghastly?"

God's answer was gentle. "Do you really think you would have wanted to send Andy back if it had been wonderful?" he chuckled. "I mean, that breakfast buffet. Come on."

"Where's Jesus?" It came out louder than I had intended, in a shrill tumble. There, I thought. This is it. The biggie. The make-or-break theological puzzle no one's been able to solve. Would God? Because unless he could answer this one adequately, Heaven and Peter and the angels and Judas and the bloody Gideon Bible would never make any sort of sense. Ever. And I didn't think my mind and my heart could survive living in a senseless Heaven – more senseless than it already was – without going eternally insane.

The Almighty's unexpected response was to take both my hands and grasp them firmly with his own. They were strong and warm, and in that moment I felt safer than I ever have before or since. And then, as he squeezed his palms against mine, I registered the relief of raised, rough scar tissue.

We sat close together for a long minute as, with more love and tenderness than there is in the whole world, God waited until my heart understood as far as it was able. Then he gently withdrew his hands and spoke again. "The lover, the beloved, the love. Like a cost-saving three-in-one kitchen appliance, only more useful, and slightly easier to wash."

I felt momentarily dizzy. I took a breath and asked my penultimate question, desperate but terrified to hear the answer. "I promised Andy I would wait here for her. Will I be allowed to Go On, eventually? To the real Heaven? Or at least … a better one? Or … am I stuck here forever?" The last words were a whisper. Of all the questions I had asked, this one was the most terrifying.

The divine smile widened. God raised his right hand and placed it firmly on my heart, and it was as if I was dying all over again, but I felt too damn wonderful to care.

"It may be time, my dear author, to finish your novel," said God. "Depending on how it ends, you may find that the real Heaven is in here." He pressed, and my soul gasped.

I didn't understand, but I didn't need to. I felt still and clear. I had just one more question.

"Why was everything yellow?"

God shrugged. "I like Coldplay, and bananas. What can I say? But I'm fine with the change. As good as a holiday, right?" He stood and stretched a little.

"I'll be back," he said. "I'm not sure when." He made for the door, but just before opening it he turned back. "I'll keep an eye on her, Maurice." He winked. "Even if she does become a lawyer."

And he was gone.

When I woke there was a pad of paper and a pen on the bedside table. The first page of the pad had several lines of writing on it. I recognised the handwriting, and the words. They were mine. It was the first paragraph of my novel; the first words I had written all those years ago in my tiny university flat, the first brave steps of an odyssey that would ultimately lead me here, to this strange and marvellous Heaven. I picked up the pen and I started to write, my memory piecing together long-abandoned words and phrases and sections, like the painstaking repair of a ripped and precious tapestry. I've filled ten pages already.

Will I ever Go On? Has God declared the deal I made in order to save your life null and void? I don't know. All I know is that one day, you will come. The universe will deliver you to me, just like your letters. And until that day, I am willing to wait.

Just like *Waiting for Godot*, but with a better ending.

Love,

Dad x

Epilogue

… but the end
comes gently, on tiny padded paws.
It nudges once, twice.
Hello. I am here. It's OK.
My fighting fist sighs open
and trembles on whispery velvet.
It reminds me
of the downy head of my baby daughter
as she suckles at my newly clumsy breast, her wise little hand clenching
and caressing,
my mother-ness an other-ness
not yet comprehended;
and of the exquisite fragility of love,
and new beginnings.

– from the poem "Letters to my Father" (*Without a Drop Being Spilt: Selected Poems and Short Stories*), by Andrea Toogood-Hardacre

Note from the author

This novel was inspired, in part, by Kate Bush's music, particularly the songs "Lily" from the album *The Red Shoes*, and "Among Angels" from *50 Words for Snow*. If you do a search on YouTube you will find "Among Angels" set to a short animated film called *Father and Daughter*, by Dutch film maker Michael Dudok de Wit. My words may be the flesh and bones of this story … but Bush's song and Dudok de Wit's film are its heart and soul.

Acknowledgements

Ella, my beloved daughter, the day you were born was the start of the best story ever written. Thank you for being my biggest fan and my frankest critic.

Peter, my dear friend and co-parent, thank you for your quiet, unwavering support.

Dad, thank you for passing on to me your love of stories, your passion for book hoarding, and your (slightly warped) Irish sense of humour. All those Sunday mornings spent sitting in the front pew, listening to your sermons and flicking through the Bible when I was bored and trying desperately not to laugh when we caught each other's eye, clearly paid off.

My proofreading and editing clients, I have learnt something from working with each and every one of you. Thank you for helping me to be a better writer. I still have much to learn.

My fellow book club members, thank you for never putting forward *The Time Traveler's Wife*.

James George, very early on you helped me believe that this novel was worth writing. Thank you for your kindness and wisdom.

Jo Frew, thank you for being my first beta reader. Your thoughtful and honest feedback was hugely helpful. Felicity Boyd, thank you for being my second, and for your wonderful friendship. Also, thank you for being nothing like Felicity Bonmot.

My friends at Cloud Ink Press, thank you for taking a punt on "the one about the ghastly but hilarious Hi-de-Hi heavenly holding pen", and for all you have done behind the scenes to support me.

Nikki Crutchley, thank you for your eagle eye and kind feedback.

Karen McKenzie, amazing person and PR guru, you are so generous with your time and skill. I owe you a huge debt of gratitude.

Craig Violich, thank you for the gorgeous cover design (and the banana peel email debates).

Lynn Charlton, thank you for walking with me through my own story, showing me that it's possible to change the narrative, and for never giving up on me.

And finally, to my mother: At the end of everything, there is only love left, and human hearts to feel it. Despite everything, and perhaps also because of everything: Thank you for being my mum.

About the author

Patricia Bell is a writer, editor, and proofreader. Her short stories, poems, and non-fiction articles have been published in anthologies, literary journals, and online. Her short story "Dandelion Clocks" won first prize in the 2021 New Zealand Society of Authors Graeme Lay Short Story Competition, and her fiction has twice been highly commended in national competitions.

Patricia has a widely read author website (www.patriciabellauthor.com) where she shares some of her creative writing and offers writing advice, as well as musings on language, reading, and the writing process.

Patricia was born in Northern Ireland to a Presbyterian minister from Belfast and a teacher from Motherwell, Scotland, which probably explains a lot. She now lives with her daughter in Auckland, New Zealand. She is a trained singer and musical theatre performer, a bird nerd and conservation advocate, a proudly loud feminist, and a born-again agnostic.

The Library of Unfinished Business is her first novel.